Loving You Twice

Andaleeb Wajid is a hybrid author, having published 40 novels in the past 14 years. She enjoys writing in a number of different genres such as young adult, romance, and horror. She lives and writes in Bengaluru.

·JASMINE VILLA SERIES·

ANDALEEB WAJID

Loving You Twice

First published by Westland Books, a division of Nasadiya Technologies Private Limited, in 2023

No. 269/2B, First Floor, 'Irai Arul', Vimalraj Street, Nethaji Nagar, Allappakkam Main Road, Maduravoyal, Chennai 600095

Westland and the Westland logo are the trademarks of Nasadiya Technologies Private Limited, or its affiliates.

ISBN: 9789395767910

10 9 8 7 6 5 4 3 2 1

This is a work of fiction. Names, characters, organisations, places, events and incidents are either products of the author's imagination or used fictitiously.

Typeset by SÜRYA, New Delhi
Printed at Nutech Print Services-India

ONE

Ana Hasan was having a really good day. She smiled to herself as she tucked her luggage in the overhead compartment and sat down quickly so that other passengers could walk down the aisle to their seats. She was nervous but she hoped it didn't show on her face and she tried to pretend she had been flying all her life. After all, she was good at that. Pretending.

Taking a deep breath, she observed the other passengers as they found their seats. The flight to Kuala Lumpur was filling up slowly, with families and businessmen who would be changing flights to travel on ahead to other destinations.

She still couldn't believe she was doing this. Her father had been wary and not willing to give in when she had spoken to him about it. It had been just a few months since she had got a job as a behavioural counsellor at an international school and she knew it had been a stroke of luck that she had been chosen to attend this conference.

'Abbu, please. It's a great opportunity,' she had told him. He had looked at her, helpless and uneasy.

'You'll be travelling alone, out of the country,' he murmured.

'So? It's fine. I'll be fine. Everything is taken care of,'

she told him. She had turned to her older sister Tehzeeb who was visiting them with her six-month-old son Aslan and beseeched her to make a case in her favour.

'Abbu, she's right. She may not get such an opportunity again,' Tehzeeb said. Abbu seemed cornered and he turned to Athiya, her younger sister who was a spitfire and was probably jealous too. To her surprise, Athiya too took her side.

'Why are we even discussing this? If Ana Api had been a boy, you would have sent her without even thinking twice no? Why can't she go just because she's a girl?' she asked as she bent and took Aslan from Tehzeeb, cooing to him.

Sighing, Abbu capitulated. 'Okay, fine,' he said. He looked lost and worried and Ana had to reassure him that everything would be fine.

'But why isn't anyone travelling with you?' he asked.

'Why would they?' she asked him, surprised.

'Aren't other people going to this conference?'

'Yes, but they're from all parts of the country and other institutions. Why did you think everyone would be going from Bangalore?' Ana asked.

She smiled now at the memory and blinked when she realised that the plane was full. Her silver jhumkis clinked as she caught her reflection in the window of the plane. She had been given a window seat, although it wouldn't do much good to look out because it was night. The seat next to her was still empty. She looked out of the window, not really listening to the flight attendant who was giving instructions about seatbelts and safety.

She sensed some sort of disturbance at the entrance and someone apologising profusely. The flight attendant paused and then began again. Ana couldn't see what the fuss was about and she went back to looking outside, wondering what Abbu and Athiya were doing. She pulled out her phone and sent a quick message to her sisters that she had boarded and the flight would take off soon.

The excitement inside her had finally kicked off. Until this moment, she was worried that something would go wrong, someone would intervene and she would be deprived of this experience. She knew her father was getting calls from that pesky Taskeen Auntie who was trying to send rishtas for her, and Abbu could deflect only so much.

One of these days, he was going to relent. She knew this was a possibility that she had to be prepared for and deep in her heart, she had accepted it. Not everyone was as lucky as Tehzeeb to fall madly in love with her husband, to have him love her back just as passionately, to live such a charmed life.

She was no longer jealous of her sister and she knew that Tehzeeb deserved every bit of happiness. She smiled to herself, thinking that she was going to stop thinking about annoying people like Taskeen Auntie and what waited for her back in India. She was going to live in the moment and enjoy what life gave her *now.*

She continued to look out into the darkness when, suddenly, there was movement beside her. She realised that the person occupying the middle seat had arrived and she turned the slightest bit to see. Her breath caught in her throat.

Luqman was shoving his backpack into the overhead compartment and dusting his hands. He smiled at the person sitting in the aisle seat, asking them if they could get up so he could sit down on the middle seat. Ana turned away swiftly, looking out of the window as her heart pounded and sweat made her palms clammy. Luqman was going to be seated next to her for the duration of this flight? Oh no! Oh yes, her mind warred. No. What did it matter?

But she couldn't possibly sit like this until the plane landed. It hadn't even taken off yet. She felt a sort of prickly undercurrent radiating from his arm when it brushed hers and she took a deep breath. He hadn't seen her yet but she knew she had to face him soon.

The air around her seemed to have thickened. She swallowed nervously. It had to be done now. She had to turn around, feign surprise and say hello to him. She looked down first. He was wearing jeans and his shoes were a little scruffy. Lifting her head, she straightened up in her seat and felt him stiffen.

He had seen her now. Keeping her face expressionless, she looked ahead for a few seconds as the boarding was completed and the plane began to move. She had never flown before and it was then that the reality of the situation struck her. She gripped the armrest tightly and shut her eyes, icy fear flooding her insides, turning them cold.

Suddenly, she was glad Luqman was sitting beside her. She turned to him and smiled tremulously, taking in his chiselled clean looks in a quick appraisal.

'Hi,' she said, forgetting her plan to act surprised. He smiled back so warmly that she knew she wasn't just glad he was sitting beside her. She was very, very glad.

TWO

Luqman's day had just gotten a hundred times better. He couldn't believe that Ana was sitting next to him on this last minute flight he was taking. It was a connecting flight for him onwards to San Francisco but … he stopped thinking altogether as he examined her closely. She was radiant and there was a light in her eyes that made him want to keep looking. Her smile was heart-stopping for the barest of moments, but within seconds, she was looking panicky.

'First time?' he asked her in a low voice. The plane roared as it gathered speed on its journey down the runway and she gripped the armrest tighter, her throat working and she shut her eyes. She nodded and without thinking, he covered her hand with his. She was in a dark green shalwar kameez, a wispy chiffon dupatta covering her shoulders. He could see the rise and fall of her chest and he looked away immediately. Not when she was scared out of her wits.

Her hand was cold and shaky. Lifting it, he rubbed it with both of his palms, leaning close to her.

'Listen. This lasts for not even a minute. We'll be fine once we're airborne,' he said.

She opened her eyes and nodded. 'I feel so stupid,' she muttered.

'No, it's fine. Lots of people are scared of flying and if it's your first time … it's always a bit scary,' he said, smiling.

She took a deep breath but it didn't seem to help. 'Talk to me,' she said, turning to him.

He stared back at her, thinking of how she had never strayed too far from his thoughts. Although he hadn't met her since the day she had walked into Ayub's office to return Tehzeeb's things to him, he was reminded of her whenever he spoke to Ayub, or met him, or when he had visited them when Ayub's son was born. Each time, he had hoped Ana would be around but why would she be in her sister's in-laws' home?

To think that he had almost missed this flight! And that he hadn't wanted to go in the first place. He decided to tell her that, if only to make her smile.

'I almost missed this flight,' he remarked.

She nodded. Her face was still pale and beads of sweat had popped up on her forehead.

'I wasn't even going to go for this project actually,' he said.

She frowned. 'Why?'

'I'm tired of all this travelling. I spoke to my boss and told him that I'd rather stay in Bangalore or the company should send me out to one of the branches abroad and let me just stay there. For good,' he said.

'And you'd be okay with that? Never coming back?' she asked softly.

He shrugged. 'I don't know. I thought I could do it for at least three to five years. By then, my brothers will be married and my mother will start harassing me about getting married too,' he said. Why did he have to bring up marriage, he thought. He noticed how she stiffened at the mention of it.

'So are you going to KL alone?' he asked. She nodded.

'I'm attending a conference there,' she explained. 'I work with young adults and adolescents and there's a new study that has been conducted that correlates privilege and pressure that they face. The school where I work was very keen to get a representative to this conference which explores this paper.'

'That's good,' he said, clearly impressed. He looked out over her shoulder at the runway. The plane tilted as it was about to take off. She held his hand even more tightly and her eyes widened.

'Just breathe. Focus on your breathing,' he said softly. She nodded, still looking at him. Her eyes were the most alluring shape, he thought.

'And that's it. We're airborne,' he said.

She pursed her lips and only then realised she was holding his hand too tightly. Embarrassed, she tried to tug away her hand and he let her because it was kind of strange to keep holding on to her hand now when she didn't need it.

'Sorry,' she whispered.

'No worries. Look,' he said, indicating the window. She turned away from him, all too eager to look at the lit-up city they were leaving.

When the plane had ascended higher and they were swept in the dark masses of clouds, she turned back. She pressed her head back on the headrest and he wondered if she was going to sleep. He had actually planned to catch a few winks on this flight but now …

'You were the last person I thought I'd see here,' she said softly, leaning forward and picking up the inflight magazine.

He smiled. 'Same here. It's just … so …'

He trailed off because he couldn't think of an appropriate word. Serendipitous? But she was engrossed in turning the pages of the glossy magazine and he looked away. He didn't want to stare at her no matter how much he wanted to. She'd be creeped out and rightly so.

'So, where are you headed in KL?' she asked him. He detected a cautious sort of casualness to her question and that made him feel better.

'Um, no. KL is my transit. I'm headed to San Francisco,' he explained. He wished he was looking at her face to see if she was disappointed. Hell, he was disappointed too. Why couldn't he have had his work here in Malaysia? She could have attended the conference and in the evening, they could have gone out together. He would have shown her the sights. She would have let him hold her hand and they would have walked past the Petronas Towers. He would have taken her right up to the viewing deck where they could look out at the glittering city.

He shook his head. He was being silly, daydreaming over a girl who … he forgot his thoughts when she turned to him. She leaned close and whispered. 'I'm sorry you're not going to be in KL,' she said.

Her softly-spoken words were like a punch to his gut. Straightening in his seat, he smiled. 'Why?' he asked. She shrugged and didn't answer.

'How long are you here in Kuala Lumpur?' he asked, hoping it wouldn't sound too intrusive.

'Just for around four days,' she said.

He sighed. 'Well, if not four days, then I'm happy we at least got four hours together,' he said.

She looked down at her lap and he could see that her face

had turned pink. It didn't feel like they were surrounded by other people, by a couple of crying kids somewhere at the back, by flight attendants who were rolling down the service trolley. It felt like they were somewhere alone. Somewhere together.

'I'm happy too,' she said, looking at him shyly.

THREE

When the tray tables had been shut and most other people had dozed off, Ana and Luqman still continued talking softly. Ana had never felt this alive. She wanted to prolong the feeling and not waste even a minute of her time with Luqman. She was conscious of herself and she was relieved she had taken care of her appearance before leaving home.

He laughed easily, his eyes crinkling almost adorably. What Ana enjoyed was that he made her laugh too. She spoke about her sisters fondly, about Tehzeeb and how much she admired her, and about Athiya who annoyed her. He spoke about his brothers – he was the youngest. His older brother was dignified and quiet and nothing like him, apparently. She sensed that he hero-worshipped him.

'What about your middle brother?' she asked with a smile. She was the middle child and she knew how infuriating it could be at times.

'He's a stodgy buffoon,' Luqman said, making her laugh. 'No, really. He's so prim and proper and I used to enjoy getting him in trouble when we were kids.'

When the cabin lights were dimmed once more, she wondered if he would sleep but he turned to her and asked her something she would never have expected.

'Did you go to Maira's wedding?'

She was a bit taken aback at the question and even surprised. Tehzeeb's sister-in-law Maira had been in love with Luqman for years. Or so she claimed. Ana was still embarrassed when she thought of that day when she had gone with Tehzeeb to speak to Luqman, to convince him of Maira's love for him.

'No, did you?' Ana asked. He shuddered. Luqman had been trying to get rid of Maira's unwanted advances for years and he used that opportunity to convince Maira that he was in love with someone else. Tehzeeb had taken photos of the two of them – Ana and Luqman sitting together, supposedly gazing dreamily into each other's eyes and blurred out Ana's image before showing it to Maira.

'No way. My mother went, of course. I was glad I wasn't in India then,' Luqman said.

Ana nodded. She felt awkward at this reminder and she didn't know what it meant going forward with their conversation.

'I hope she's happy,' Luqman added with a smile. 'She was always like a little sister to me.'

Ana stayed silent. According to Tehzeeb, Maira was quite happy. Her husband and in-laws lived in Dubai and she had moved there as well. Her wedding had been fixed a few months ago and she got married just after Aslan had been born.

'I … I'm sorry again for putting you in a spot that time,' Luqman said.

'It's old news,' she said quickly.

She turned to him to smile and assure him that it was fine but she lost track of her thoughts. He was looking at her intently, and it was doing all sorts of things to her. The fluttering in her belly increased and she felt herself change in that moment, reminding her of the crazy thoughts during that photo session. She had wanted to lean in closer to him, to touch him. And kiss him. She felt the same sensations once more and it was all the more pronounced because they were alone together, even with more than a hundred people on the plane with them.

Gulping, she looked away quickly, before he could read it on her face. She was in over her head. She was having that same feeling once more, of wanting to touch his cheek, hold his face and bring him closer to her and she didn't know how she could face him. She felt an intense need inside her, something that wanted to reach out to him. To make him stay with her. To make him belong to her. She wanted his smiles. She wanted that look in his eyes. For herself.

'Hey … everything okay?' he asked, touching her arm lightly.

Inhaling deeply, she nodded and turned to him. 'Yeah. I'm a little tired. I think I should take a nap before we land,' she said quickly, without meeting his eyes.

'Oh. Right. Of course,' he said. She kept her face averted and shivered the slightest bit when his arm brushed against hers. Clearly, he wasn't suffering from the same symptoms as her. He was absolutely fine. She had to bring her emotions under control and soon.

She shut her eyes, and for the next ten minutes, she tried to imprint everything about the conversation they'd just had, the moments they'd shared together, the laughter, his eyes, his smile.

She felt something warm glide over her and she opened her eyes a fraction. It was a blanket. He was covering her and he looked surprised at finding her awake.

'I thought you were feeling cold,' he said. She nodded.

'Thanks,' she murmured and turned away, touched by his thoughtfulness. She began to wonder if this is what Maira had felt too. This surge of emotion, this emptiness at the thought of not knowing when she would meet him again, this … ache inside. How she had disregarded that poor girl's feelings for him. And here she was, in the same boat, because he seemed to have that effect for some reason.

He probably had that effect on all women. Shards of jealousy sprung up inside her and she pushed them back down, knowing it was pointless. She was not going to be another Maira, another petty annoyance for him. Even now, she berated herself for opening up so much, for talking freely and laughing. He probably thought she had a crush on him already.

It wasn't a crush. She was quite sure she was in love.

She squeezed her eyes shut tightly. This was dumb. This was ridiculous. People didn't fall in love at the drop of a hat. Look at Api and Ayub Bhai, her mind whispered. She refused to think of her sister and brother-in-law who had fallen in love with each other almost instantly. They both had felt it together. Not like this.

'Did I do something?' he asked softly. She opened her eyes and shifted so she could look at him without moving too much.

'What?'

He shrugged. 'We were getting along fine until … I don't know what happened. What happened?' he asked, sounding confused.

You're too you, she thought. She tried to find a way to put her thoughts into words, something that wouldn't make him want to run away.

'We're good,' she said. How could she tell him that she couldn't look at him without wanting to launch herself into his arms and kiss him senseless? How could she tell him that she hated this sudden loss of control over her emotions? He would think she was another Maira certainly. And she didn't want that.

'Did I upset you for some reason?' he asked, as though he was still trying to figure out what was happening. If she had been like Maira, or any other girl, she might have told him a version of the truth at least, about some of the things she was beginning to feel for him. But not her.

'Not at all. I think you're overthinking this,' she said curtly and turned away.

'Fine,' he muttered and sighed. She wanted the easy banter they'd shared just half an hour ago. The laughter, the smiles that he seemed to bestow on her so easily. Why did things have to change? Why did she have this upsurge of feeling towards him?

There was another hour and a half before the plane landed. She could have spent it talking to him, laughing at his jokes and his self-deprecating humour. But instead, she was trying to get comfy on a plane seat, wishing he hadn't been thoughtful with the blanket, wishing he hadn't been on this flight with her, sitting so close to her, taking up her mind and stealing her heart.

FOUR

The plane dipped and shuddered a little and Ana awoke, acutely aware of the crick in her neck. She remembered where she was and who was sitting with her. She turned to see if Luqman was awake almost too quickly and her neck hurt. Biting back a gasp of pain, she tried to unobtrusively rub her neck without moving too much in the seat. Outside, the night sky had lightened, giving way to a pink sky.

He was sleeping. She stared at him for the briefest of seconds and then looked away, knowing she had to bring her emotions under control because she was being stupid. She knew that. And yet, a part of her wanted to throw caution to the wind and tell him of this acute connection she felt with him. She shushed that part away and asked it to leave.

The lights in the cabin blinked, became brighter and an announcement informed them that the plane would land in the next twenty minutes. She looked out of the window when she sensed him wake up. He made no attempt to talk to her and it hurt but she knew she had been the one to rebuff him earlier.

As the plane landed, she shut her eyes tightly. He had held her hand during the take off and his presence had comforted her greatly. To her surprise, she felt his warm hand cover hers once more and squeeze gently. She opened her eyes and turned to look at him. He stared back at her. They didn't exchange any words. They didn't need to.

She barely noticed the bump or the scrape of the wheels as the plane touched the ground. She was staring back at him mesmerised, wishing she hadn't shut him down earlier, wishing they had stayed up the rest of the flight, talking. When the plane had finished taxiing on the runway and came to a halt, she swallowed and pulled out her hand from his.

'Thanks,' she muttered.

He nodded. She wanted to get away as soon as she could. She wanted to bring some sort of normalcy to her life, to make it go back to what it had been before she had stepped on this plane. She wanted him to go away so she could heal because her heart felt like it had been trampled relentlessly. She wanted him to sit by her side for the rest of her life.

God, she was so dumb. How had she evaded fuckboys all her life and fallen for one in the span of two hours? Because that was what he was. He'd have been happy to flirt with her more, and she was sure he would have taken things forward if she'd shown a little more interest. And then? He'd give her the whole spiel about having two older brothers and how he was not interested in commitment. He'd already told her about his plans to move away from India.

When they were finally allowed to disembark from the plane, she waited for him to get up and leave and she continued to sit on her seat. He turned to her in surprise.

'Um, aren't you getting up?' he asked as he took down his backpack from the overhead compartment. She nodded.

'Yes, in a bit,' she said. He waited for her and then the people around him nudged him since he had already moved into the aisle. Confused, he nodded and joined the people walking towards the exit. Feeling a rush of disappointment and relief, she got up, removed her carry-on luggage from the overhead compartment and walked towards the exit as well.

At the end of the aerobridge, her heart jolted when she realised that he was waiting for her. She took him in completely then because when he had been sitting next to her, she hadn't been able to focus on him entirely. Not like this. She'd been too focused on his proximity.

He looked younger than Ayub Bhai, although she knew they were the same age. His white shirt was crumpled a little but he looked fine. There was the beginning of stubble on his face. He smiled at her broadly. She smiled back uncertainly, hating herself for having these reactions to him.

'I just thought I'd say goodbye,' he commented as she neared him. 'I have to head this way for my next flight.' He indicated another corridor. She nodded.

'It was really nice meeting you,' he added.

'Yes. It was nice,' she said. What else could she say? The person who had been sitting on the aisle seat in her row walked past them and apparently, he too was headed for a connecting flight. He glanced at the two of them and shook his head. She wondered what he had thought of the two of them when they had continued whispering and talking in the cabin, lost to the world.

'I hope we can catch up in Bangalore,' he said and to her shock and surprise, leaned forward and hugged her lightly. She stepped back, her heart beating erratically.

'I hope n-not,' she stammered and walked away, knowing that she didn't have time to relish the look of confusion on his face. She kept her back straight as she wheeled her carry-on luggage with her, heading towards the exit.

She really didn't want to see him again. If she cared for her sanity and for her mental peace, it was best if she never met him again. Sharing the flight with him, seated so close to him had shredded her nerves and she never wanted to go through that experience again. She knew she was lying to herself but what was the alternative? She definitely didn't want to become one of the many girls who mooned over him and wanted something more while he made excuses.

This trip had gotten off to an awful start. She didn't have time to dwell on him or whatever this shit was. Why did this have to happen to her *now*? She'd been excited and gung-ho about everything – the job, the chance to prove herself to her peers, the school and she'd been so excited about the conference.

Straightening up, she shook her head. She was not going to let one man derail her like this. She was going to put him out of her mind firmly and not think of him. Ever. Again.

FIVE

Confused and stung, Luqman watched her leave. He wanted to call out to her and ask her to explain but he knew that wasn't possible. Everything had been going so well and suddenly, he didn't know why, she had just shut down and closed herself off from him. She insisted that he had done nothing, but what else could it be? How had he offended her?

He'd fallen asleep after she had, after staring at her near-perfect features for a few minutes, waiting to see if maybe she was playing a trick or joking with him. But then her breathing had regulated and even though she was asleep, he didn't want her to think that he was creepy. So he had looked away, shut his eyes and fallen asleep.

Shaking his head, he adjusted his backpack and walked away towards the connecting flight. The man who had been sitting next to him on the aisle was walking on ahead. He knew he had a long flight now and he didn't look forward to being on it at all. All sorts of emotions warred inside him. This was more than the passing interest he normally felt towards girls who were attracted to him.

He remembered the moment he'd seen her, that feeling of being in the right place had been all too real. It was almost a physical feeling, that happiness he'd felt at knowing that he would be spending four hours with her.

He checked the boarding pass for his connecting flight details and then walked over to the gate where he was supposed to wait for another two hours. Still feeling shitty, he hoisted his backpack again and sat down on a chair. He wondered what she was doing right now. Picking up luggage? Would someone from the conference be there to meet her? Would she go to the hotel and crash for some time or would she take a hot shower and head to work?

Why couldn't he stop thinking about her, dammit? Why had he let her snub him that way? He realised foolishly then that he hadn't even taken her number. He had thought there would be time, that before they departed, he would ask for her number so they could stay in touch when he returned to Bangalore.

He was still ruing his foolishness, wondering if it would be all right to ask Ayub for Ana's number. Ayub would definitely know something was up, and maybe it was. Deciding to get some coffee, he got up, walked towards the nearest café and bought a cappuccino for himself. He looked up and saw the man who had been seated next to him. He was buying a coffee for himself too. He caught Luqman's gaze and smiling, walked towards him.

'My flight is in less than an hour and my gate is pretty far from here. But I wanted coffee and I'm so glad I bumped into you here,' he said.

Luqman nodded curtly. He wasn't in the mood to talk to people at the moment but the man didn't take the hint. He was well-dressed, wearing formal trousers and a grey shirt. He seemed to be a little older than him because he had a few greys in his hair, but they only made him look distinguished.

'I'm Haroun,' he said, offering his hand to Luqman. Luqman shook it reluctantly.

'Luqman,' he said.

'I know,' the man said. Huh?

'Do I know you from somewhere?' Luqman asked him, stepping back and looking at the man up and down.

'Um, no. But … I'm sorry. I didn't want to listen, but the two of you were whispering and talking and I sort of overheard everything,' the man said sheepishly.

Embarrassed, Luqman nodded. He'd forgotten about other passengers the moment he'd settled into the seat and noticed that Ana was his co-passenger. He'd just assumed no one would listen to them talk.

'Look, it's cool, man. Don't be embarrassed. A pretty girl like her, anyone would want to spend the entire flight just talking to her,' he said.

A flush crept up Luqman's cheeks. 'Yeah, whatever,' he said, not meeting Haroun's gaze.

'Okay, I have to go now, but I just thought I'd tell you that the two of you were very entertaining,' Haroun said. Luqman looked up at him, annoyed. He wanted to make a scathing remark but Haroun continued to speak. 'What I didn't get is … she was totally into you, man. Why didn't you do anything?'

What?

'What do you mean?' Luqman asked him. Haroun shrugged.

'Her body language, her tone of voice … everything suggested she was taken in by you,' Haroun said.

Shut up, Luqman wanted to tell him. Who was this man and what did he think of himself? And what could he possibly do on a plane? And how was it any of his business? What a douche, Luqman thought.

'I got to go now. Good luck and I hope you can get hold of her back in Bangalore,' Haroun said, picking up his laptop case and walking away from there. Luqman stared at the back of the man, shocked and angry. He had intruded into their personal space and he was giving him advice? How dare he?

But he redirected his anger towards himself. He had been an idiot. Even a stranger had been able to ascertain that Ana had been interested in him and what had he done? Just sat like an idiot and watched her walk away from him.

Suddenly, he didn't feel like having the coffee. He was already jittery. Should he ask for her number from Ayub right away? Should he call her now? But what would he tell her? Maybe it would be best to take her number from Ayub when he went back home. The three-week assignment now seemed three years long to him. Why had he said yes to it? But then if he hadn't, he would not have met her on the flight.

He walked back to the gate and took a sip of his rapidly cooling coffee. He wondered what she was doing, if she was thinking of him too, if she was missing him as acutely as he was missing her. He sighed. He'd been a complete idiot but he was going to go back to Bangalore and ask if he could meet her. He didn't care if he had two brothers ahead of him, waiting to get married. He could ask Ana to wait awhile. Hell, he could get Ayub to speak to Ana's father, to assure him that he was perfect for Ana.

SIX

Two weeks later

Ana stared at her father and shook her head slowly. Abbu mirrored her actions as well.

'Look,' he said, holding her shoulders.

'Abbu, please,' she said. This wasn't fair. She had just started her job here. 'I don't want to think of marriage yet!'

'But beta, when you get proposals like this, you don't turn them away,' Abbu said. He sighed and looked defeated. 'I worry about you all. I worry about this house and what's going to happen to it when I'm gone and ...'

'Abbu!' Ana said sharply. She wanted to call Tehzeeb and talk to her, ask her if she could intervene on her behalf. But she needed to make Abbu understand.

'What do you even know about these people?' she asked. 'Why do you think they're so perfect for me?'

'Their family is respectable and I have heard of them. They don't even want to come and see you at home because ...'

'Because?' Ana asked suspiciously.

'Apparently, the lady saw you at Tehzeeb's wedding. So she likes you already. They've asked us to come and see the boy and I'll be taking Ayub and a few of your uncles with me tomorrow. Once we've seen him and if we like him, we'll take things forward.'

Ana sighed and walked away to her room and then turned around when a thought struck her.

'Was this Taskeen Auntie's doing?' she asked. Abbu shook his head.

'No, no. Not at all. She had nothing to do with this. It's almost providential how this proposal came to us, beta. That's why I'm keen to see if it could be the right thing for you,' Abbu said.

'But Abbu, what about my job? You know how hard I've worked to get it and I can't abandon it just because … just because I'm getting married,' she said.

'No one is asking you to abandon the job. At least not yet,' Abbu said with a smile. 'Why don't you just continue doing what you do and if things work out here, then well and good.'

Nodding, Ana went to her room to get ready for school. She was late today but Abbu had caught her off-guard when he spoke about the proposal he had received for her.

Stop thinking about Luqman, she told herself furiously. He didn't deserve even a single thought. But sometimes when she wasn't really focusing on anything, he would creep into her head and remind her about that flight, those moments they had spent whispering and talking to each other, how magical and right it had all felt.

To her. It had felt that way *to her.* He hadn't felt that way or maybe he had but had decided that she wasn't worth pursuing. She dressed quickly, shoving him out of her mind because she had missed the 7 a.m. bus thanks to Abbu. Now there was a good chance she could be late and that was a problem, because the school valued discipline and tardiness among teachers or students was frowned upon.

Athiya was asleep. She had her periods and her cramps were pretty awful so she had decided to bunk college that day. She murmured sleepily as Ana raced about fixing her appearance and rummaging for her shoes. She glanced at her sister and felt a moment's envy for how ignorant she was of everything that was happening.

She had to call Tehzeeb and speak to her or she'd go crazy. She had to process these feelings for Luqman so she could put them away somewhere. She had to figure out a way to deal with the thoughts of him that appeared out of nowhere so she could accept whatever happened in her life. Her father was making plans for her marriage. She had to go along and pretend that she was okay with everything.

She had to pretend until it became true.

'Abbu! I'm leaving!' she called out and didn't wait for his answer. She hurried out of the house, pushed at the rusty gate and walked down the leafy lane. Around them, there were several developments coming up, houses being torn down and converted into apartments. She shivered when she saw the ruins of a house whose owners had tied up with a real estate company and had decided to build a monstrous-looking apartment in its place.

She reached the bus stop and was in time for the seven-thirty bus, thankfully. Hopefully, she'd be only ten minutes late for school today. She settled into a window seat and looked out as the bus trundled along. The school was far, almost at the other end of the world. Her house, Jasmine Villa, was in Fraser Town while the school was in Sarjapur Road, where most of the international schools could be found. It took an hour to reach there with no traffic but on most days, it took her just short of two hours. She hoped the commute wouldn't be longer than that today.

She picked up her phone and contemplated calling Tehzeeb but resisted the urge. Ever since Aslan had been born, Api didn't get to sleep properly at night and since she was still on maternity leave from work, she was most likely catching up on sleep at the moment.

She shut her eyes briefly and Luqman's face flooded her mind's eye.

Go, she told him firmly. You're not needed here. He didn't reply. He just gave her that charming grin of his and brought his face close to hers. She opened her eyes and he disappeared from view.

She focused on the plan for the day, the meetings she had scheduled with some of the students and the report she'd been compiling about the conference. The bus lurched and dipped as it went over a pothole and with its many stops, it soon started filling up. By the time she reached the school, she felt like she'd been through the wringer.

She checked the time on her mobile. It was a few minutes to nine. She was late but not too late. Heaving a sigh, she pulled out her ID card and flashed it at the security guard, who let her inside. Her day was full and she had no time to think of Luqman or even the proposal her father had received.

She was thankful that she had an office to herself as the counsellor and that she could relax a little before her workday began. But before anything else, she quickly typed out a message to Tehzeeb, asking if they could talk sometime soon. Tehzeeb replied almost immediately saying she was free to talk whenever Ana was free.

'Great. I'll call you during my lunchtime,' Ana texted back.

'Is this because of the proposal Abbu has arranged for you?' Tehzeeb replied.

Ana frowned at the screen. She wanted to tell her sister about Luqman but she also knew her sister would try to intervene. There was nothing to do there. So why bother? But who else could she tell about the feelings he'd inspired? Ana rubbed the back of her neck. These feelings were annoying and troublesome and she had to bury them somewhere deep inside.

'No, just like that,' she typed back.

'Sure. Aslan sends his drooly kisses,' Tehzeeb's message came up with a photo of Aslan's face, smiling his gummy smile at her.

Ana grinned, unable to stop the beam of happiness that she felt when she saw her nephew.

'Squish him on my behalf, please,' she replied.

SEVEN

Ayub looked at his father-in-law nervously. He and Tehzeeb had been married for more than a year now, but he was still awkward around her father. He knew Abbu still had some sort of resentment over his own father's machinations and how it had led Tehzeeb away from him. Tehzeeb assured him that it wasn't the case but he still felt like he was being judged in his presence.

He cleared his throat and smiled as they waited outside someone's house. He switched off the engine and turned to Abbu and realised he didn't have anything to talk to him about. But he was certainly glad that he had been recruited for this.

'So, um, Abbu, is Ana okay with this?' he asked finally. He cleared his throat again.

'I think she is,' Abbu said slowly, looking straight ahead.

'Um, uh, if you could give me the address,' he said as a burly uncle stepped outside his house and walked up to his car. They had to pick up another of Tehzeeb's uncles from nearby and then they would be going to see this prospective groom for Ana.

He had dropped Tehzeeb and Aslan at Jasmine Villa and picked up Abbu from there. He had been eager to join in, help in any sort of way and wished that the wrinkles from that one week of their life could be smoothed over completely until they were forgotten. This was a step in that direction.

'Yes, beta,' Abbu said, pulling out a piece of paper and squinting at it. He gave up finally and handed it to Ayub just as the uncle opened the door at the back and sat inside. Ayub said salaam and smiled and looked at the paper. It was an address in HRBR Layout, not too far from there. Since it was Saturday evening, there was a fair bit of traffic though.

Nodding, they drove to another uncle's house and once they were all accounted for, they started the drive down to Ana's prospective in-laws' home. Abbu was silent on the way and Ayub didn't know what to say. Finally, when they reached the turn off from the main road, he checked the address again.

'So, who are these people uncle-Abbu,' he amended quickly. Abbu turned to him and nodded.

'They actually, the mother I mean, she saw Ana at your wedding. So maybe they're people you know,' he said.

'Oh! What is the boy's name?' Ayub asked, surprised. Tehzeeb hadn't told him this. Maybe she herself hadn't known.

'Um,' Abbu squinted as though recalling the name and then straightened. 'Farhaan. Yes, that's his name.'

'Farhaan Ahmed? And his family runs a real estate company?' Ayub asked, even more surprised.

'Why, yes. Do you know them?' Abbu asked.

'Yes! I do! Farhaan's youngest brother Luqman is my childhood friend. My best friend actually,' Ayub said excitedly. This was so cool! Ana would be getting married to Farhaan!

'Oh! So you must be knowing everything about them!' one uncle said from the back seat.

Ayub looked at Abbu as he continued to drive. He knew the way now. He didn't need to rely on the paper.

'Well, I know Luqman and he's a gem. His brothers are also great. The family is good,' Ayub said happily. Luqman had been telling him that his mother was on the look out for a girl for his older brother. This was fantastic, he thought. Luqman's family was a much more conservative family than his own. They were honest, hardworking people as far as he knew. They wouldn't have been able to handle Athiya and her firebrand attitude, but soft-spoken and pretty Ana would fit right in.

Abbu listened quietly as he told them what he knew of Farhaan. Farhaan had done his MBA and then he had started helping in the family business and his younger brother Nouman had joined them after he finished his studies. Luqman was considered the black sheep of the family because he hadn't joined them and had instead done his master's in engineering and was working at a top IT firm in Bangalore.

'Farhaan changed the way the family was doing business. He brought it up to the next level. His father died when he was quite young but he took over the reins and has been responsible for their success,' Ayub said, praising his best friend's brother effusively. Abbu looked pleased.

'This is good. Now going and meeting them can be just a formality,' he said, folding his hands and placing them over his lap as Ayub brought his car to a halt outside Luqman's home. He wondered if his friend was in India.

As Abbu and the others stepped outside, he typed a quick message to him.

'Where are you? In India?' he hit send and then put the phone away. He'd know soon enough where he was, once he went inside the house.

Abbu perused the façade of the house and they pushed open the gates and walked inside. It was a stately mansion, smaller than his own but still magnificent when compared to Jasmine Villa. Ayub knew their house was a sore point for Tehzeeb's family – they loved it and they were a little embarrassed about it. But the love won over more often than not. He had come to feel a similar sense of fondness for the rundown house because it was where Tehzeeb had grown up. It had shaped her into the woman she was. Tehzeeb had tried explaining what the house meant to her but she couldn't express it.

'It's like a person, like my mother is still there. I can feel it,' she said. Ayub didn't know what that meant but he had held her close, because she always got emotional when she spoke of her mother and during her pregnancy, she was almost always emotional. Things were looking a little brighter now that Aslan was born. He smiled automatically when he thought of his son and his wife and then his phone beeped. He looked at the screen. It was a message from Luqman.

'No, dude. Not in India at the moment but coming back next week. I was going to text you actually,' Luqman had replied.

Ayub knew it would be rude to text but as they waited for the door to be opened, he swiftly typed out a text to his friend – 'You won't believe this but let me text you once this is done,' he said.

'Once what's done?' Luqman asked. Ayub smiled and put the phone away. If it was 5.30 p.m. here, it was most likely early morning for Luqman wherever he was. Let him sleep for a bit. He'd message him with the good news as soon as they finished here, he thought as the door was opened by Nouman.

Nouman was not as distinguished-looking as Farhaan and neither did he have Luqman's sharp good looks. He was slightly portly and had a somewhat snivelling air about him. He looked at Ayub in surprise and then at Abbu and the others.

'Oh! Ayub! What are you doing here?' he asked. But he seemed to understand what was happening and he pulled the door open further. Ayub smiled and patted Nouman's shoulder as they walked inside.

EIGHT

Ana was waiting for a chance to speak to Tehzeeb alone. Well, they were alone at home finally now. Athiya had gone to a friend's house and she and Tehzeeb were waiting for Ayub and Abbu to return. Ana felt something heavy settle in her stomach. She wasn't very happy at how fast things were progressing. What if Abbu liked the boy he had gone to see? What would she do if Abbu gave the go-ahead? She would have to just go along.

But did she want to? Tehzeeb was feeding Aslan in their bedroom and she was sitting outside in the living room. She hoped Api would put him to sleep and come outside so they could talk before Abbu returned. She was still not sure how much to tell her about Luqman. The phone call they had promised each other hadn't happened and Ana had let it be because Tehzeeb had texted her that she would be coming over with Ayub when he went to see the boy.

For the past two weeks since she had returned from Malaysia, she hadn't been able to completely push him away from her thoughts. She hated herself for being so helpless when it came to her emotions. Why did he affect her so much? And why couldn't she get rid of the thoughts about him?

Tehzeeb stepped outside the room and shut the door gently. She collapsed on the sofa beside her and put her head back on the headrest.

'Exhausted?' Ana asked.

'You have no idea,' she said, wincing as she fixed her bra. 'Stupid boobs start leaking if I don't feed him on time and sometimes even after I'm done feeding him.'

'Ugh. TMI,' Ana said, shuddering a little but she glanced at her sister who looked content. 'You're happy no?'

'Very. Alhamdulillah. It's hard to even put it in words,' she said, patting Ana's hand.

Ana smiled. She wanted that too but every time she thought of the future, Luqman's name or face appeared before her. She sighed deeply. It was time to tell Tehzeeb some of the truth maybe. To gauge her reaction. Even then, what did it matter? Why tell her sister about her heartbreak because Luqman was never going to be in the picture?

'Tell me what's on your mind. You've been very quiet since I got here and we never got to talk on the phone too. Something's bothering you,' Tehzeeb said.

Ana looked at her sister's face and the shadows under her eyes and sighed.

'So, remember when I went to Kuala Lumpur?' Ana began. Her stomach started contracting, the moment the thoughts of Luqman came. Her mouth dried. She realised she was eager to share what she had felt with someone finally and she was glad it was her sister.

'Yeah, of course I remember. I'm so proud of you,' Tehzeeb said patting her hand.

'Of what? Travelling alone?' Ana scoffed. Tehzeeb cocked her head and looked at her sister.

'I meant attending the conference, representing your school,' Tehzeeb added.

Ana nodded. 'Okay, so …' she took a deep breath. Here goes nothing.

'So?'

'So, you wouldn't believe who was on the flight with me,' she said.

Tehzeeb's brow furrowed. 'Who?' she asked.

Ana realised she had to clear her throat once. And then once more, because his name kept getting stuck in her throat.

'Luqman,' she said.

Tehzeeb's eyes grew wide. 'What? How come you didn't tell me?'

Ana shrugged, deciding to play it cool. 'I, well, um, it didn't seem that important,' she said. Her face was pink.

'Liar,' Tehzeeb said, smiling. 'So what happened?'

'Nothing. He was actually sitting right next to me on the flight,' Ana said quickly, looking down. The scarred wooden coffee table in front of her suddenly seemed to be more interesting.

'Ana, what aren't you telling me?' Tehzeeb asked her sister quietly.

When it came to saying the actual words, it sounded so silly and rubbish, Ana thought frantically. How did they make it look so easy in the movies and books?

'It was … nice, sitting with him, talking,' Ana said finally. Nice? Was that what it was? It was much more than that.

'Okay?' Tehzeeb was still looking at her in a scrutinizing manner. Ana's heart was beating fast. What should she tell her?

'And that's it. It was, he was …' Ana swallowed.

'He was what?' Tehzeeb asked sharply. 'Did he misbehave with you?'

Ana shook her head frantically. 'No, he didn't. He was really nice Api. He … I was nervous about flying for the first time and h-he held my hand for a bit.'

'Oh. He did?' Tehzeeb asked, her eyes narrowed.

'Shit. What is this even?' Ana asked, covering her eyes and shaking her head. 'I can't believe I'm saying this but I think I know why Maira was so torn up over him.'

Tehzeeb inhaled. 'Are you saying …'

Ana tried to swallow again but her mouth was dry and her throat felt poky and strange.

She nodded. 'I just … I think I have a crush on him.'

Whew. She had said it.

'And what about him?' Tehzeeb asked. Ana looked at her unhappily.

'I don't know. We shared a moment, actually many moments but he kind of, I don't know, I realised he wasn't that into me. I froze after that and I told him I was sleepy and I tried to ignore him for the rest of the flight,' Ana said.

Tehzeeb looked anxious. 'Why didn't you tell me after you came back Ana? Why are you saying this now? Abbu has gone with Ayub to see a boy for you. How can you be okay with that, especially if you feel this way about Luqman?'

Ana winced. 'What does it matter, Api? It was just a stupid crush. He didn't feel the same and I definitely didn't want to be another Maira who took so long to get over him.'

'Are you sure?' Tehzeeb asked, placing her hand on Ana's.

Ana shrugged. 'Like I said, what does it matter? He's got that way about him. I think women just succumb to his charms wherever he goes. I don't want to be yet another notch in his belt or whatever.'

Tehzeeb sighed. 'I don't know about that. What if he

felt something too? Was he staying in Malaysia? Did you meet him after that?' Ana shook her head.

'No, he was headed to the US from there. He's still there, I think. He didn't even bother to take my number so there's *definitely* no interest from his side.'

'It's just so weird. I wish you didn't have to go through this,' Tehzeeb sighed.

'I wish that too. Every time I think about him, I go hot and cold and I get all sorts of weird and inappropriate thoughts,' Ana said.

Tehzeeb smiled and shook her head. 'I remember that stage when I met Ayub for the first time,' she said.

Ana shook her head vehemently. 'This isn't the same. You two felt something together and that brought you to each other. Here, I'm just another stupid dumb girl who got a crush on him just because he sat next to me on the flight.'

Tehzeeb nodded and patted her hand. 'Well, I'm glad you told me sweetie. It's okay. If luck will have it, you'll never see him again in your life.'

'That's what I'm counting on too,' Ana said, and hugged her sister impulsively. She was glad she had confessed this to her. It had been eating away at her all these days. Aslan woke up then and rolling her eyes, Tehzeeb went inside to fetch him.

They sat outside, in the living room, playing with him, and Ana thought that maybe, just maybe if she went into her marriage with her eyes wide open, she may not have Tehzeeb Api and Ayub Bhai's epic love story, but she'd be able to manage just fine.

NINE

Luqman sat up in his bed and yawned. The utilitarian apartment where he was staying was occupied by him and another techie from Hyderabad who kept to himself. Luqman couldn't wait to finish working on the release and return to Bangalore. He had been a fool not to take Ana's phone number from her or even from Ayub.

He picked up his phone once more and frowned. It was now 8 a.m. on a Saturday which meant that in India it was probably Saturday night. What had Ayub meant when he texted him? He had waited for Ayub to reply but when he hadn't, Luqman had dozed off, dreaming about Ana, her eyes, the shape of her mouth, the feel of her soft hands in his.

Now he turned his phone in his hand absently, wondering if he should call Ayub and talk to him. But first, should he call Ammi and speak to her? She had called him twice yesterday when he was stuck in an end-of-the-week meeting and he hadn't been able to call her back and talk to her.

His indecisive mood was cut short when his phone rang once more. It was Ammi. Smiling, he answered the phone and he realised she was chattering away excitedly like he already knew what she was talking about.

'Slow down Ammi. What are you saying?' he said, standing up and stretching. He'd better go to the gym nearby and work off some of this listlessness, he thought, as Ammi went on about fixing his older brother Farhaan's marriage.

'Oh wow! That's wonderful,' Luqman said, turning to the mirror and staring at his body. Finally, one down, one more to go and maybe if things worked out, he could … he could ask for Ana's hand. But he wanted to be with her even before that. And he wanted to get her number from Ayub, so he had to focus and listen to what Ammi was saying.

'The girl's family left just sometime ago. We have had all the important discussions and we have even fixed the engagement date for next month. You better be in India then,' Ammi said, chiding him.

'Yes, yes, Ammi. Obviously, I'm going to be there for Farhaan Bhai's engagement. I hope he's happy,' he added.

'Of course. I'm so glad I had this brainwave,' Ammi said.

'Brainwave?' Luqman asked, pushing up his vest and splaying his hand on his abs. He pulled down the vest and was about to topple back into bed when Ammi's next words froze him.

'Yes! I had already seen her at Ayub's wedding and then at his house as well during his wife's baby shower. So we did away with all the formal girl-seeing thing that people do,' Ammi babbled on.

'Er, who is this family? Who's this girl?' Luqman asked. He felt a strange sensation in his stomach, a kind of knotting and unknotting that made him want to throw up. He gripped his phone tightly in his hands. Surely Ammi didn't mean …

'Ayub's sister-in-law, Ana,' Ammi said, laughing effusively. Luqman was still looking at his face in the mirror and he saw his expression change. He was taking shallow breaths and his mind was racing furiously. What the fuck? What had just happened?

He couldn't speak. His tongue had frozen.

'Luqman? Are you still there?' Ammi asked, her voice rising with maternal concern.

He still couldn't answer her. Breathing heavily, he ended the call and threw the phone on the bed where it bounced once and nearly fell on the floor. The phone started ringing once more but he ignored it and sat down staring into space.

Fuck. He had to put a stop to this. But how? Ammi said the engagement had been decided already. If he intervened, Ammi would be shocked and she was so old-fashioned, she would blame Ana somehow and never agree to him marrying her.

His phone stopped ringing and he picked it up immediately. He had to talk to Ayub before his mother called him again. He dialled Ayub's number but it was engaged. Sweat streamed down his face and with shaky hands, he hit the redial button and kept it up until the call connected.

'Where are you?' he asked Ayub as soon as he answered.

'Going back home. Why?' Ayub asked, sounding surprised. 'Everything okay?'

'No, it's not okay,' Luqman said. He couldn't speak at all.

'Listen, man, you're on speakerphone and Tehzeeb is with me,' Ayub said. Oh shit.

'Maybe we should talk later,' Luqman said. He couldn't bring himself to talk about Ana in front of her sister. What could he say?

'No, talk. I know something is up. Tehzeeb is also looking anxious but she wouldn't tell me anything until we got in the car,' Ayub said.

'Luqman, if you liked Ana why didn't you say something? Why didn't you ask for her number?' Tehzeeb's soft, firm voice came through and he winced, shutting his eyes.

'What?' Ayub asked. Suddenly, there was the sound of a baby crying and Tehzeeb was murmuring soft words of endearment to quieten the baby. 'Wait, I'm stopping the car for a bit.'

'Okay,' Luqman said. He felt sick. Physically sick. Suddenly, Ayub's voice sounded louder and he realised he'd been taken off speakerphone.

'You idiot. You fool. Why didn't you say anything?' Ayub said.

'I …'

'Man, this is a mess. I also had no idea about … when did they meet?' Ayub had apparently asked the question to Tehzeeb.

'Shit. And Ana told you today?' he continued the conversation with his wife.

Luqman's stomach was cramping badly. He couldn't talk to Ayub like this. He had to speak to him face to face.

'Listen, I'm coming back right away. I can't wait another week,' Luqman said, walking to his laptop and opening a website to book his ticket.

Ayub exhaled. 'Maybe that's for the best. We'll talk when you get here,' he said.

Luqman wanted to ask him for Ana's number but now … it seemed even more presumptuous. He ended the call and looked at the earliest flight that could take him back to Bangalore.

When he finished paying for it, he realised he hadn't asked permission from his boss, Akshay, about coming back a week early. Screw that, he thought savagely. He typed out an email on his laptop, stating that there was a family emergency and he had to go back.

His phone rang again. Ammi. He didn't want to tell her that he was returning a week early. She'd be happy but suspicious. He let the phone ring for a few seconds and then answered wearily, knowing she would get worried.

'Are you all right?' she asked him sharply.

'Yes. I was feeling a little faint,' he said.

'Oh, mera baccha!' Ammi said. He winced and shut his eyes. 'Hating the food there? Is it too hot there?'

How was he expected to talk about mundane things like food and weather when his heart was on the verge of breaking?

He suddenly stopped short when another realisation hit him hard. Was it possible that Ana knew then that his older brother was the prospective groom her father had just met? Was she okay with it? How much had she told Tehzeeb?

TEN

Ana's nightmare began when Ayub and her father had returned home, laughing and talking and she and Tehzeeb looked at each other. Tehzeeb smiled and nodded and patted her hand gently. 'It's going to be okay,' she said to her softly.

Ayub walked inside and settled down on the sofa, a wide smile on his face.

'You will not believe whose house we just visited,' he said to Tehzeeb. Ana wondered if she was expected to act like a shy bride and disappear inside her room. Nonsense. She would do no such thing. She continued to sit there and wondered where Abbu was. He had gone to his room apparently.

'What's Abbu doing?' she whispered, getting up to see. She saw him emerge from his bathroom and unfold the prayer mat.

'Abbu said he wanted to read shukrana namaz because he's so happy with this proposal,' Ayub said, taking Aslan in his arms and looking down at his son.

'You were saying something,' Tehzeeb reminded him and Ayub, who was making his son gurgle, looked up at them and nodded.

'Yes! I couldn't believe it! We'd gone to Luqman's house to see the groom,' Ayub said. Ana looked at him, startled.

'What?' Tehzeeb asked, glancing at her quickly. She tried to keep her face impassive but Ayub, who was holding on to a squirming Aslan, hadn't noticed.

Ayub nodded, standing up and shaking his head when Tehzeeb tried to take the baby back.

'No, no, I can manage,' he said. 'So yeah, Ana's getting married to Luqman's older brother, Farhaan.'

Ana felt the blood drain away from her face. No, no, this couldn't be happening. Tehzeeb looked at her shocked. She seemed confused and Ayub hadn't understood what a bombshell he had just delivered. Thoughts crowded her head and they were replaced by images – of Luqman, sitting next to her, holding her hand, leaning close to her and she shut her eyes to blink them away.

Before she or Tehzeeb could say anything to Ayub, Abbu walked outside and he looked so happy that Ana froze. She stood up and he pulled her close and embraced her.

'My darling Ana. I'm so happy today. They seem to be such a nice and warm family and I really like this boy, Farhaan,' Abbu said.

Ana felt like the ground beneath her feet had cracked open. She wished she could just sway and faint like a Bollywood film heroine. Maybe this nightmare would stop then. She had just hoped that she would never see Luqman again. Maybe then she would have been able to eventually put him out of her mind, treat him like a crush; someone she had been mildly infatuated with for a little while. But if she was going to get married to his older brother, how on earth could she cope with living in the same house as him?

She extricated herself from Abbu's embrace and sharing

a pained glance with Tehzeeb, cleared her throat but found that she couldn't speak. She couldn't do anything. How could she say anything to Abbu? How could she ask him to reject this proposal because she had idiotically fallen in love with not just someone else, but the youngest brother of the prospective bridegroom?

Tehzeeb looked at her, concerned, and Ana couldn't take it anymore. She excused herself and walked away to her room, her steps quick, and sat down on the bed. She heard footsteps and looked up. Tehzeeb sat down beside her.

'This is not good,' she whispered. Ana nodded.

'But what can we do Api?' she asked.

Tehzeeb worried her lower lip with her teeth and expelled a breath. 'I'll speak to Ayub,' she said.

Ana shook her head. 'But what will you tell him? Oh god, this is so embarrassing!'

'It's not embarrassing!' Tehzeeb protested. 'Look, none of us had any idea this would happen!'

Ana covered her face with her hands and shook her head. 'I wish I'd never met him!'

'Don't say that. Everything happens for a reason,' Tehzeeb said gently. She pulled Ana into her arms and they hugged. Ana wanted to cry but her eyes would become red and Abbu would get suspicious.

'I don't know what to do!' Ana whispered into her sister's neck. Tehzeeb patted her back and sat back to examine her face.

'Listen, don't worry. Just stay put. I'll talk to Ayub. I'll tell him what happened,' Tehzeeb said.

'But that's the thing! Nothing happened! What can we possibly tell Ayub Bhai? That I fell in love with him just like Maira and now, I have to face him all my life as my brother-in-law? The worse part is that he doesn't feel anything for me,' Ana said, anguished.

'Are you sure about that?' Tehzeeb asked her. Ana looked up at her sister.

'What does it matter now? He could have taken my number, or gotten in touch if he was interested in me. Now I'll be his Bhabhi,' Ana said bitterly. 'I'm worse than any cliché in the world.'

'Nonsense. I will tell Ayub everything. Maybe ...' Tehzeeb looked into the distance, her face troubled.

'There's nothing anyone can do now,' Ana said.

'Don't say that. We can do plenty even now,' Tehzeeb said.

'Yes, but what excuse will we give Luqman's family? And did you see Abbu? He was looking so happy at this proposal working out. How will we be able to tell him anything?' Ana shook her head miserably.

'Ana, we'll figure something out. I'm with you,' Tehzeeb said as she got up. Ana nodded but didn't look at her sister as she left. She knew she ought to go outside and say goodbye to them because they were leaving. But she couldn't get up from the bed. She couldn't even cry.

Why did this happen to her? Her thoughts were anguished and churning and she tried to sleep but couldn't. She knew Athiya would come back and demand to know everything that happened and she wouldn't be able to hide anything from her sister.

After listlessly trying to sleep, she sat up and picked up her phone because it was ringing. It was Tehzeeb. She answered the phone but she didn't want to talk to anyone.

'Can we talk tomorrow?' she asked Tehzeeb. She looked out of the small window and saw that it was dark. She didn't know the time but it was probably late and she sighed, knowing it was time to make dinner.

'No, this can't wait,' Tehzeeb said. Ana heard some shuffling sounds in the background and then Tehzeeb's voice came clearer to her.

'Aslan, no. Yes, stay with your father,' Tehzeeb ordered. Despite her heavy heart, Ana smiled. Tehzeeb spoke to Aslan like he could understand everything she said. He was only six months old!

'What is it, Api?'

'Ana, Luqman just called us when we were coming back home in the car,' Tehzeeb said. Ana's heartbeat quickened.

'What?'

'Yes, and he was very disturbed at this proposal. He likes you too, Ana.'

Ana didn't know what to think but the room felt like it was spinning. She sat up on the bed, the slightest bit of hope growing inside her.

'But …'

'He's an idiot who thought he had all the time in the world. But he's leaving right away. He was supposed to come back next week but will be returning to Bangalore tomorrow.'

'Oh. But …'

'Listen, let him come back first. Let's see what he has to say. We can figure something out, surely,' Tehzeeb said.

Ana ended the call after that but she didn't allow herself to feel too hopeful. What could he do now? Still, she went to sleep, aware that she would most likely dream of him and if he had said that he liked her too, maybe, just maybe there was still a chance for them.

ELEVEN

Tehzeeb turned to her husband who was lying on the bed and staring at the ceiling. Aslan was asleep in his cot nearby and she moved close to Ayub, craving his touch. He put his arm around her shoulder as she snuggled near him but kept gazing upwards. The room was semi-dark, a night light now a permanent fixture since she had to wake up at odd times to feed Aslan or change his diaper.

'What's going to happen?' she whispered as she splayed her palm on Ayub's chest. She felt sick at heart. This would never have happened if she hadn't taken Ana along with her to meet Luqman. Ana wouldn't have developed these feelings for him and the situation could have been averted.

Ayub sighed, running his hand through her hair. 'I don't know, darling. I wish I'd known something at least. If only Luqman had told me or if Ana had told you earlier. I genuinely thought it was such a good proposal that I praised Farhaan even more in front of Abbu. This is all such a big mess.'

Tehzeeb closed her eyes. She couldn't get Ana's image out of her mind. Sad, devastated and shocked that this was happening to her. She couldn't imagine going through something like that.

'We have to stop the wedding,' she murmured. Ayub rubbed her arm briskly and turned so they lay facing each other.

'We can but ...'

'But?' she asked, looking at him intently. He shrugged.

'They already liked Ana. Abbu and your uncles liked Farhaan. They took the matter forward, setting an engagement date with plans to have the wedding in less than six months.' Tehzeeb's stomach roiled when she heard these words.

'What if we tell Farhaan's family that we don't want to get Ana married to him?' Tehzeeb asked.

Ayub pushed her hair back from her face and feeling emotional, she kissed the centre of his palm. 'That's the problem. How can we tell them such a thing? What reason will we give them? And how can we get Luqman married to Ana after that?' he asked softly.

'This is all my fault,' she said, knowing that somehow, she had set things in motion by breaking Maira's heart.

Ayub shook his head. 'No, it's not your fault. How were you to know that they'd sit together on the plane? Or that they would start liking each other? Either of them should have said something. Instead of just ...'

Tehzeeb looked at him intently. She realised then how lucky the two of them were, to have found each other despite everything. She thought of how foolishly she had almost thrown it away when she met Ayub before their engagement, thinking that they should call it off. She was glad he had persisted. Happy that she had found love with him in a way she had never thought possible. She wanted that happiness for her sisters. She didn't want despair in their lives.

'What are you thinking?' Ayub asked her softly. She shook her head, not sure she'd be able to tell him without tears welling up in her eyes. The emotional stress she had been feeling constantly during her pregnancy was less now but it hadn't completely disappeared.

'I want—' she took a deep breath. 'I want my sisters to be happy.'

'I want them to be happy too,' Ayub said, pulling her close.

'But how? How will we do this?' she asked, her breath hitching. She put herself in Ana's place and the very thought was horrifying.

'Let Luqman come back. We'll meet him and discuss. There must be some way in which we can salvage this,' Ayub said, kissing her lightly.

All her emotions rose to the surface and she held his head and kissed him back hungrily. If he was surprised, he didn't let on but he let her straddle him and she kissed his bare chest. He was breathing heavily, his arms running down her back.

'I love you, Ayub,' she whispered. It became too much for her suddenly, and she burst into tears.

'Shh,' he consoled her as she covered her face with her hands. Why was she crying? She had everything she wanted and yet, she couldn't guarantee the same happiness for her sister.

When her sobbing subsided, she put her arms around his neck and he sat up, bringing her up with her.

'I love you, Tehzeeb. I will do whatever I can to ensure that Ana is happy,' he said, cupping her face and kissing her. He wiped away the tear tracks from her face, pushed the sheets away from the bed and pulled her close until there was no space between them. They swapped places and he entered her, holding her hands above her head.

She whimpered a little. Ayub slowed down and kissed her. He was still inside her, poised above her and she touched his face, knowing how much she loved him. She was surrounded by him and his scent, and her body jerked a little when his hand travelled down to touch her between her legs. She clamped harder around him and he groaned.

She pushed at the sweat slicked hair on his forehead and he did the same to her. He smiled and she traced his smile with her finger. They knew they barely had time for leisurely lovemaking now, thanks to Aslan who woke up every now and then. But it didn't matter. The urgency, the need to slip into each other was stronger, now that their freedom was curtailed.

'Don't think. Just feel,' he whispered as he pushed her over the edge. She clung to him, her body shuddering in release, her mouth dry, her skin slick with sweat. He strained and then covered her body with his, trying to slow down his panting breath.

Later, when he had fallen asleep, his arm around her waist and leg thrown over hers possessively, she thought once more of her sister. She gently extricated herself from him, got down from the bed and padded towards Aslan who had started whimpering. Her breasts were tingling already and she knew it was time to feed him. As she settled down on the sofa with Aslan in her arms, he latched on to her breast hungrily. She stroked his soft, tiny back, rubbed her thumb over his barely-there eyebrows, and thought of how protective she felt towards him. She felt the same towards her sister.

TWELVE

Luqman was exhausted and his eyes burned as he struggled to stay awake on Sunday evening. He hadn't gone home yet but had instead checked into a hotel because he wanted to figure out what to do. He had called up Ayub on the way back from the airport and asked if they could meet. Ayub had been subdued and had agreed to come to the hotel directly so that Luqman could just crash after he spoke with him.

He paced his room, wondering how he had let all of this happen. He had met Ana a total of four times – at Ayub's engagement, when she had visited with Tehzeeb to speak about Maira, at Ayub's office and now, on the flight to Malaysia. Each time, he had been struck by her decisiveness, her clarity and her beauty. If he had been harbouring any doubts about what he felt for her, spending time with her on the flight had only made him realise that his feelings for her were real and very strong.

He cursed himself again for having thought that even if Ana got married off to someone, he'd be able to live with it. But the moment he thought of Ana with his older brother Farhaan, he felt sick enough to throw up. That was when the realisation struck that he didn't want Ana with anyone else. He wanted her for himself.

There was a knock on the door and he walked up and opened it. Ayub walked inside.

'Why are you in a hotel?' he asked looking around.

'I can't face my family yet,' Luqman replied, pushing his hair back from his forehead. Ayub looked relaxed and not worried at all. It was the complete opposite of the panic he was feeling.

'What do I do?' he asked Ayub who had settled himself into the single-seater in the room. Ayub shrugged.

'Come clean,' he said.

'What?' Luqman was horrified at the thought of doing that.

Ayub leaned forward and steepled his fingers. 'Look, there's no other way to get out of this situation. Go and speak to your mother and tell her that you saw Ana at my engagement and you really liked her. You do … you do feel something for her right? Or you wouldn't have …' Ayub trailed away.

Luqman took a deep breath. 'I love her,' he said. 'It took me a while to realise it but it's the truth. But talking to Ammi will be … I don't know if I can do it.' He shook his head.

Ayub frowned. 'There is literally no other way,' he said.

'What about Ana? Does she also?' he looked at Ayub hopefully. Ayub stared back at him and then sighed.

'Ana decided to tell Tehzeeb about her feelings for you yesterday, as something to get off her chest probably because she thought you weren't interested. She probably wanted to go into a new relationship with a clean slate. So you can imagine her shock when she found out who her prospective in-laws were.'

Luqman winced but he plunged ahead, knowing he

would lose courage if he didn't ask now. 'Can I have her number?' he asked.

Ayub looked conflicted. 'I have to ask Tehzeeb. And I have to ask Ana if she wants to talk to you.'

'But you said she had feelings for me,' Luqman asked, confused. Ayub shrugged.

'In the time I've been married to Tehzeeb, I've come to know her sisters pretty well. Ana thought you weren't interested and she decided to push you out of her mind.'

Luqman felt his throat dry up. 'Yes, but I realised my mistake and I want to rectify it,' he said.

'Whatever rectification you have to do, it has to be with your mother first,' Ayub insisted. Luqman stopped pacing and sat down on the bed, holding his head in his hands.

'You know how I feel about talking to Ammi about these things,' he muttered. He thought of his mother whom he always tried to protect from everything bad or ugly. He always felt that she had suffered enough when his father passed away around ten years ago.

'But this is your life. And Ana's,' Ayub said. He was right.

'Why does life have to be such a mess?' Luqman asked, exhaling loudly. He hadn't slept at all and now the jet lag was catching up with him. He felt nauseous and the thought of talking to his mother, telling her that the girl she had chosen for his older brother was the girl he loved, made him want to puke.

He glanced at Ayub who was texting on his phone. 'Seriously? My life is falling apart and you're ...'

'Asking Tehzeeb if I can share Ana's number with you,' Ayub completed, raising an eyebrow but still not looking up from his phone.

'Oh,' Luqman said. He had a lot of messes to clean up

and he didn't know where to begin. 'What did she say?'

His own phone beeped and he picked it up from the nightstand. Ayub had sent him Ana's number. He stared at the number for a few long seconds before adding it to his contacts. He looked up at Ayub and shook his head.

'Man, you had it easy,' he said. Ayub rolled his eyes.

'It's not like we didn't have our own problems,' Ayub reminded him. Luqman brushed it off.

'But you got married to her. The two of you fell in love with each other. You can handle anything if you have each other,' he said.

'True,' Ayub said, feeling grateful. 'I thank Allah every day for bringing us together.'

Luqman had stopped listening to him. He was looking at Ana's Whatsapp profile photo, a quote on a black background that said, *'When life gives you lemons, grab the tequila and salt'*. His finger hovered over the screen, wondering what he should tell her. 'Hi' sounded redundant. He had so much to discuss with her and he didn't know where to begin.

He realised Ayub had walked up to him when he put his hand on his shoulder. 'I'm off now. My advice - talk to Ana. Don't text her,' he said. 'But also talk to your mother. Or this is all going to become even messier.'

Luqman nodded and stood up. He hugged his friend impulsively. 'I just feel like I missed the most important bus of my life,' he said.

Ayub shook his head and patted his back. 'No, you didn't. There's still time. Just make sure you don't mess things up further,' he said.

Luqman watched Ayub leave, and uneasiness rattled around inside him. The next few days were going to be absolutely painful.

THIRTEEN

'Who's the good-looking dude standing outside talking to Abbu?' Athiya asked as she came inside the room. Ana turned to her in surprise. She had been sitting by the window, looking out and wondering what was going to happen. Her phone was on the bed nearby and she had been waiting for Luqman to call her all day. Then she realised she didn't know what time his flight arrived and where he was. Would he speak to his mother right away? How was this going to play out?

'Who?' she asked her sister who dropped her college bag on the bed and started stripping out of her clothes as she headed into her shower.

'I don't know. Some tall guy, stepped out of his car and Abbu was just returning from his walk and they were standing outside talking to each other,' Athiya called out over her shoulder. The shower started running and Ana walked outside curiously. Abbu hadn't come inside. Who was he speaking to? She went to the doorstep and paused as she looked out towards the gate. Abbu was indeed talking to someone just inside the gate. It was a very familiar someone, whose side profile she could see and her heart skipped a beat. It was Luqman.

What was he doing here? Was he speaking to Abbu before speaking to her? What was wrong with him? Why hadn't he called her first? She rushed outside to see if she could prevent some big disaster from happening. What would she tell Abbu? That she was in love with him? Perspiration dotted her upper lip. It was a sultry evening and there was no breeze.

Abbu saw her coming out of the house and he smiled. The garden was filled with the perfume of the jasmine flowers that gave their house its name. At the moment, it felt stifling to her. She felt hot and sticky and uncomfortable with what she was about to do.

'Um, what are you doing Ana?' he asked. Luqman turned around swiftly and Ana stopped short. It wasn't Luqman. It was someone who looked eerily a lot like him but he wore glasses and his hair was cut differently in a shorter and starker style. The difference in features registered rapidly on her mind and she realised she was staring at Luqman's brother, Farhaan, her soon-to-be betrothed. Shit.

'I … er … sorry,' she stammered and walked away from there.

'No wait!' Abbu called out. She paused, her face turning pink. Her heart was racing now and she licked her lips.

'Yes, Abbu?' she said, turning around slowly, keeping her gaze lowered.

'This is Farhaan,' Abbu said with a smile. I know, she wanted to say. She nodded and said salaam quietly.

He replied similarly in a deep voice. She pursed her lips, not wanting to run away like a shy bride but not knowing what else to do. She didn't know what he was doing here. Why had he come here? Was he spying on them? Had he been checking out their house and Abbu caught him while he was at it?

'I asked him to come here,' Abbu said and Ana looked at him, surprised. Why? Her face turned warm even though she knew Farhaan wasn't staring at her and she nodded and turned away.

'Please make tea for us,' Abbu requested. Straightening her back, supremely aware of how she looked, she nodded and went into the house. She rushed to her room where Athiya was sitting at the dressing table, drying her hair.

'The good-looking guy outside is Farhaan,' Ana announced and Athiya turned around surprised. She was wearing a light yellow cotton top that she had paired with a flared white shalwar and she looked like she was ten years old.

'You mean Farhaan as in ...' she asked, getting up and coming to sit with her on the bed.

Ana nodded. She sat down on the bed, aware that Athiya would be very angry with her if she didn't tell her about Luqman. But what was there to tell? And there was no knowing what Athiya would do if she found out the truth.

'Oho, I see someone's feeling very shy,' Athiya said, poking her shoulder with a finger and Ana looked up at her and shook her head.

'Shut up. Abbu is inviting him inside and he wants tea,' Ana said.

'So you go and make it,' Athiya said, sitting cross-legged and getting comfortable.

'Please make it?' Ana said, reaching for her phone. The notification light was blinking on it.

Athiya sighed. 'Fine. You owe me one. Or actually, you owe me a lot considering the number of times you've fobbed off tea-making duty to me,' she said, getting up.

'Wear your dupatta and go!' Ana said, her eyes widening

when she saw that her sister was walking outside as she was. She looked like a ten-year-old only because she was short and her features seemed younger and unrefined. But you just had to look at her bust, and well, you'd know she wasn't a child.

'Fuck the dupatta man,' she said as she went to the kitchen just as Abbu opened the door of the house and stepped inside with Farhaan.

Ana stood at the doorway of her room, and she could see Abbu lead Farhaan into the hall after which she couldn't see them so she stepped into the narrow corridor.

What was Abbu doing? Why had he asked Farhaan to come here? The two of them kept up a quiet conversation and despite trying her best to overhear them, she couldn't understand what they were speaking about.

'Sure, uncle,' she finally heard Farhaan say. What? What had Abbu asked him to do? She still couldn't hear anything clearly. When she looked up after a few minutes, she saw that Athiya was holding the tea tray at the threshold of the kitchen, a wry look on her face.

'Shit,' Ana muttered. She knew her sister had walked out of the room without her dupatta on purpose. So she would come and take the tea and go outside. Idiot girl.

Ana walked up to the kitchen, took the tea tray from Athiya's hands and made a face at her. 'This isn't funny you know,' she said.

'Why? You could have also brought my dupatta to me,' Athiya countered. Glowering at her because she was right, Ana walked outside, trying to keep her face blank.

Farhaan looked up when she walked into the hall and kept the tray on the coffee table before them. Abbu smiled at her almost beatifically but she didn't stay there. She walked away from there quickly, back to her room, her heart pounding.

This was not good. Whatever Abbu's reasons for calling Farhaan here, she knew that his heart would break if she told him that she couldn't marry him. Abbu looked completely at ease with Farhaan, even more than he did with Ayub Bhai which was quite maddening. Ayub Bhai was such a wonderful person but she had not seen her father warm up to him like he had with Farhaan.

She picked up her phone and stared at it. There were four missed calls and one message from the same number. She tapped it open and it felt like the world outside had receded altogether. It was from Luqman.

'Can we talk?' it said.

Her stomach cramped almost painfully as she considered her options. Luqman's brother was outside, getting friendly with her father. Her sister could come inside any moment and she wouldn't be able to hide the truth from her.

'Not now,' she typed back and hit send. She saved his number and opened Whatsapp, refreshing it. He was online and her heart started racing once more. She tapped open his profile photo and stared at it. He had that same jaunty expression on his face, a smile that stopped her heart and almost made her smile back in response until she remembered that Farhaan was still sitting in her living room.

FOURTEEN

Farhaan shifted in his seat uncomfortably. He had been taken aback when he got the phone call from Mr Yusuf earlier this evening. Some instinct told him not to mention the call to his brother, Nouman, who was leaving for home just then. Nouman was a blabbermouth and he would have told Ammi, who would have called him and then there was no saying how she would have reacted.

He looked around at the living room where he was seated on a sofa that had seen better days. Mr Yusuf – he couldn't bring himself to call him anything else, was looking at him quietly as they sat sipping tea. So this was his future in-law's home.

The tea was good, he realised as he took a sip. It was strong, kadak, just the way he liked it, and the ginger didn't overpower it but lifted it to a different level. Had Ana made it? He had seen her for the first time today and he had been pleasantly surprised to see how pretty she was. He had just gone along with whatever Ammi asked him because that was what he did all the time. Ammi said she had seen Ana twice earlier and that she was perfect for him and he'd said, sure, okay, fine, whatever.

He was thirty-one years old. People younger than him

were already married and had two kids, at least, to show for it. He had been so busy with expanding his father's business that he hadn't focused on himself, hadn't even thought about marriage until Ammi spoke to him earlier this year. He had realised just then that he was watching life from outside, like a spectator and not really living it.

Sometimes he envied Luqman who had walked away from the family business because he could, because he was the youngest, because no one had any expectations from him. But being the oldest meant that everyone looked up to him, all his actions were scrutinised and he had given no reason to anybody to disrespect him.

He took another sip of the tea and settled back into the sofa. Mr Yusuf had called him to ask him if he would assess the land. Was he planning to sell it? Maybe he thought that since he, Farhaan was in real estate, he would have an idea. Well, it was prime land and it would easily go for at least three crores, he thought.

The house had been painted recently but it was already showing signs of wear. The flooring was red oxide and it was pitted and scarred in places. He looked up and just then glimpsed someone in yellow who made a dash for the room beyond. Amused, he wondered who it was. It couldn't be Ana since she was wearing something in dark pink. Maybe it had been the girl who had come inside the house when he had just arrived.

He hadn't taken a proper look at her because he was talking to Mr Yusuf. He probably should connect with Ayub if they were going to become brothers, he thought. It wasn't a very comforting thought. Ayub was like Luqman, handsome, a little brash and a sense of living life to the fullest while he, he knew what they thought of him. Dull and boring.

Maybe this was all meant to happen, he thought brightly. Maybe his life would change for the better once he got married to Ana. He had met Ayub two days ago when they had visited his house. He had been warm and friendly and that had surprised him. Maybe he needed to reconnect with his own friends too. He had let everything slide since he had taken over the reins at the business.

He had been finishing his undergraduate studies when Abba had died.

He cleared his throat when he finished drinking the tea and placed the cup back on the tray on the coffee table. Mr Yusuf had finished his tea too.

'So, um, what exactly do you need my help in, Mr … um … uncle?' he asked, smiling slightly.

'See, the land was under dispute for many years which is why I couldn't touch it then. But the case was resolved two years ago. I have been contemplating what to do ever since then. I first thought I'd sell the house and divide the proceeds among my children but at the same time, I never want them to feel like they don't have a home to come back to.'

Farhaan listened to him in silence and nodded. Mr Yusuf continued.

'I had been contemplating getting into a joint development project with some builders but I was worried about what it would mean for us, what I would get out of it and how I would be able to justify it to my daughters.'

'Then what do you want to do?' Farhaan asked. Joint development projects were lucrative and this was a good piece of prime land.

'I wanted to ask you if *you* would be open to doing a joint development project with me because I can trust you.

You are, after all, going to be my son-in-law,' Mr Yusuf said.

Farhaan straightened and nodded. This was tricky and he had to navigate it properly.

'Of course. I need some time to evaluate everything and to discuss it in the office and we can work on it together, uncle,' he said.

Mr Yusuf smiled then and Farhaan was taken aback at how much warmth there was in his eyes and his smile. It reached out to him, to his heart and opened the fist that he had closed around it so tightly all those years ago since his father had died. For the first time in the longest while, Farhaan felt a different sort of happiness and it was like he couldn't contain it within himself. He stood up.

'Call me Abbu,' Mr Yusuf said as he stood up too and patted his shoulder. He pulled him into a warm embrace. That infinitesimal change inside him expanded and threatened to overpower him, making him want to cry like a baby. He had better get away from there, he thought nervously. He looked up and saw that yellow streak was actually the young woman who had come into the house when he had arrived. She stood just at the threshold of the living room, as though about to enter it but had stopped on seeing him hug her father.

That was probably Ana's younger sister, he thought as he stepped back and smiled at Mr Yusuf.

'Okay Abbu,' he said. The words didn't stick in his throat as he thought they would. When he looked up, the woman was gone.

FIFTEEN

Luqman rubbed his eyes as the fatigue of the past two days overtook him. He had fallen asleep waiting for Ana's phone call but it never came. Or maybe it had and he had been asleep, he thought as he tried to force his eyes open long enough to squint at his phone's screen. Shit, yes, she had. Three times. He glanced at the time. It was 3 a.m.

Obviously not the time to speak to her but he texted her quickly, apologising, saying he had fallen asleep because he was tired. To his surprise, she texted back, asking if he was awake and they could talk now.

He dashed into the bathroom, splashed some water on his face and rubbed his eyes again. He looked at his face in the mirror and winced. He looked dreadful but it was okay. It wasn't like they were getting on a video call.

'Coming,' he whispered as his phone began to ring. He grabbed it off the nightstand and swiped the screen to answer it.

'Hello,' her voice was soft, whispery and it sent an ache straight into his heart. He wanted that voice, the speaker of that voice for himself.

Gulping, he cleared his throat. 'Hi,' he said. There was silence as they both didn't know what to say to each other. He wanted to tell her that he loved her but it seemed strange to begin the conversation with that.

'Ana, I'm sorry for this mess,' he said finally.

'Why are you sorry? It's not your fault,' she said.

'In a way, it is. If I had taken initiative, none of this would have happened,' he said, lying down in the bed and looking at the ceiling above.

'Yes, but how would you have known this would happen? But ...'

'But?'

'But if I had known that ... that you liked me or anything of that sort, I wouldn't have given the go-ahead to Abbu to go to your house,' she said.

He shut his eyes. That was on him. She continued speaking. 'I couldn't bring myself to tell anything to Abbu because I didn't think there was anything here between us,' she said.

He cut her off. 'You really think that? After that flight, you really think there's nothing happening between us?'

'I ...' she paused but went on, her voice suddenly stronger. 'Well, *I* certainly felt something but I had no clue you felt it too.'

'You were the one who went to sleep,' he countered. Why was he arguing with her? He wanted her, didn't he?

'I'm sorry, I didn't mean to get aggressive,' he said and exhaled loudly.

'I went to sleep because I couldn't take it any longer,' she said.

'Couldn't take what any longer?' he asked, surprised. He glanced out of the windows and saw that it was dark but a fat moon hung in the sky, like it was waiting for something.

'Sitting so close to you,' she said finally. His eyes widened and he sat up immediately. Blood rushed to his head and he shook his head a little.

'Anyway,' was she going to go on like she hadn't just said something so important?

'No what did you mean by that?' he stopped her.

'Nothing, I just …' she trailed off.

'Ana, now's the time we need to be honest with each other and come clean about our feelings,' he said.

'But to what end Luqman? What does it matter what I feel for you? Our families have met and they're taking things forward, setting an engagement for next month and organising the wedding within the next six months,' she spoke fiercely.

'I will take care of it,' he said, not knowing how he was going to do that.

'How?' she asked. It was a valid question and he didn't know the answer to that. Ayub's words came back to him. 'I'll speak to my mother about us.'

'She will hate me,' Ana said simply. She was right. Ammi would think Ana was very forward and she would not be happy at all about Luqman wanting to marry his older brother's intended bride.

'I will tell her that I saw you and fell in love with you and you had nothing to do with this,' he said. There was silence on the other end.

'Ana?' he asked.

'Fell in love?' she whispered. He winced. He hadn't intended to blurt it out like that, like it was a cheap trick, like it didn't mean anything to him. He swallowed and then took a deep breath.

'It's true, Ana. I'm in love with you and I should have told you something on the flight but I didn't. I let my usual insecurity about Farhaan Bhai get in the way, thinking that there was no way Ammi would agree to me marrying you when he wasn't yet married,' he said. 'But when I heard that Ammi wanted to get you married to him, I realised then ...'

'Luqman, what if I was getting married to someone else? Would you have been okay with that?' she asked. 'Or would you have realised that you loved me then?' Luqman flattened his hair with his hand, in exasperation.

'I don't know the answer to that Ana and the truth is, I don't know anything anymore. I've never felt this way about anyone and I just want to embrace that. Live with that. Live with you. Marry you,' he said. She gasped softly.

'I'm sorry I'm just saying all these things to you without any prelude, without making it into a special occasion, which you completely deserve, by the way, but I've already delayed everything and I feel like I'm making mistakes no matter what I do. I just needed you to know these things before anything else,' he said.

She sighed. 'Your brother had come home earlier, when you called me. He was sitting outside talking to Abbu,' she said.

What?

'Farhaan Bhai?' he asked, in shock. His blood froze but strangely, sweat broke out on his forehead. He hadn't considered Farhaan Bhai's feelings in all of this. What if Farhaan Bhai had taken one look at Ana and fallen in love with her? Much like what had happened with Ayub and Tehzeeb?

'Yes. Apparently, Abbu had asked him to come. When he left, Abbu told us that he wants to do a joint development project with ... with Farhaan because he trusts him and since he's going to be his son-in-law,' Ana said.

Shit. This just kept getting even more difficult, Luqman thought frantically.

'Did you talk to him?' Luqman asked.

'No. But I don't know what to do, Luqman,' she said, sounding distressed. 'I mean, my father is genuinely happy about this proposal.'

'I'll speak to Ammi when I go home today,' he said, feeling resolute.

'And until then?'

'Until then, just don't say anything to anyone. We'll sort this out. *I'll* sort this out. Promise,' he said huskily.

'Okay,' she said softly. 'I think I should hang up now.'

'No, wait. You said something earlier,' Luqman reminded her. He rubbed the stubble on his chin roughly.

'What?' she asked, surprised.

'About why you went to sleep,' Luqman said. 'On the plane.'

'Oh. Um, I …' she was stalling.

'What did you mean by that? Because I was sitting so close?' he insisted.

'I wanted to kiss you,' she said, shocking the hell out of him. 'But you kept talking about your brothers and I decided you were never going to make a move. That's it.'

'That's it?' he repeated incredulously. Despite everything that was going to shit around them, despite all the hurdles that lay ahead, he felt stupendously happy in this very moment.

'Yes, I …' she tried to sound suitably pissed off but he couldn't stop grinning.

'We should have had this conversation in person,' he said.

'Oh god. Why did I have to say all that to you?' she groaned.

'I'm the world's biggest idiot to not have realised what you wanted,' he said.

'That you are,' she agreed readily.

'But I promise I'll make amends,' he said.

'You'd better. Or I'll become your Bhabhi in a few months,' she said.

Yuck. Thank goodness she didn't say that she'd be kissing Farhaan instead of him, he thought with a shudder.

'Not going to happen,' he promised her.

'I'll hold you to it,' she said. 'Okay, I have to go now. Bye.'

But she didn't end the call. He could still hear her breathing softly and he realised he was wildly turned on at the thought of Ana wanting to kiss him.

'I want to kiss you too,' he said.

'I know,' she replied promptly and giggled. The sound warmed his heart. He really was feeling a lot better now that he had spoken to her. To his surprise, she expressed the same thing.

'I've been feeling awful since I came back from Malaysia and worse since the past two days,' she said. 'But talking to you has made me feel so much better.'

'I feel better too,' he admitted.

'I love you, Luqman,' she said suddenly and his face turned warm. Dammit. Why were they speaking on the phone? 'I hope I don't get married to your brother. I don't want to be with him when I'm in love with you.'

He drew in a breath. 'Don't. Don't even joke about it,' he said.

'I'm not joking. I'm very serious. Okay, I'm really going now. I can hear Athiya getting up,' Ana said hurriedly and she ended the call this time.

Luqman stared at his phone for the longest time before he fell asleep once more.

SIXTEEN

Athiya knew something was going on with her sister. She was behaving strange and there was a sadness to her face that was worrying her. Why wouldn't she tell her anything? She was sure that Ana would have told Tehzeeb whatever it was that was troubling her. The two of them had always been closer to each other, treating her like a baby, protecting her and while it annoyed her, it also made her feel left out.

She woke up when she felt Ana get out of bed in the middle of the night. She fumbled around for her phone and squinted at it to see the time. What was Ana doing? She peered through the darkness and saw her sister leave the room and she got down too, her heart thumping painfully.

She knew something had been going on the past two days. Ever since Abbu came back with Ayub Bhai, Ana had been withdrawn, like she wasn't happy with the proposal. She should have told Abbu something if she wasn't happy, right? Why was she going through with it? To be fair, that Farhaan was quite the looker, although he seemed like the broody sort. He would actually be perfect for Ana, because she was also not very vocal. They'd get along beautifully, she thought.

As she walked towards the door, she tried to keep her

footfall soft and low and she strained to hear what was happening. Ana was talking to someone on the phone. Who would she talk to at this time of the night? Did Ana, of all people, have a boyfriend? She was always the stickler and the straight arrow of the family, never one to break any rules. And if she had a boyfriend, what was she doing, agreeing to marry Farhaan? Also, why hadn't she told *her*?

Or wait. What if Ana was secretly talking to Farhaan now? But why so late at night? She could have spoken to him at any time. Athiya smiled to herself. She was the sort of person who liked or disliked people immediately and often didn't give second chances to people. If she hated someone on sight, then that person would always be at the bottom of her list. If she liked someone, she'd find ways to defend them, no matter what. Thankfully, she had liked Farhaan. Just like she had liked Ayub Bhai, she thought.

She leaned in closer to try and hear better. She could only get snatches of the conversation. Ana sounded upset and it made Athiya want to run in and confront her. What was going on? Had Farhaan said something to anger her?

'I wanted to kiss you.'

Athiya's jaw dropped open. This was *her* sister? The one who gave Tehzeeb hell for sneaking off with Ayub Bhai on their engagement? The two of them thought she didn't know but she knew everything. Payback's a bitch, she thought gleefully.

Athiya wanted to go back to her room and plot ways on how to let her sister know she knew everything. Maybe her sister had already met Farhaan somewhere and had fallen in love with him. It wasn't hard to imagine it. He had that aloof vibe about him, the kind that made the girls crazy because they wanted to be the ones to break through the outer shell and bring out the inner lover boy. Or caveman. Whatever, she thought.

But she didn't go to her room. She hung around, hoping to hear more nuggets that she could use as leverage sometime later. She heard the word 'Bhabhi' and then 'Malaysia' and she frowned. What was that all about? Athiya felt a little uneasy inside. She stepped out, as far as she could without alerting Ana. She knew she had to hear more.

Ana's voice wasn't soft now but it was firmer, like there was a conviction to her words.

'I love you, Luqman. I hope I don't get married to your brother. I don't want to be with him when I'm in love with you.'

Athiya felt like her heart had stopped beating. Her skin felt clammy and cold and her mouth had dried up quickly. She tried to take in a breath and instead let out a squeak. Fucking hell. What was really going on? She realised that the sound she had made had probably reached Ana so she quickly went back to the room and lay down, her mind racing.

Ana was in love with Farhaan's younger brother Luqman? Shit. Shit. Shit. Had she met him in Malaysia? Was that where she had fallen in love with him? Oh god, this was such a mess! She knew she was breathing too heavily to pretend like she had been asleep. So she got up and went to the bathroom. When she came out, Ana was lying on the bed in her usual place.

She wanted to confront her sister and ask her outright what she was doing. But she wanted Ana to tell her everything on her own too. It hurt that her sister wouldn't confide in her.

She faked a yawn and then padded back to bed. 'Where

were you?' she asked Ana as she settled down beside her to sleep.

There was a pause and it looked as though Ana was contemplating her choices. Tell me the truth. I can try and help you, Athiya thought. Above all, she wanted her sister to be happy. She realised that while she knew nothing about this Luqman, she didn't want poor Farhaan to be trapped in a loveless marriage either. He didn't deserve that, surely.

'Just stepped out to get a drink of water,' Ana replied, her voice sleepy. Athiya stared at the ceiling in anger. She kept a tight rein on her emotions and it wasn't easy. She was always prone to temper outbursts and she was dying to give her sister a piece of her mind but she didn't say anything. Why should she? Her sister should have trusted her enough to tell her the truth.

Athiya thought of her father who had started making arrangements for the engagement. When he told them about the joint development idea, Athiya had hated it entirely. Why should they do this? The house was good enough as it was. But Abbu explained to them that this was for the best. The house was breaking down, and there was no saying when it would collapse. He couldn't afford to build something new on his own. Not now, at his age. But this way, they would all have a bit of Jasmine Villa for themselves.

Ana's breathing had become soft and regulated. Had she fallen asleep so easily? Her thoughts turned to Farhaan, the young man who had visited their home just hours earlier. She had spotted him embracing Abbu and she had been arrested by the look on his face – wonder, surprise and she saw a glint there, like there were tears in his eyes. She had walked away from there when he had noticed her.

For some reason, she couldn't get that image out of her mind. Farhaan didn't deserve this shit. If her sister didn't do anything and let the engagement carry on as usual, she was going to do something about it. She would go and tell Farhaan everything.

She felt sick at the thought of betraying her sister. But at the same time she felt angry towards her for not confiding in her. If Ana had told her something, anything, they could have called Tehzeeb too and they could have worked it out together. Instead, her sister was being secretive as usual.

We'll see about it, Athiya thought decisively.

SEVENTEEN

Luqman was feeling cheerful. Despite all the ways that things could go wrong in his life, there was a spring to his step. Ana loved him. She wanted to kiss him. Damn, he wanted to do much more than that to her. He knew he had to talk to his mother now.

His enthusiasm slightly dampened as he checked out of the hotel. His mother liked to behave like her sons were still teenagers. She didn't like anything that contradicted that viewpoint. But he had told Ana the truth. He was going to speak to his mother and tell her that he wanted to marry Ana. Surely, they could find another suitable girl for Farhaan Bhai?

He wheeled his luggage outside the hotel, adjusted his backpack which had his laptop and other stuff and then checked his phone to see if the cab had arrived. It was on its way. Excitement and dread warred inside him but he couldn't wait to meet his family, couldn't wait to see Ana again, and he really couldn't wait to make the two of them official. He didn't care what his mother had to say about this but he was determined now. Ana could not marry Farhaan Bhai.

The cab arrived and once his luggage was inside the

boot compartment, he settled down into the seat at the back. The driver, a young boy not older than twenty-two or twenty-three started driving and Luqman's phone pinged. It was Ayub. He wanted to know what he was doing.

Luqman contemplated calling up Ayub and telling him everything, about the phone call with Ana last night, about what they'd discussed but he stopped himself in time. It would be a better idea to have the discussion with Ammi first. Then he would talk to Ana and then call up Ayub and tell him that they were going to be related. They were going to be brothers now. He smiled to himself at that thought.

The cab moved along at snail's pace at first because of the traffic. He had booked into a hotel in Indiranagar and now had to head to HRBR Layout. His house was actually quite close to the airport but he had needed some time to figure things out. Anyhow, it shouldn't take long to reach home either, once the traffic let up, he thought. He had got caught in the morning commute traffic since it was a Monday. When they were on the relatively free Baiyappanahalli Road, the cab sped up.

He exhaled and looked out of the window. He wondered what his mother's reaction was going to be like. Would she start crying? Would she tell him he was being an ungrateful son? He was used to all the things she used to say to emotionally manipulate all three of them. While he and Farhaan Bhai knew it, Nouman always fell for it and was thus her favourite son because he capitulated to her demands all the time.

As they reached the HRBR Main Road, his anxiety ratcheted up a little. He sat straighter. He was twenty-nine. He was old enough to face his mother and tell her that he loved a girl. Even if that girl had been chosen for his brother. It was never a question of being afraid of his mother, but more of trying to live up to her standards and not disappoint her. Especially him. No matter what he did, he was never good enough.

His phone pinged again. It was Ayub once more asking if he was okay.

Rolling his eyes, he was just searching Ayub's number to call him as they crossed an intersection when a car from the other end jumped the signal and crashed into their cab. The phone slipped from Luqman's hand as the cab spun and hit the car that was behind them. There was a sickening crunch, the sound of metal scraping, a man shouting hoarsely, and people screamed even as a bike rider tried hard to brake but couldn't stop his vehicle from crashing into the car.

Luqman had been slammed into the side of the cab on the first impact and while he tried to protect his head, they were slammed twice more. His head hit the window as it crashed and shattered, he felt the metallic smell of blood fill inside.

He was going to die, he thought, horrified. He had no idea what had happened just now, except that his head felt like a squashed watermelon and the pain in his leg was excruciating. The cab had stopped spinning and he could hear people trying to extricate him and the driver from the cab.

Blood ran into his eyes and he blinked, trying to lift his hand to wipe it away but his arm couldn't move. His breathing was shallow and even though the cab wasn't moving, he still felt like they were spinning around. He welcomed the blackness when it enveloped him completely.

When he opened his eyes, he realised he was being taken in an ambulance. He wondered if he would survive the trip to the hospital. He wanted to talk to his mother before he died. He had to tell her. Something.

What was he going to tell his mother? He couldn't remember what it was. His BP was falling, someone called out and he blacked out once more.

When he regained consciousness, he was thankful that he was still alive. Doctors surrounded him and the pain in his leg was intense. His head ached and everything hurt. He remembered snatches of something, an important meeting, a discussion. With whom? Had he just finished it or was he going for it? Someone had better call his office and tell them that he couldn't make it to work today. Why was he in a cab? Why wasn't he in his own car?

Much later, when he opened his eyes, he saw nurses walking around. Various machines beeped and he was on a bed. Nearby, there were other beds as well. He realised he was in the ICU. When they saw he was awake, the nurse called up and spoke to someone, presumably a doctor.

Luqman was relieved he was still alive. When his mother came inside the ICU, she burst into tears and the nurses looked at her disapprovingly. He frowned, or tried to. He remembered that he had been anxious that his mother would cry. But why? He hadn't known he would be in an accident, surely.

She came up to him and stood near his side for the longest while. She patted his arm and kept looking at his head.

'Have they shaved my head?' he asked. 'Or is there a big hole there?'

'Shush! Bewakoof bacha,' Ammi said, wiping at the tears running down her face. She turned around to go and Luqman wanted to call out to her. He had to talk to her. But she shook her head and left. Luqman wanted to sleep but just then, Farhaan came inside.

His normally silent brother was also quite overcome with emotion.

'Give it to me straight. Have they cut off my leg? It's hurting like hell. So it's still there right? If I can feel it?' Luqman asked. The questions tired him. He was thirsty but no one was giving him water.

'You fool,' his brother muttered, wiping his eyes. 'They haven't cut off anything and there's no hole in your head. You're lucky you survived the accident because the cab driver didn't.'

Luqman felt a deep sense of sadness for the young boy who had been driving the cab. He hadn't even bothered to ask his name when he usually struck up a conversation with cab drivers whenever they took him to the airport.

Airport. He was returning from the airport. Where was his luggage?

'Bhai, my laptop,' he said suddenly.

'It's gone. Crushed in the accident. So is your phone,' Farhaan Bhai said.

Luqman nodded or tried to, and only then realised his neck was in a brace. Shit.

'I'll live, right?' he asked, suddenly.

'Of course you will. You're too stubborn to die just like that,' Farhaan said but his face crumpled even as he said the words.

'Let the patient rest,' a nurse came and admonished Farhaan. Nodding, he left. Luqman was alone in the ICU once more, a nagging feeling like there was something he was missing out, something he couldn't remember.

As he fell into a drugged sleep, he recalled a pair of almond eyes, wide and beautiful.

EIGHTEEN

Ana was in school when the phone call came. She ignored it of course, because she was at work but when the phone kept ringing, she picked it up, annoyed. If it was Athiya calling her to tell her about some stupid crisis that could have waited until later, she was going to get it from her. But Athiya never called her at work. No one did.

Anxious, she peered at the screen. It was Tehzeeb. Worry gnawed at her insides as she answered the call. Was it Abbu? Was he all right? Why was Tehzeeb calling her in the middle of the day? Was it Aslan?

'Hello?' she said, nervously.

'Ana, I need you to come home,' Tehzeeb said without any preliminaries and Ana felt as though the wind had been knocked out from her chest. Something was wrong.

'What is it? What happened? Is it Abbu?' she asked, getting up from her chair and collecting things, putting them inside her handbag.

Tehzeeb paused for a few seconds. 'No, it's not Abbu. It's Luqman. He met with an accident this morning as he was going home,' she said.

Ana's blood froze. She felt paralysed, like she couldn't move.

'What?' she whispered. Her head felt like it was spinning. This couldn't be happening. She had spoken to Luqman just last night and they had exchanged words of love. Please don't be dead, she screamed in her mind.

'It was a horrible car accident. The driver died on the spot but Luqman survived. He's had a head injury and he's fractured his leg. Thankfully, it happened very close to his house and Farhaan was at home when it happened. They took him to the hospital right away but he's slipping in and out of consciousness. He's in the ICU,' Api said.

Ana felt like there were ants crawling over her scalp. She wanted to tear out her hair but breathing heavily, she controlled herself. Luqman was alive. She could live with this. Tears were running down her face and sniffling, she wiped them away.

'I want to see him,' she whispered.

'I know, but you can't go to see him alone. You have to come with me. We have to make it look like a courtesy visit,' Tehzeeb said.

Fuck courtesy, she wanted to shout at her sister. But she knew Tehzeeb was right. Luqman was supposed to speak to his mother about them but he'd obviously had the accident before that. His mother would think that she was there because they had heard about the accident. What other reason would they have for being there?

'Ana, are you there?' Tehzeeb asked. Her voice sounded strained. Ana wanted to break down and cry but she had to hold herself together.

'We spoke last night,' she whispered as she picked up her handbag and adjusted the strap on her shoulder.

'Oh, and?' Tehzeeb asked.

Ana took a deep breath. 'We both love each other, Api.

He was going to speak to his mother about us,' she said. The tears started again, if they had ever stopped.

'I'm so sorry, sweetie. Come home and we'll go together. You really shouldn't be going alone,' Tehzeeb said.

'No, Api, I can't come to your house. Not right now. I'm a mess,' she said.

Tehzeeb was silent for a bit. 'Okay, I'll come and pick you up from Jasmine Villa. Can you wait for me there?' she asked.

Sniffling, Ana agreed and then ended the call. She realised she had no friends other than her sisters, at least not anyone with whom she wanted to share this momentous and life-changing news. She wanted to call Athiya and tell her but this wasn't the right time. She should have told Athiya about Luqman last night when she asked her.

Her heart felt like it was crowded inside her chest and was desperately trying to break free. She gathered her things and then left, after informing the staff room that there was a family crisis and she needed to go. No one seemed too concerned except one of the teachers who would often strike up a conversation with her whenever they met each other.

'I hope it's nothing serious,' Minimol said.

Ana was on the verge of breaking down but she shook her head and walked away, knowing she didn't want to make a scene. The school was off Sarjapur Road, almost near Electronic City and she needed to reach the main road before she could get an auto. She couldn't bear waiting around for an Uber.

As she walked, she tried to recall the words they had spoken, the tenor of his voice, his laugh and she kept a litany of prayer in her head that he be healed soon. She had lost her mother a few years ago to cancer but that had been different. It had slowly eaten away at her, and at them too. The knowledge that Ammi would no longer be with them soon had devastated Athiya but Ana had bottled her feelings and pushed them down, thinking that it was for the best. Ammi had suffered and if she had found release in death, then Ana was glad that she no longer had to endure more pain.

But when Ammi had actually breathed her last, Ana had been shocked at the intensity of her feelings and her emotions. Despite Ammi's agony coming to an end, Ana had realised that she would miss her mother in their everyday lives, something she had already been missing for nearly a year since she had fallen seriously sick.

Luqman's accident had just jolted her back into that dark place which she had kept pushed away into a corner of her mind. She finally found an auto on the main road and she got inside, knowing it would take at least an hour to reach home. She pulled out her phone and looked at Luqman's Whatsapp profile photo, her eyes blurring with tears that she wiped away.

Why had this happened? As it was, things were difficult for them to get together because of the proposal from his family. And now, she decided she didn't want to think about that yet. She just wanted Luqman to survive and to get well soon. She wanted to think of nothing but his well-being at the moment.

The auto stalled in traffic and took its own sweet time to reach home. Ana had managed to school her expression suitably and only then realised that Abbu would think it odd that she had come back home. What could she tell him? This much concern for her intended husband's younger brother would not be appropriate, she thought.

Then she decided she wasn't going to care. Let Abbu think what he wanted to. She just hoped Tehzeeb wouldn't take too long in coming. Her house was close by. When she reached home, thankfully, Tehzeeb had already arrived and told Abbu about the accident.

Abbu was coming with them too, she discovered, aghast.

'Poor boy,' Abbu muttered as he got into the car that Tehzeeb had brought with her along with one of their family drivers. Aslan was in Tehzeeb's house with her mother-in-law.

'Where's Ayub?' Abbu asked Tehzeeb who was in the back with Ana. She reached out and held Ana's hand and squeezed it tightly. Ana looked out of the window, not sure if she could manage talking to anyone at the moment.

'He's already in the hospital, Abbu,' Tehzeeb said.

Ana turned to Tehzeeb, her face pale and eyes worried. She typed out a message on her phone and gave it to Tehzeeb who took it, surprised.

'He'll be fine, no?' she had asked.

'He will,' Tehzeeb typed in response and handed the phone back to her.

NINETEEN

Luqman's body felt like it was on fire. He wanted to scream but found that he couldn't. Tears fell rapidly from his eyes as he focused on breathing, on trying to take his mind off from the pain. Nurses hovered by his side and he resisted the urge to ask them for a painkiller injection. Those came with sedatives and knocked him out and he didn't want to feel disoriented. But his expression, and most likely his vitals, which were broadcast on the monitor behind and above him on the wall, had been an indicator of his pain because one of the nurses checked in on him, switched his saline drips and gave him an injection after which he lapsed into sleep again.

When he came to, he had no idea of the time. The ICU was a form of hell invented by humans, he pondered. With the constant bright lights inside, beeping machines and soft footfalls of doctors and nurses, it was impossible to guess what was happening outside in the world. Ayub came to see him, his face drawn and worried.

'What's the time?' Luqman asked.

'Around 6 p.m.' Ayub said. He pointed to the large clock on the wall and Luqman felt like an idiot for not having noticed it before.

Ayub didn't say anything but kept looking at him. 'What is it? I already know I don't have a hole in my head,' Luqman asked.

He shook his head. 'We were texting right before the crash happened,' Ayub said finally.

'Oh. What about? Were we making plans to catch up?' Luqman asked.

'No, I was waiting for you to text me back. I …' Ayub swallowed but kept quiet.

'You always had an uncanny way of knowing when I'm in town, dude,' Luqman said.

'Luqman what do you remember about coming back from the US?' Ayub said suddenly.

There it was again. That void in his memory, the strange feeling that he was forgetting something important. But he didn't want to tell that to anyone. He didn't want them to be more worried.

'I was getting back from the airport when the accident happened, right?' he asked. Ayub looked at him anxiously and he wondered if he had said the wrong thing.

'Do you remember anything about Farhaan's engagement?' Ayub asked.

'What? Farhaan Bhai got engaged? To whom? Why am I hearing about this just now?' Luqman asked. His mouth felt dry. Why had his family hidden something so important from him?

Ayub looked perplexed but the nurse came and shooed him off. He went away regretfully, saying he was right outside, waiting with Ammi and his brothers.

Luqman had no clue what was happening outside the ICU and he had an urge to rip off all the tubes and go join his family and ask them what was happening. Farhaan couldn't have gotten engaged already. Right? They would have waited for him to join them.

Who was he getting engaged to?

He hated being sick and this was much worse. For a moment, he thought about the poor cab driver who had died. When Farhaan came inside again to see him, he was going to ask him to ask around about the driver's family and see if they could help them in any way.

*

Ana and Tehzeeb walked behind Abbu, deliberately slowing down so they could talk as he walked ahead of them to reach the ICU.

'Ayub's here. He texted me some time back that Luqman is conscious and he's talking. He's going to be fine soon. Nothing to worry about, Ana,' Tehzeeb said.

Ana nodded but her throat was tight with worry. She would believe that he was fine only when she saw him with her own eyes. The ICU floor was full of people waiting outside the doors to see their loved ones. There were chairs and a TV on the wall, and people sat down and waited while others haggled with the security guard, trying to coax him to let them visit the patients inside.

Ayub met them and Abbu hugged him. 'I'm sorry to hear about your friend,' he said. Ayub nodded but stayed quiet. He looked over at the two of them and indicated slightly with his head that they should step away so they could talk. Abbu had spotted Farhaan and he made a beeline for him. Ana wished her eyes could bore through the doors so she could see him right away. She could almost hear the thundering sound of her heartbeat.

Farhaan looked over at them just as Abbu embraced him. Ana noticed another young man and a familiar looking woman standing beside them. She looked anguished as Abbu turned to talk to her but she nodded her head.

'He's going to be fine,' Ayub said when they had stepped aside, a little away from the rest of Luqman's family.

Ana looked at Ayub and she could see that he was not telling them everything. Tehzeeb had guessed it correctly too.

'But?' Ana asked. Ayub looked conflicted.

'I went in and spoke to him. He looks bad at the moment because of the neck brace and the bandages around his head and his leg is in a cast. But what's important is that he's alive and well and will heal soon,' Ayub said.

'But you're not telling us something,' Tehzeeb said.

Ayub sighed. 'His mind is a little muddled right now,' he said.

'What do you mean?' Ana asked.

'He thinks he got back from the US today and was on the way back from the airport when the accident happened,' Ayub said.

Oh. But…

Just as Ana wanted to ask him what he meant, Abbu beckoned them over and they walked towards him. Ana's heart was pounding. She had been waiting to meet Luqman again but she had never expected it would happen like this, with him in the ICU and her coming to see him.

Ana kept quiet as Tehzeeb spoke with Luqman's mother who was crying and she hugged Tehzeeb. She then noticed Ana too and pulled her into her embrace.

'Thank you for coming, beta,' she whispered.

Farhaan looked uncomfortable, so he stepped away to join Ayub.

'I want to see him, Api,' Ana whispered to Tehzeeb. She didn't give a fuck if anyone thought it was inappropriate. Tehzeeb nodded.

'Can we see him?' she asked Luqman's mother.

'Visiting hours are over but the security guard lets people inside if we plead with him enough,' she said and asking both of them to follow her, she went to the entrance of the ICU.

Ana didn't care what it looked like to the world. Luqman was alive and she was going to see him now. That's all that mattered. After fifteen minutes of cajoling, the security guard agreed to let them inside but for just two minutes.

Ana and Tehzeeb stepped inside the ICU, glad that Luqman's mother hadn't joined them. They removed their slippers and padded down the narrow hallway that led to the double doors that opened inside.

The area inside was painfully bright. There were people lying on beds, hooked up to machines and nurses walked around busily. One of them looked up, annoyed at seeing them.

'Visiting hours are over,' she said brusquely.

'Just two minutes,' Tehzeeb said as they looked for Luqman. When they reached his bed, Ana went up to him to stand near him, her stomach contracting painfully. It hurt so much to look at him like this as he slept. She wanted to remain there as long as she could.

She thought back to that flight when he had been so vibrant and full of life, making her laugh, making her feel everything so intensely. Tehzeeb stood at a distance as Ana stared down at him, willing him to wake up. She would feel reassured only when she heard him talk.

There were cuts on his face and she wanted to kiss every one of them. His hand was bandaged too, and his leg was in a cast. She muttered a prayer for him, her heart full.

'Ana, we should go,' Tehzeeb said. Ana didn't look up but she stood still as tears fell from her eyes. She didn't want to leave his side.

'Ana,' Tehzeeb repeated in a soft and patient voice. Nodding, Ana reached out and touched his cheek gently. She couldn't breathe. She looked at the vitals being monitored on the screen above and saw that his heart rate was good. He was going to be all right.

'Can't we stay until a nurse kicks us out? I want to talk to him,' she asked Tehzeeb in a wavering voice. Tehzeeb shook her head immediately.

'It's not a good idea. Come, let's go,' she said. Ana bent down and kissed his cheek lightly, breathing him in, even though the antiseptic smells of the hospital were overpowering. She got up and walked away from there, tears falling from her eyes.

'Tehzeeb?'

Ana turned around. He was awake! Tehzeeb and she turned back to talk to him but a nurse frowned.

'Please, just one minute,' Ana said and evaded the nurse and walked back to Luqman's bed. He looked at her confused. She wanted to hold his hand, hug him actually, but she restrained herself.

'Luqman,' she said.

He looked over at Tehzeeb and then back at Ana and then again to Tehzeeb. 'This is your sister, right?' he asked. Ana froze.

Tehzeeb looked at him, aghast. 'Yes, my sister, Ana,' she said. Ana stared at Luqman. What did this mean? The two of them had opened their hearts to each other just last night. They had made plans. They were in love.

'Thank you for coming to see me,' he whispered, shut his eyes and fell asleep once more.

TWENTY

Tehzeeb wanted to hold Ana tight and never let go. Her sister looked devastated as they left the ICU and her heart ached for her. What the hell had just happened? Was this what Ayub meant when he said that Luqman's mind was a little muddled? This was definitely more than that.

'He's forgotten everything about me,' Ana stated. Her voice came out hoarse, as though she was choking.

'No, but …' Tehzeeb didn't know what to say. Ana was right. 'Listen, you need to compose your face before you leave the ICU.' Ana was putting on her slippers, her expression rather lifeless.

'You know, I don't really care about what his mother thinks?' Ana snapped.

'You do. You care about what Abbu thinks also, remember? He's happy with the proposal with Farhaan and you told me that Farhaan had come yesterday because Abbu asked him,' Tehzeeb reminded her, wearing her slippers as well.

Ana rubbed her eyes, her face crumpling. 'Api, I just want to scream. I want to let this out. I'm tired of holding it all inside,' she said.

Tehzeeb pulled her into her arms for a hug. She rubbed

Ana's back gently. 'Come and stay with me for a couple of days,' she said. Ana shook her head.

'I can't.'

'Why not? You know Abba and Ammi won't mind. You stayed with me after Aslan was born and I returned from Jasmine Villa after the delivery,' Tehzeeb said.

'Api, I can't right now. I'm a mess,' she said.

'That's why, come and stay with us. We have a guestroom where you can stay, and you can cry all you want. You won't have to explain anything to anyone. We could tell Abbu and Athiya that I asked you to come and stay to help out a little with Aslan.'

Ana was near the door of the ICU. Tehzeeb continued speaking. 'You can talk to us. We're the only ones who know about you and Luqman. You'll feel better when you can talk about this instead of bottling it all inside,' she said.

'I'll think about it,' Ana said as she pushed the door open and stepped outside.

The security guard glowered at them because they had certainly taken longer than five minutes inside. Ana walked straight ahead without looking at anyone and Tehzeeb glanced at her husband, hoping he would understand what to do. Thankfully, he did. He nodded to Ana and led her away from there.

'She hates hospitals, Auntie,' Tehzeeb said, turning to Luqman's mother who looked curiously as Ana walked away from there.

'Oh and she still made an effort to come and see her devar,' Auntie said. Yikes. Tehzeeb nodded and then noticed that Abbu was still talking to Farhaan. She excused herself and told Abbu she was going to get some fresh air and he could join them when he was done.

Ayub and Ana hadn't got too far. They were standing in front of a lift as she joined them. Ayub's eyes brightened when he saw her and he smiled at her slightly. Tehzeeb's breath caught in her throat. That was the look Ana had been hoping to see in Luqman's eyes too.

The lift arrived and the three of them got inside. Instead of going downstairs, Ayub pressed the button for the fifth floor.

'There's a canteen sort of thing there. Let's get some coffee,' he said. Tehzeeb nodded. Ana looked down, not meeting their gaze. The lift had a couple of other people, visitors, probably, and a nurse in scrubs who was texting on her phone furiously.

When the lift stopped at the fifth floor, they got out and walked towards the canteen where Ana sat down at the first empty table she spotted. Ayub went to get them coffee while Tehzeeb sat down opposite her.

'Listen. Ayub is going to be here. He'll talk to Luqman's doctors and find out if his memory has been affected. We'll … fix this,' Tehzeeb said.

'Fix what?' Ayub asked as he placed a tray with three cups of coffee on the table and sat down next to Tehzeeb.

'Luqman has forgotten me,' Ana said. Ayub looked shocked.

'What?'

Ana nodded, tears forming in her eyes. 'He was asleep when we went there but he woke as we were leaving. He looked at me and he asked if I was Api's sister. That's it.'

'Shit,' Ayub said, his face looking drawn and worried.

'Do you think Luqman has some sort of amnesia?' Tehzeeb asked but Ayub looked uncertain.

'I don't know. But I'll try and speak to his doctor.

He remembers everything else, except the last couple of days,' Ayub said. 'Like he was surprised when I mentioned Farhaan's engagement. That's why I thought...'

'What do I do?' Ana asked, wiping at the tears falling from her eyes. 'I feel so helpless and I have no control over anything. I hate this. I wish I'd never met him.'

'You don't mean that,' Tehzeeb said gently, reaching out and covering her sister's hand with her own.

Ana pulled out her hand from under and wiped her face, sniffling. Ayub held Tehzeeb's other hand and squeezed gently before letting go. Tehzeeb's mind was spinning. Why was this happening to her sister? Momentarily, she was reminded of the horrible thing Maira had said when she had seen Luqman's photo with Ana, without knowing it was her. She had said that she hoped the girl in the photo would never find any happiness.

'What do I do?' Ana asked again. 'He was supposed to speak to his mother about us today.'

'Maybe I should speak to Auntie,' Ayub suggested. Tehzeeb thought it was a terrible idea and Ana echoed her thoughts.

'No, Ayub Bhai. If he doesn't think of me as anything other than Api's sister, you will just make a mess by talking to Auntie about us. You would need him to back you up and if he has no clue about what we shared, why would he?' Ana said. She took a sip of the coffee and put the cup down.

'Maybe his memory will just come back,' Tehzeeb said. She wasn't feeling entirely optimistic, but wasn't that how it worked in movies? Lost memories reappeared suddenly.

'His memory is intact. I'm just someone who fell through his memory when the accident happened,' Ana said bitterly.

'Um, that's not how it works,' Ayub said gently.

'Of course I know that's not how it works,' Ana said, annoyed. 'I'm just trying to make sense of everything. Why me? Why has he forgotten only me?'

'I'll speak to the doctor and see what he has to say,' Ayub said, just as Abbu called Tehzeeb on her phone to see where she was.

'We have to go now,' she said, getting up from there. Ana stood up too. Tehzeeb turned to her husband and thought she would go crazy if her husband failed to recognise her. 'I've asked Ana to come and stay with us for some days.'

'Excellent idea,' Ayub said as he got up and they walked out.

'I don't want to,' Ana said as she followed them out slowly. 'I have school and ...'

'You can go to school from here. Problem solved,' Tehzeeb said.

Ana looked away unhappily. Poor thing really looked like she needed a place to vent, a place where she could let go of her feelings and have a good, solid cry.

'I'm with you Ana,' Tehzeeb said, in the lift as they travelled down to the ground floor where Abbu was waiting.

Ana nodded, her face still bleak.

TWENTY-ONE

Luqman was shifted to a private room after a day in the ICU. He realised it was going to take time for him to heal and while he was impatient to get back to life, he decided to let things happen at their own pace. He mostly slept but would get up whenever that nagging feeling would come back to him, a feeling that he was missing something important. He knew he'd lost the work which had been in his laptop, so maybe that was it.

His colleagues came to visit him and one of them said something strange. Sunil, one of his teammates said that he had left the San Francisco project in a mess and it was actually a good thing he was in the hospital or Akshay would have fired his ass long ago.

'I never leave any project in a mess,' Luqman said indignantly. 'You know I'm a thorough professional.'

'Dude, that's what the people from San Francisco said. And what Akshay also told us when he said you had an accident. Didn't you email Akshay on Saturday to tell him there was some family emergency and you had to leave early?'

Luqman stared back at Sunil's placid face in shock. He had no idea. It was like the two days before his accident were completely missing.

'What's the date?' he asked Sunil who rolled his eyes at him.

'It's the twelfth of March,' Sunil replied.

Luqman clearly remembered that his ticket back to India had been booked for seventeenth March. So what was he doing back here a week early? He nodded slowly, knowing that he couldn't show any sign of confusion to Sunil, who would report everything to Akshay.

When Sunil left after sometime, Luqman tried to sleep again but those eyes kept haunting him. Who did they belong to? Why was he dreaming about the eyes and why couldn't he see this person's face? It was all a mystery to him. He remembered then that Ayub said they had been texting just before he had his accident. Would Ayub know what the gaps in his memory were?

He wished he had his phone so he could call Ayub but Farhaan Bhai had promised to get him a new one when he visited today. They were taking turns to be with him – Ammi, Farhaan and Nouman. Usually, Ammi was with him during the day, sitting on the attendant bed, reading the Quran softly. She barely spoke and whenever she looked up at him, tears would fill in her eyes because she kept thinking of how he had nearly died.

So he avoided talking to Ammi as far as possible. He knew he had to wait until Farhaan visited him in the evening. Every time he tried to think of the past two days, his head started hurting so he stopped. Then he thought of the strange scene in the ICU when Tehzeeb had come to visit him.

Why had she brought her sister with her? What was her name again? Ana?

Strangely, when he thought of her, something weird

happened inside, like the precursor to a stomach-ache. Maybe it was her perfume that made him feel like that. He remembered the drawn look on her face. He remembered waking up to something feather soft and light touching his cheek and he had opened his eyes to see two people walking away. He recognised Tehzeeb but he didn't know who was with her. He wanted her to turn around but when she did, nothing happened.

When Farhaan visited him that evening, he brought him a new phone as promised and he had saved some contacts on it already. Thankfully, Ayub's was also there.

'I didn't know you had Ayub's phone number,' Luqman said as he explored the phone.

'I didn't. But you know…with the…' Farhaan trailed off and Luqman looked at him.

'With the what?' he asked.

Farhaan smiled the slightest bit. 'Well, I'm getting married to Tehzeeb's sister, so Ayub and I are going to be related now,' he said.

'Oh! I didn't know this,' Luqman said, surprised. Ana was getting married to Farhaan? For some reason, his stomach churned again. Just talking about her was enough to elicit this weird reaction, he mused, annoyed.

'Luqman, Ammi called and told you about this when you were in San Francisco,' Farhaan said patiently.

Luqman made a face. 'I don't remember, Farhaan Bhai,' he said, turning his face away. He didn't want to talk right now. He knew he should be happy for Farhaan. Ana was pretty enough and … and … he remembered sitting close to her when they took that photo to fool Maira. Right. That's where he remembered her from. She had been with Tehzeeb at that time too.

He didn't want to think of her. The uneasy feeling inside him grew for some reason and he dialled Ayub's number. Ammi had said that Ayub had been with them since he heard of the accident and he had gone home only after he had been shifted out of the ICU. He wanted to talk to Ayub, ask him what he knew about his plans to return to India. Why was he here a week before he was supposed to be?

Ayub answered the call and they got talking. 'So when are you coming to see me?' Luqman asked.

'Soon. I'll come see you on my way home,' he assured him.

'Okay. I need to talk to you,' Luqman said.

'About?' Ayub asked him sharply.

'Just this and that?' Luqman replied, trying to stave off that strange sensation that was floating around inside him once more.

'Sure,' Ayub sighed. They spoke a little more and then ended the call. Farhaan was staring at him as he put away the phone.

'What was that about?' he asked.

Luqman wondered if he should tell Farhaan something about the missing gap in his memories. But he didn't want to worry Farhaan. And hadn't he just told him that he didn't remember what Ammi said about his marriage plans?

'Nothing. I'm bored. How long will I be in the hospital?' he asked.

'I have no idea. It's going to be a few days, maybe even weeks,' Farhaan said. 'You need to heal.'

Luqman told him to try and find out about the cab driver who had died and to see if they could help his family.

'Already done,' Farhaan assured him. He sighed as he

got up, walked to the window and looked out. Luqman realised he would never take something as simple as walking for granted. Or even going to the loo. Simple things like taking a piss or just wandering around were things he couldn't do yet and it worried the hell out of him. He wanted reassurance that he could do all this again. But Farhaan was looking out of the window and he turned to speak to him.

'So, the family was devastated of course. He was the only bread winner in the family. He has two younger sisters and I have promised to help them as much as we can,' Farhaan said.

'Thank you, Bhai,' Luqman said, feeling sick because of the relief he had felt when he realised how close he had been to dying. Someone else had died. Someone else's family was suffering.

'No need to thank me,' Farhaan said, taking out his glasses, wiping them, with a soft cloth he kept in his pocket, and putting them back on.

'You rest now. I'll be sitting right here,' Farhaan said, taking up the chair near his bed.

Luqman couldn't sleep. He was waiting for Ayub to come.

TWENTY-TWO

Ayub managed to track down Luqman's doctor while he was in the middle of his rounds. The doctor, who was in his fifties with a head full of shaggy hair, looked rather unkempt and annoyed.

'Who are you?' he asked Ayub imperiously as he glared at one of the junior doctors hovering near him. The young man paled as he checked the sheets of paper in his hand.

'One of your patients is my friend Luqman. He was in an accident two days ago on Monday morning. He's hurt his head so I wanted to know if it would affect his memory in anyway,' Ayub asked. The doctor looked at him and snorted.

'You think this is some sort of movie is it?' he asked.

Ayub was trying to keep his temper so he smiled tightly as he shook his head. 'He seems to be a little mixed up about the events of the days leading up to the accident,' he said.

'Says who?' the doctor asked, putting a finger inside the collar of his shirt and pulling it back, like he needed air.

'I'm saying that, based on a conversation I had with him. I just want to know if it's possible to selectively forget a few things and remember everything else?' Ayub asked.

'Look, I don't have time to get into this. I have been

checking that patient and he seems to be fine,' the doctor said.

'Yes, he is. But I wanted to know if it was possible and why it would happen?' Ayub asked.

'The internet is your doctor these days, right? Check for yourself,' he replied. Ayub walked away from there angrily. He had already looked up selective amnesia on the internet but he had wanted to speak to Luqman's doctor and find out just what was possible and not.

'Never mind,' he muttered to himself as he climbed the stairs to the second floor to Luqman's room. His jaw clenched when he thought of how exasperating the doctor was but he schooled his expression into one of nonchalance as he walked down the corridor.

Ana was staying with them, rather reluctantly. She seemed to be doing all right but one just had to look at her sad eyes to know what she was going through. She stayed shut in the guest bedroom most of the time, emerging only at mealtimes and Ammi had been getting curious.

Tehzeeb, on the other hand, seemed to think this was all her fault. She kept talking about some divine retribution, about how hurting Maira had brought this about. Ayub tried to pacify her but she wouldn't listen. Maybe he should call up Maira and tell her the truth about what had happened. Maybe then Tehzeeb would believe it wasn't somehow her own fault that her sister was suffering.

Ayub reached Luqman's room, knocked on the door and pushed it open. Farhaan saw him, smiled and got up. They shook hands and even did a one-arm hug and Ayub felt pained at how clueless Farhaan was in all of this. Luqman, who was lying on the bed, stared at them and made a face but didn't say anything.

Farhaan said that he would go home and bring his mother who wanted to see Luqman and then he would stay back with him for the night.

'Sure,' Ayub said. Farhaan collected a few of the things that needed to be taken back home and left. Ayub pulled the chair closer to Luqman and sat down near him. Luqman turned to him, looking worried.

'What?' Ayub asked. 'Are you all right?'

'I don't know. The pain is always there. But there's something else,' Luqman said.

Ayub leaned in closer. 'You can tell me, Luqman,' he said.

'I feel like I'm forgetting something important,' he whispered.

Not something. Someone, Ayub thought but kept quiet. He didn't know how head injuries acted out and how the human brain worked and that asshole doctor hadn't even elaborated on whether it was all right to push Luqman and try to make him remember. He didn't want to make things worse for him.

Based on what he'd read on the internet, stress did cause people to forget certain things and Luqman had been worried about talking to his mother about Ana. Ayub came to the reluctant conclusion that maybe, just maybe, the stress of that upcoming talk had just deleted itself from Luqman's brain along with any associated memories. He could be totally wrong.

'Like what?' he asked. When he had discussed his theory with Ana, she had become even more upset. She thought that it was best to leave Luqman to heal at his own pace. Pushing him to remember her could cause more harm than anything.

'That's what I don't know,' Luqman sighed. 'Every time I try to think of it, I just draw a blank. And I get this nervous feeling in the pit of my stomach.'

Ayub listened in silence. Luqman had been through a lot and there was no way he could hurry him along.

'I have a feeling it could be about my work. My laptop was destroyed in the accident,' Luqman said, looking at Ayub with hopeful eyes.

'Hmm,' Ayub crossed his arms, knowing that they had to wait for Luqman to try and figure things out himself. He knew it wasn't easy and it wasn't going to happen instantly, but one could hope.

'Why do you think that?' he asked.

'I don't know. There's another thing that is worrying me. I clearly remember getting tickets for the seventeenth of March and if I was in the accident a couple of days ago, why had I left San Francisco a week early? And according to my colleague Sunil, I left the project in a mess over there. None of that makes sense you know?' Luqman said. He looked worried and strained. Ayub remained silent.

'You said you were texting me when I had the accident. So you knew I was in Bangalore? How?' Luqman asked.

Ayub didn't know how he could explain this to Luqman without telling him about what happened with Ana. He shrugged.

'I was just guessing to see if you were back,' he said finally. Luqman didn't look convinced.

'But why was I back a week early? Why did I leave the project in a mess?' he asked.

Because you fell in love with my sister-in-law Ana, Ayub thought. But he stayed quiet.

'Maybe you'll remember everything eventually,' Ayub said finally.

'I'm worried I'm losing my mind,' Luqman whispered.

'What? Why?' Ayub asked, frowning.

'I have this uncanny feeling that there's something important that I need to talk about with someone. I just don't know what it is and with whom I'm supposed to speak. It's frustrating. And I haven't told this to anyone, like Ammi or Farhaan because they will get worried. I can trust you right?' he asked.

Ayub sighed. 'Of course,' he said. The gap in Luqman's memory had to be filled naturally. It was best not to rush the process. No matter how much it hurt Ana. But he had to try at least once.

'Have I shown you Aslan's latest photo?' Ayub asked, pulling out his phone. Luqman smiled and took the phone from him, wincing a little because of pain.

He stared at the screen. Ayub had taken a photo of Ana holding Aslan and that photo was on the screen. He hoped to jog his memory at least a little.

'Sweet,' Luqman said and handed the phone back. Nothing. Ayub hid his disappointment. Maybe Luqman had never loved Ana and so maybe this was for the best if they were going to make such a big mistake. Maybe the accident, however horrible it had been, had happened for a reason.

'That's my sister-in-law, Ana,' Ayub offered as he put the phone in his pocket.

'I know,' Luqman said, resting his hand on his stomach lightly. He winced again.

'What is it?' Ayub asked. 'Should I call a nurse?'

Luqman shook his head. 'No. I get this weird funny feeling in my stomach whenever I see her, Ayub. I don't know why,' Luqman said.

Ayub's mouth dropped open. 'What do you mean? What

does Ana have to do with anything?' he asked, holding his breath. Did this mean that his body remembered Ana even though his mind had blanked her out? Did this mean that he did indeed love her?

'I don't know. My stomach starts churning and I just want to think about something else immediately,' he said.

'Oh. That *is* weird,' Ayub said. But he knew it wasn't. Luqman's mind was just trying to protect him from more hurt but how would forgetting the girl he loved help him?

TWENTY-THREE

Ana was ready to go back to Jasmine Villa. She was actually glad Tehzeeb had asked her to stay here for a couple of days because at home, she would have to hide her true feelings. She wondered what Athiya had made of it all. She knew her sister was self-absorbed but sometimes she could be uncannily perceptive. She was just surprised that Athiya hadn't texted or called her when she'd found out that Ana was staying in Tehzeeb's house. Normally, she would have wanted to come over and stay too so she could spend time with Aslan.

Ayub came back every day after visiting Luqman and his recovery was encouraging. Except for the part where he had completely forgotten about her. It hurt so much. She cried into the pillow every night as she slept, thinking, wondering why this had happened. Why did she have to fall in love with him when she was expected to marry Farhaan? Why did he have to forget her? Did she mean so little to him?

She knew that they had to call off the wedding and do it soon. Abbu was getting too attached to the idea of Farhaan as his son-in-law and she needed to tell him that she wasn't ready to get married yet. She felt better as soon as she came to this decision.

She packed her things and kept them ready, planning to get an auto soon. Luqman's accident had taken place five days ago and she had been here since then. Ayub Bhai came back every day with reports of his recovery and she could read his expression every single time. Luqman still hadn't remembered her. Maybe he never would.

Perhaps this had all been for the best. What if the accident had been a way to show them that they were not meant to be together? The thought squeezed her chest until she felt like she couldn't breathe.

She left the guest bedroom and went looking for Tehzeeb who was taking a nap with Aslan. She knocked on her door and then stepped inside. The room was a little dark and it was quiet. Tehzeeb was lying on the bed, sleeping peacefully, while Aslan was awake in his cot. He was quietly staring at the crib mobile that hung above him and gently tinkled. He looked at her when she leaned down to pick him up and he smiled his gummy smile.

Ana felt her heart overflow with emotion as she held him in her arms and walked softly to the sofa where she sat down with him. He gurgled and waved his hands around, clutching a lock of her hair, letting it go and doing so all over again. He was such an adorable baby.

Tehzeeb stirred on the bed and she woke up. 'Hey,' she said sleepily. 'He's awake?'

'Yes. He was awake but he was quietly looking around like a good little boy. Weren't you?' she cooed. He cooed back at her and she smiled. When she was with Aslan, she could almost forget the pain that lanced through her heart every now and then.

Tehzeeb sighed. Sitting up, she leaned over to fill a glass of water from the jug by the nightstand and sipped it. 'I had no idea breastfeeding would leave me so thirsty all the time,' she said.

Ana didn't reply. She had felt a little icky at first whenever her sister would talk about all that she had gone through – the labour pain, the delivery, and all those gross things and then after he was born, she talked about breastfeeding, trying to get the baby to latch on to her nipple and even more gross things. But she listened because she knew that Api needed to talk about all this to someone. They didn't have Ammi. They only had each other.

'Shit. I've started leaking. Here, hand him to me,' she said as she sat back and adjusted her clothes. Ana gave Aslan over to her and he squirmed a little as Tehzeeb arranged him properly. Ana wanted to leave but Tehzeeb shook her head.

'Sit. Talk to me,' she said firmly.

'What's there to talk about?' Ana said, even as she sat down on the sofa. She looked out at the balcony door that was shut.

'Well, what are we going to tell Abbu?' Tehzeeb asked. 'We *have* to think of some reason to break off the wedding.'

'I don't know. I don't want to think about it,' Ana lied. It was all she could think about. She tried to think of all the different ways she could break this off but nothing stuck. There was nothing wrong with Farhaan and there was nothing wrong with her. Except that she loved his brother.

'Ana,' Tehzeeb said gently. 'What if we … what if we tell Abbu the truth?'

Ana looked up, shocked. She shook her head. 'No. No way. I can't,' she said.

'What's the worst that can happen?' Tehzeeb asked.

'Please Api, I can't tell Abbu. He'll think that I …'

'You won't know what he'll think until you tell him,' Tehzeeb said.

Ana shook her head again. 'I can't have him think of me as being immoral and …'

'Immoral?' Tehzeeb scoffed. 'What nonsense!'

'Well, he'll think I'm forward or, or …' Ana trailed off. She couldn't explain it. Tehzeeb was the beautiful one who got away with everything, and Athiya was the headstrong and impulsive one. She was the good one, the one with the moral compass. The grounded one. Abbu would be heartbroken if he found that she had … what had she done exactly, she wondered. She hadn't done anything wrong. She had just fallen in love.

Tehzeeb saw the doubt on her sister's face and went in for the kill. 'Come on! What's the worse that can happen? Abbu will be a little upset but he'll get over it eventually. It's not like you even got engaged to Farhaan.'

Api was right, Ana thought. Even if Luqman never remembered her, she could probably survive it if she didn't have to see him ever again. She knew she was lying to herself. It was all she could do to not run to the hospital and be with him every day. She was dying to see him again. Her heart ached every time she thought of him in pain. She wanted to be the one to comfort him, hold his hand, kiss his forehead, wipe the tears of pain from his eyes. And it was killing her that she couldn't do any of this.

'Okay,' she said finally.

'Okay what?' Tehzeeb asked, taking Aslan off her breast and switching sides. She sighed as he started suckling loudly. 'Ouch.'

'What happened?' Ana asked and realised too late that she didn't want to know.

'Little rascal bit me,' Tehzeeb said.

'He doesn't have teeth!'

'He bit me with his gums. Uff,' Tehzeeb said as she settled back into the mound of pillows behind her. 'All this is so much discomfort, ya.'

Ana sighed as she got up to go. 'Yes, but it's worth it, I suppose. Eventually.'

'Who knows?' Tehzeeb said, grinning.

'Listen, Api, I'm going home now. I've packed my stuff and everything,' Ana said.

'What? Why? Stay here, no? It's the weekend anyway,' Tehzeeb protested.

Ana shook her head. 'Thanks for letting me stay here and decompress. It helped more than I could have thought possible. But now it's time to go and face reality,' she said.

'You're going to talk to Abbu?' Tehzeeb asked. Ana nodded.

'Yes. I think you're right. It's best we break this off right now,' Ana said.

'Good. It *is* for the best,' Tehzeeb said. What remained unsaid was what Ana was going to do now. Would she be okay with another family coming to 'see' her and select her as their bride? Would she be able to convince her father that she didn't want to get married? Maybe Tehzeeb thought that she would get over Luqman in a few months or years. Ana knew that wasn't going to happen.

But she had to speak to Abbu first and break this off.

TWENTY-FOUR

When Ana reached Jasmine Villa, she was surprised to find only Athiya sitting in the living room. Athiya was reading a book and barely looked up when she walked inside the house. She knew she had to talk to her sister and tell her everything. But she dreaded it. Athiya was rash and got angry at the drop of a hat.

'Where's Abbu?' she asked her as she unpacked her clothes from the overnight bag she'd taken to Tehzeeb's house, put them inside her cupboard and came back out to the living room.

'What do you care?' Athiya asked, biting into an apple loudly.

'Don't be stupid,' Ana admonished her out of habit. Athiya looked up at her, eyes flashing angrily but didn't say anything.

'He didn't tell me where he was going except that it was important,' she said, her nostrils flaring as she shut her book and stood up.

'Sit. I want to talk to you,' Ana said. Athiya glared at her.

'Athiya, sit. Please. I'm sorry I haven't been around much lately but my life is going to shit and I …'

'… need me to figure out a way to make things easy for you?' Athiya asked, sitting back down.

Ana sat back on the sofa and sighed. 'You won't believe what the past few days have been like for me.'

'How would I know unless you tell me?' Athiya asked.

Ana paused for a moment, trying to understand why Athiya was so angry. It hit her just then. Athiya knew more than she was letting on.

'You know, don't you?' she asked, looking at her sister whose jaw was set squarely.

'About you and Luqman? Yes,' she said, crossing her arms. Ana sighed again.

'My life is so messed up ...' she began but Athiya stopped her by lifting her hand, her eyes narrowed.

'You brought this mess upon yourself. Have you even thought of what poor Farhaan is going to feel?' she asked.

'I ... yes, but ...'

'No, you haven't. When are you planning to tell Abbu? After your engagement?' Athiya asked.

'There's nothing to tell,' Ana said, her voice flat. She wished she could push away all her emotions somewhere and lock them up.

'Lying to me again!' Athiya spat out angrily.

'Listen. Yes, there was something between Luqman and me and he was going to meet his mother to tell her about us,' Ana began, getting angry herself. She hadn't been expecting to get into a fight with Athiya the moment she returned home. She didn't have the energy for it.

Athiya was listening to her in silence. 'But then he had the accident and now he doesn't remember me,' Ana said.

'What?' Athiya looked shocked. Then to her horror, she started laughing.

'I'm not joking Athiya!' Ana said angrily. Athiya shook her head and kept laughing.

'He *forgot* you? Selective amnesia? Oh god, that's rich,' Athiya said. Ana stared back at her sister, wondering how she and Tehzeeb could be so different. Where Tehzeeb felt everything keenly, Athiya, it seemed, cared only about herself.

'Maybe there was a reason why I didn't want to tell you any of this,' Ana said softly as she got up. Athiya stopped laughing.

'Right. Blame me for hiding things from me. You and Tehzeeb Api always get together and leave me out. Even in this,' Athiya said, her anger back.

'Look, I'm going through hell right now. I don't expect you to understand. I had planned to tell you everything but then I thought I'd wait till Luqman spoke to his mother. I didn't know this was going to happen. I saw him in the ICU …' Ana stopped as she choked on the words. She remembered Luqman, how vulnerable he had looked and how she had felt helpless about everything. 'He woke up and I was so happy then to just see him, you know? But he looked at me blankly and asked Api if I was her sister. And then Ayub Bhai spoke to him a couple of days later and he doesn't recall how we met on the plane to Malaysia, how we …' Ana stopped as tears flowed down her eyes.

Athiya was silent as Ana sniffled. 'This is all so messed up. I'm going to speak to Abbu to tell him to call off the wedding,' she said.

'You just want everyone to feel sorry for you,' Athiya said, narrowing her eyes. Ana looked up at her in surprise.

'That's not true,' she said. Did her sister really think that? 'I don't want anyone's pity. I just want to lead a normal life.'

'Fine,' Athiya said, getting up from there and going to the bedroom. Ana shut her eyes, wondering why she had thought that talking to Athiya would make her feel better. She wiped away the tears from her face and straightened up the hall. In the few days she hadn't been at home, Athiya had let the house become a pigsty. If Ammi had been here ...

If Ammi had been here, would she have told her everything? Would Ammi have spoken to Abbu on her behalf, told him that this was all a mistake?

She heard the door unlock and open and Abbu called out to Athiya. Ana rose and went to him. He looked surprised and happy on seeing her and hugged her.

'I'm glad you're back, Ana beta. I have some really good news that I want to share with you first,' he said.

'What good news, Abbu?' Ana asked, doubtfully. She had just noticed that he was holding a folder in his hands.

He waved the folder to her and sat down on the sofa. Athiya came outside and looked at him curiously.

'I wish Tehzeeb were here too. But we'll call her to celebrate later,' he said.

'Celebrate what?' Ana asked, getting a bad feeling about this. Lately, whatever made Abbu happy had been no good for her.

Abbu showed them the folder. With shaky hands, Ana took it and opened it. There was a legal agreement inside and she skimmed it, her heart sinking rapidly.

'What is it?' Athiya asked impatiently.

'I just signed the joint development agreement with Farhaan today. I also had the chance to speak to his mother on the phone. Given that Luqman is still recovering, his mother didn't want an engagement, so we have decided to do away with it and directly arrange the wedding in August. We have finalized the date too,' he said with a smile.

Ana tried hard to keep her face blank. She didn't even look at Athiya because she didn't know what she would do if her sister gloated. She felt like she had been on a spinning top and someone had just brought it to a halt. She felt dizzy and faint and blood roared in her ears.

She looked up at Athiya then, who looked shocked. She looked like she was going to say something when Ana shook her head.

'No,' she mouthed.

TWENTY-FIVE

Two weeks after his accident, Luqman was discharged from the hospital. His leg was still in a cast but otherwise, he was recovering quite well. He was anxious to get back to work, at least from home at first because Akshay had visited him a few days ago and told him to take his time. That was never good. Akshay had appeared sympathetic, so much that Ammi had gushed over how kind he had seemed after he left, but Luqman had been able to read him like a book. His boss was pissed with him on several counts.

The pain in his head had receded and if he tried to think of normal, happy things, he could almost forget Ana's face. He felt guilty whenever he thought about her. Why the hell was he obsessed with her face, he wondered. The initial discomfort that he felt when he thought of her had given way to something else now, a morbid sort of curiosity about her. Morbid because she was going to marry his brother this August. The curiosity was prompted by a memory of hers that had suddenly flashed in his head – when she had come to Ayub's office to return some of Tehzeeb's things and to tell him that her sister still loved Ayub.

He recalled how decisive she had appeared then and it triggered something else but he couldn't pin it down.

A couple of days ago, when Ayub had visited him in the hospital, he had said that Maira wanted to talk to him and he had connected the call. Luqman had taken the phone from him uneasily, spoke to his sister and was surprised that she just sounded genuinely worried for him due to the accident. When the call had ended, Ayub continued to look at him almost speculatively.

'She's over you, so you can relax. In case you don't remember, she's married now and in Dubai,' he said. That startled him.

'Why wouldn't I remember it?' he lied, his heart racing. 'And why would you say that I wouldn't remember it? What else have I forgotten?'

Ayub had just looked at him contemplatively but hadn't said anything. Since that moment, another memory of Ana had resurfaced and this one made him feel something other than the discomfort he felt when he thought of her. He remembered sitting next to her at a coffee shop. Where the hell was that? Why had he been sitting next to her? And then, he remembered the soft feel of her hands in his as he held them.

He had to stop thinking of her. This was no good. He couldn't have all these weird thoughts about the woman who was going to be his Bhabhi in a few months. Every time he thought of her as his Bhabhi though, he felt like puking. He wished he could understand why he was having all these strange reactions.

At home, Ammi had moved his things downstairs to the guest bedroom because he couldn't walk upstairs with the cast. He was itching to move around, for life to get back to normal but he knew it would take time.

When he looked at his face in the mirror in the guest

bedroom, he was shocked. He looked haggard and pale, nothing like his usual self. Despite feeling exhausted by the simple act of shaving his face, he persisted, feeling much more human as his face emerged from under the growth of facial hair.

Nouman hadn't gone to the office after Farhaan had dropped him home. He had said he would stick around in case Luqman needed any help. While he didn't say it out aloud, Luqman was glad of his brother's presence. For one, it kept away any thoughts of Ana. And secondly, Nouman talked too much. His constant chatter kept his mind occupied and he was thankful for that. In fact, he had nearly lulled himself to sleep even as Nouman continued to speak, until he heard the name 'Jasmine Villa'.

He cracked open an eye and looked at him curiously. 'What's this Jasmine Villa?' he asked Nouman.

His brother looked perturbed. 'I wish Farhaan Bhai had consulted with me before signing the papers for this joint development deal with his father-in-law. Jasmine Villa is the name of the house where Ana lives,' he explained. Luqman's eyes narrowed and his heart rate picked up a notch.

'What do you mean?'

'Well, first of all, it's not a good idea to do business with your prospective in-laws. And he didn't even let me inspect the house and the land like he normally does. He said he had done it himself but I think he's so taken in by his future wife Ana that I'm sure he hasn't done a very good assessment job either.'

Luqman's heart did that strange swooping thing again but he kept his face impassive. 'Why? It's not a good deal?'

Nouman shook his head. 'I don't like how he has made

the agreement. For that size of land, we usually build around six apartments, three floors, two on each floor. He's giving them two floors,' he said.

Luqman had never gotten into the nitty gritty of his family's real estate business and even now he wasn't interested but he understood how this appeared. Ana's family would be getting the larger share of apartments without investing any money in the venture. No wonder Nouman was a bit pissed.

'Has Farhaan Bhai met Ana? What makes you think he's taken in with her?' Luqman asked suddenly.

'I don't know. I think he met her at her house when he went there for the first time. Maybe they've been in touch since then. It's annoying how a man will change when there's a pretty girl in the picture,' Nouman said.

'Is Ammi okay with all this?' Luqman asked. Nouman shrugged.

'You know that Farhaan Bhai is the boss and he does what he thinks is right. He never asks for our opinion. Just ploughs along,' he said bitterly.

Luqman wondered about the equation between his brothers and how it worked out for them when they were in the office. Farhaan was quiet but very assertive. Just one look from him and everyone would fall silent. Nouman, on the other hand, kept up a constant stream of words and people avoided being with him in the same room for too long because they never got their work done.

'Ammi also really likes this Ana. I can't believe that insufferable friend of yours is going to become a part of our family,' Nouman said, sniffing. Luqman smiled the slightest bit. Nouman had hated Ayub right from school because Ayub loved to pull his leg all the time. Nouman liked to take himself seriously and didn't enjoy it when others didn't and thought he was inadvertently funny.

Luqman shut his eyes and opened them immediately. The eyes he kept seeing whenever he tried to fall asleep – they were Ana's, he realised. This jolted him even more. The thoughts that just the mere mention of Ana's name inspired were not appropriate at all, he acknowledged.

He had to do something. He had to stop obsessing over his brother's fiancée.

'I'm tired. I want to sleep for some time,' he told Nouman, his throat suddenly dry.

'Sure. I have some work to catch up on. I'll come and see if you need anything in a bit,' Nouman said as he rose and left.

TWENTY-SIX

Ana leaned over him and he opened his eyes, startling her. Her pretty face flushed pink and he smiled, pulling her hand towards him.

'Where were you all this while?' he asked her. She tried to remove her hand from his but he wouldn't let go. So she gave up squirming after that and moved closer to him. He realised he was lying on the hospital bed and wondered why he was still there. Hadn't he been discharged? But he stopped thinking when she splayed her hands on his chest and snuggled close to him.

She looked at him and pressed closer to kiss his chin. 'I was here. Watching over you,' she whispered.

His life was perfect, Luqman thought, his happiness bubbling over inside as he clutched her wrist.

'Don't let go of me,' he told her, looking into her eyes. Her eyes that had captivated him the moment he had seen her.

She shook her head and the silver jhumkis in her ears clinked. He touched one of the jhumkis, his fingers exploring the delicate shell of her ear, and she closed her eyes and sighed.

She said something but he couldn't hear her. 'You need to come closer,' he said. She looked at him shyly.

'I'm close enough already,' she said, rubbing his chest and leaning down to kiss the centre.

Luqman closed his eyes and groaned as he cupped her face and kissed her. She kissed him back, holding the back of his head and he felt that same sense of rightness. He smiled and she lifted her head and traced his smile.

'You beat me to it,' she whispered, her breath warm on his lips.

'Beat you to what?' he asked, puzzled, as he settled deeper into the bed and pulled her on top of him. She threw her arms around him and pushed her face into his neck and he ran his hands down her back. Her deep green shalwar kameez was in the way. He wanted to pull it aside, to touch her skin, to taste her, every inch of her.

She lifted her head and her throat worked. 'I wanted to kiss you,' she said and moved closer. But what was this? Why couldn't he feel anything? A beautiful girl like Ana was sprawled over him and he felt numb. Only his heart raced. He still had his legs, didn't he? The accident came back to him in a rush but Ana's face swam before him and he tried to put aside the thoughts of the crash.

His mouth dry, he watched as she brought her lips to touch his. He felt that same anxiousness that had been plaguing him for days now. It twisted inside his stomach, and he tried to push it away, tried to feel what was happening to him. He opened his mouth to say something but she pushed her tongue in and he froze.

'What is it?' she asked, smoothing his eyebrows with her thumbs, still kissing his jaw, his neck.

'Nothing. Why are we on a hospital bed?' he asked, knowing he was asking a stupid question. What did it matter where they were?

She looked down and he followed her gaze but when he looked back up, she wasn't there and he opened his eyes, horrified.

He was in his house, lying on the bed in the guestroom, while Nouman dozed in a chair. He looked outside, wondering what time it was. It was evening. He wiped his mouth with the back of his hand, as though it would erase what it had done just now in his dream. He had kissed Ana, had wanted to make love with her and she had seemed keen and eager for his touch. What the fuck was the matter with him? She was going to be his Bhabhi.

Fuck no, the thought erupted. But she was going to be in just a few months. How would he ever face her? Why was he lusting after her? He barely knew her.

His throat felt dry and he cleared it. Nouman sat up and yawned. 'What do you need?' he asked.

'Just some water. I can get it. You go to your room and sleep,' he told him.

'You sure?' Nouman asked.

Luqman nodded. 'Yes, sure. Go on now,' he told him, glad that the room was dim. His brother wouldn't see the guilty expression on his face, thankfully. But to his dismay, Farhaan walked in and switched on the lights in the room. He dropped his car keys on a chest of drawers that was near the entrance to the room.

Luqman watched his brother walk with long purposeful strides. Even though he was just a little more than three years older than him, there had always been something aloof about Farhaan. Luqman admired everything about his brother and had tried to emulate him as much as possible when he had been a child. His hero worship hadn't changed now that they were grown up.

What would Farhaan do if he ever found out about the sort of dream he had just had about Ana? He shut his eyes in despair. The dream had been so vivid, so lifelike, so sweet. Even though his thoughts had moved into X-rated territory in it, there had been an undercurrent of love and an innate sense of rightness in that dream. Things had been fine when his eyes were shut. It was only when he opened them that he realised the nightmare this was.

What sort of cliché was he, falling in love with his older brother's fiancée? Because he knew that somehow he had fallen for her and the moment he had heard she was marrying his brother, he had wanted her for himself.

Imagine what Ana would think of him when she got married and started living here, he thought in horror. She would be disgusted if she got even a whiff of his feelings towards her. He knew she was upright and honest. Maybe he would get a job abroad, or ask Akshay to just send him away for good. He could probably relocate to the US or to their branch in Australia and never return.

During the few times he would visit home, she would be busy with her life, her children and he would no longer be pining after her. This was for the best, he thought, even though the thought of Ana with Farhaan made him a little dizzy.

'Are you all right?' Farhaan asked as he sat down in the chair that Nouman had just vacated.

'Yeah,' he lied.

'Don't lie to me. I always know when you're lying,' Farhaan said with a smile.

'What's my tell? Why won't you let me know?' Luqman asked. It was true. Farhaan always knew when he was lying.

His brother shook his head. 'I'm not telling. You have to stop lying,' he told Luqman. 'What's the matter?'

'Just wondering why this had to happen,' Luqman murmured. At least this was the truth. Why did this weird thing happen to him?

'The accident? Who knows? You were saved and that's the most important thing,' Farhaan said. Luqman nodded.

'Your boss, Akshay, called me,' Farhaan said suddenly. Luqman looked up at him, surprised.

'Why?'

'He didn't have your new number so I gave it to him. He wanted to send you a new company laptop but I told him you needed to rest for a few more days,' he said.

'What? Why not? I would have loved to get some work done!' Luqman protested.

'No. Not until you're fully healed. Sleep and rest. It's the best thing for you now,' Farhaan said, getting up from the chair. 'Ammi! I want tea!' he called out as he left the room.

Sleep and rest. He was tempted to close his eyes once more. Maybe he would see Ana again. And one of these days, if he ended up making love to her in his dreams, there was no way he could ever face her in real life. This was so shameful, he decided he could never talk about this to anyone at all. Not even Ayub.

TWENTY-SEVEN

Ana, Athiya and Tehzeeb were sitting in their old room in Jasmine Villa, each trying to talk over the other. Tehzeeb had left Aslan with her in-laws and she had come to discuss things with them, to talk sense into Ana actually. The fan whirred above them slowly but did nothing to dispel the heat. It didn't help that the three young women were already having a heated discussion. It was nearly April now, and summer had already begun in Bangalore.

'Didn't we discuss this last week when you were at my house? That we have to come clean to Abbu? Tell him everything,' she said. She was sitting cross-legged on the bed and Ana almost felt like it was the old days. Except it wasn't. Her heart felt like it was constantly being crushed but she was keeping a brave face and trying to behave like everything was fine.

'Yes, but that was before Abbu signed the contract with Farhaan. I looked it over, by the way, and it is a really good deal, Api,' Ana said, picking up her mobile phone and turning it this way and that. Luqman's phone had been destroyed in his accident and he'd even gotten a new number which she didn't have. She had saved his display picture from his earlier number though and she would look at it every now and then. And while she agreed this wasn't healthy, she couldn't quite help it.

'What do you mean?' Tehzeeb asked, frowning. Athiya looked at both of them, annoyed.

'She means that Farhaan is giving us a good deal because he's marrying her,' she snapped.

'Oh! I didn't know that!' Tehzeeb said. She looked at both of them and reached out to hold their hands. 'Listen Ana, you're making a mistake.'

Ana shook her head but still held Tehzeeb's hand. 'I can't do anything about it now. Anyhow, Luqman doesn't remember me. On that plane ride, he had told me that he was planning to relocate abroad and maybe he will,' she said. Her heart ached at the thought of not seeing him again. She took a deep breath. She had to stop thinking of the moments they had shared together, the quiet conversation they had, the way his eyes had travelled over her face, the way he looked when they'd locked eyes.

None of it meant anything. She promised herself she would delete his photo from her phone. Soon.

'And what if he doesn't relocate?' Tehzeeb asked.

'Or what if he remembers everything after you get married to his older brother?' Athiya asked. Ana winced. She hadn't thought of that possibility. That would be terrible, like rubbing salt into a festering wound.

She squared her jaw. 'Abbu has not been this happy in a long time. I can't bear to hurt his feelings because … because I fell in love with the wrong brother,' she said, pulling out her hand away and rubbing her face with it. Her hand trembled and both her sisters saw it. Abbu was not at home at the moment which was why they were having this conversation.

'And what about *your* feelings?' Athiya asked. Her anger was always at the tip these days, and she was ready to lash out at her for the smallest infraction.

'I'll live with it,' Ana said.

'You don't have to, you know. You don't have to be this martyr. Just come clean. If Abbu is a bit upset at first, he'll get over it,' Athiya said. Ana shook her head resolutely.

'Just yesterday, he was telling me that after I get married, Farhaan will be setting the two of you up in a small apartment somewhere until the construction here is finished. Abbu has made plans, Athiya. Long-term plans. And it's important I get married for those plans to work out,' Ana said.

Tehzeeb looked at her shrewdly. 'Tell me, how will you feel eventually when Luqman gets married and you have to see him with his wife?' she asked.

Ana's face paled. She hadn't thought of all that. But the very thought of someone else with Luqman made her feel sick. She knew it was all there on her face and her sisters could read it. Tehzeeb pressed on with her point.

'Ana, it's not too late. There is no engagement for you to break off. Just tell Abbu that you can't marry Farhaan,' she said.

Ana sighed. 'Just let me be. I don't want to create any problems for Abbu. I'm fine. Farhaan also seems like a nice person. Maybe I'll eventually fall in love with him,' she said.

Athiya snorted. 'You're such an ass. Not only are you ruining your own life as well as Luqman's, you're also ruining Farhaan's?' she asked.

'What do you care?' Ana shouted at her, then winced and lowered her tone. 'I am NOT talking to Abbu about this. If Luqman didn't have the accident and if he hadn't forgotten me, I would have considered talking to Abbu to tell him something at least. But now, I'm not doing anything. This discussion is over.'

She got up and walked out, leaving her sisters looking after her in concern. She knew they were right. In a perfect world, she would speak to Abbu, tell him to back out of the agreement and the wedding so that she could be free to live out her life just remembering those moments with Luqman. But this wasn't the perfect world.

Abbu was as excited as a little boy these days. He had already made plans to give each one of them an apartment and keep one for himself. The apartments could be rented out and would give all three sisters some sort of income, whether or not they got jobs, not that Tehzeeb Api needed any money. But Ana knew how important it was for Abbu. He knew how he felt when he was with Tehzeeb Api's in-laws; her father-in-law Bakhtiyar Ahmed had, in fact, manipulated a situation to make sure Tehzeeb married Ayub Bhai.

Ana knew that Abbu felt tons better now that he could give Tehzeeb Api an apartment; her own little legacy of the Jasmine Villa. Since Ayub Bhai was an architect, he had asked him to come up with a suitable plan for the building, and Ayub Bhai had agreed. Abbu was no doubt thrilled. One son-in-law was designing the apartment and a future son-in-law was building it. What more could he want? She had heard him say as much to someone on the phone the other day.

How could she take all of this away from him?

TWENTY-EIGHT

Four months later

Luqman had gone back to work just a few weeks after his accident. He had continued to work from home until his leg was healed although he couldn't drive yet. He was anxious about taking a cab to work but decided that he couldn't be afraid of getting into an Uber again. He threw himself into work, barely staying at home because all that was happening there were discussions about the wedding and he hated listening to them.

Ammi had gone overboard with the shopping, buying bridal finery and shoes and jewellery for Ana. One day, when he had come back from work, he saw that the house was full of relatives. Since the wedding was happening the next month, Ammi kept muttering that there was so much to do and hardly any time. She rued not having a daughter who would have at least helped her out in some of the work.

The relatives at home that day had gathered in the living room and Luqman was just on his way upstairs to his room when Ammi called out his name. He still got tired quickly because he was not taking it easy at work. His leg hurt like a bitch sometimes but he didn't say anything to anyone because it had almost healed. He did dread climbing the staircase every night because of the pain but he kept at it stoically. In fact, he welcomed the pain. It was punishment for what his mind was putting him through every single night.

The dreams about Ana hadn't stopped. In fact, they'd become worse, more intimate. He woke up almost every night, aroused, ashamed and hating himself. Why was this happening to him? Why did he have to think of her this way?

'What is it, Ammi?' he asked, exhaling loudly. His body hurt. He wanted nothing more than to get under a hot shower. He knew he was over-exerting himself but he deserved the pain.

'Come and see what we have got for your Bhabhi!' she said in a sing-song voice. Other aunties giggled as he rolled his eyes.

'Why do I need to see it?' he asked.

'Because your brother is too shy and doesn't have an opinion about this,' Ammi said. More aunties tittered. 'Here. How do you think Ana will look in this?'

She spread out the lehenga in front of her lavishly. It was an unusual colour, he had to admit. He thought all brides wore red or maroon. This was a sort of textured deep silvery grey. It glittered quietly with blue stones and the drapes fell over the sofa almost sensuously.

He could picture her in it. She would look demure and elegant but not really bride-like.

'I don't know,' he said finally. 'It doesn't look very bridal to me.'

Ammi looked at him triumphantly. She turned to the other ladies. 'See? I told you my boy had taste,' she said.

Luqman frowned. 'What do you mean?'

'This isn't the bridal ghagra. It's for the Haldi,' Ammi said.

Luqman had already turned around, tuning out the discussion. 'Fine, Ammi. Let me go up now,' he said. He overheard Ammi defending the choice of the lehenga against the other ladies who kept insisting that the Haldi outfit should be in some shade of yellow and that she needn't have bothered getting such a lavish outfit.

'The girl's side should be getting the Haldiwala outfit. Why did you spend thirty thousand on this?' one auntie asked.

'Because I want it to be special and it's my darling Farhaan's wedding. I'm so happy, I can't contain myself,' Ammi said.

Swallowing, Luqman started the painful ascent upwards to his room. The past few months had passed by in a blur. Each day had been a struggle for him to recover and heal and work had been his saviour. But each night, Ana appeared in his dreams, making him wish he never had to sleep again in his life. At the same time, he couldn't wait to shut his eyes either, because she always embraced him, held him close, murmured sweet nothings in his ear, kissed him and made him feel like nothing could go wrong.

What sort of a sick bastard was he to be lusting after this girl who was promised to his brother? He stripped out of his clothes and headed straight to the shower. But it wasn't just lust. He was in love with her and this, he felt with as much surety as the beating of his heart. Why did this have to happen to him, he thought furiously.

What should he do? How could he stay here once Farhaan got married? How could he *ever* face her? He knew the time had come to make a decision. He had to speak to Akshay about a relocation opportunity or find another job overseas and quit here. He had to get started now so he could leave immediately after Bhai's wedding, he mused as he stood under the hot shower.

He had already decided this a couple of months ago but now he was firm. He wasn't going to be swayed by anything anyone said. He shut off the tap, wrapped a towel around his hips and walked outside, wondering if he should say something to Ayub. But he had been avoiding his best friend for a while now. He knew Ayub always found out when he was lying. He was like Farhaan Bhai in that way.

He didn't want to take the chance of Ayub finding out about his feelings even accidentally. He wouldn't know how to face him. Also, every time he thought of Ayub, he automatically linked it to Tehzeeb and then, of course, to Ana. The three times he had met her were so crystal clear in his mind, but at the same time, he was afraid to probe those memories further. He felt like there was something he was forgetting, something important. But he didn't even know what he had forgotten, so how could he try to remember it?

TWENTY-NINE

Athiya couldn't even pin down her bad mood to PMS because no PMS lasted weeks and even months. She was always angry with everyone, she thought, as she stepped out of the college gates with a couple of her classmates. Even her friends were wary of her temper these days and avoided talking about anything that could create conflict and that annoyed her even more.

She was going to have to change something about herself, she thought, as they walked into the coffee shop nearby that was crowded with students and a few brave teachers. Loud music played in the background and no one could hear what anyone else was saying. Athiya and her two classmates Ashwini and Payal found an empty table and sat down. College was nearly over and they weren't required to attend classes anymore as their exams would be held in a month or so.

She barely heard what Payal was saying to her but she nodded, trying to calm her nerves. Maybe she should try yoga and meditation. But her mind would never shut up long enough for her to be any good at it. They ordered their usual coffee and sandwiches and Athiya thought of the work that was lying in wait for her once Ana got married.

Abbu had said that in less than a month after the wedding, they would have to move out to the rented apartment so that Farhaan could start demolishing their old house and begin construction. The very idea of packing all their belongings, deciding what to keep and what to discard was daunting. Even more so since they had lived at Jasmine Villa all their lives.

Her heart ached at the thought of the house being torn down. Those walls with their peeling paint, the red oxide floor, the old, rusting taps in the bathroom, the shower that sputtered more often than it worked, she would miss it all. It was home, after all, the place where Ammi had breathed her last.

Don't go there, she told herself, trying to think of something else immediately. Sometimes it worked, sometimes it didn't. She and Tehzeeb had given up trying to make Ana see what a huge mistake she was making. The wedding was happening soon and Abbu had started going on rounds for the invitations, sometimes taking Tehzeeb and sometimes that pesky Taskeen Auntie if Tehzeeb wasn't available.

If it hadn't been for all this Luqman bullshit, Athiya would have been quite pleased with how things had turned out for Ana. Taskeen Auntie had been mystified and quite astonished that her plain old Yusuf Bhai had managed to find such good matches for his daughter without her meddling.

'Never mind. I will find a boy for Athiya,' she had crooned. Athiya had shot her a look filled with so much irritation that Taskeen Auntie had looked away nervously.

The coffee arrived and the three of them got busy opening the sugar sachets and stirring it into the coffee.

Athiya had to bring herself out of this funk and control her anger. It was not going to help anyone. She remembered what the counsellor in school used to say about her anger issues, about how she used anger to stop herself from feeling anything else. She had lashed out at the poor woman, saying that she'd rather be angry than sad.

The bell above the door tinkled as someone pushed it open. Athiya sat back in surprise when she saw that it was Farhaan. She watched as he looked around, making a face when he realised that there were college students here but the person standing behind him nudged him and he walked inside with a look of suffering.

He and his companion, a middle-aged man, spotted an empty table and sat down.

He hadn't seen her, so Athiya could look at him properly for the time being. He was really good-looking in that broody, unattainable sort of way and she wondered why Ana couldn't have fallen for him. Never mind. Ana thought her feelings were like a switch. Did she actually believe that once she got married, she would be able to switch off her feelings for Luqman and activate them for Farhaan instead? What an idiot her sister was.

Farhaan inspected the menu, a frown on his forehead. The glasses made him look distinguished and neater around the edges. He smiled at the man with him and asked him to choose something. The man shook his head so Farhaan beckoned the waiter and asked for two cups of coffee. As he put down the menu card, he noticed her and their eyes met.

Athiya found that she couldn't look away. She tried to make her face smile but realised she didn't know how. Shit. Had she forgotten how to smile? He looked surprised but more in a way that looked like he was trying to recall where he had seen her. Did all the stupid men in their family have memory issues, she wondered. She looked down finally and took a sip of her coffee.

'I can't wait to get a job, Athiya. I just hope I get something decent,' Payal was saying.

'Um hmm,' Athiya said, trying hard not to look in the direction of Farhaan's table.

'Don't you think Ashwini will look nice if she dyed her hair purple?' Payal asked.

'Um, sure,' Athiya responded. Then she registered the words and put her coffee cup down.

'What?'

'See? I told you she's been distracted,' Payal said to Ashwini.

Ashwini rolled her eyes. 'What's new? The only difference is that we're not scared of telling you the truth. I think,' she added with a shudder.

Athiya looked at both of them and burst out laughing. 'Since when have you two ever been scared of me?' she asked.

'Since you've been biting off everyone's head in class for the smallest of things! And everyone has been walking around you on eggshells,' Payal said.

Athiya sighed. 'I'm sorry, guys. I never mean to get angry but sometimes it's like my default emotion. I can't seem to help myself,' she said.

'Yes, but we've known you since undergraduate college and it's never been this bad before. What's going on? You can tell us surely,' Ashwini said, putting her hand on Athiya's wrist.

Athiya sighed again and lowered her voice. 'See that

guy who just walked in and sat down on that table? Don't look *now*. You'll make it look obvious. Yeah, so he's getting married to my sister next month,' she said.

Payal and Ashwini checked him out as unobtrusively as they could.

'Wow. Nice looking guy,' Payal said. But she frowned. 'But why should that make you angry? Unless you like him or something?' She looked horrified at the thought.

Athiya's eyes widened. 'What? No, absolutely not!' she said, her voice loud and then she had to lower it again.

'That's not the issue,' she told her friends. And lowering her voice even further, she told them about Ana and Luqman.

'What the hell, man? This is like some movie. Why is your sister hell-bent on ruining her life?' Payal asked, a little too loudly.

'Shh. That's what's been making me angry these days. She's been saying that Abbu is happy and so she's willing to sacrifice her own happiness for him,' Athiya said.

'That's crazy. You'd never do that, right?' Ashwini asked.

Athiya sat back, surprised. She had never put herself before in Ana's shoes. She had just been annoyed and angry with her. She glanced at Farhaan again who was talking to the man with him, a client probably, but his eyes kept straying to her, like he was still trying to figure out who she was.

Would she have done what Ana was doing? She had seen how happy Abbu was these days as he walked around, humming to himself, making plans for the apartments and all sorts of things. But she honestly didn't know if she would have done the same thing if it was her in Ana's situation.

THIRTY

Farhaan nodded politely but he was horrified that his mind was so distracted at the moment. He had barely heard what Mr Joshi was saying. Mr Kapil Joshi was another developer with whom he was working on a project to build villas on the outskirts of Bangalore. It was a gated community project and they did one of those, every couple of years. They had had to meet a financier who lived on this side of the city and the meeting had just concluded.

Farhaan wanted to speak with Mr Joshi for a few minutes and discuss options and he thought it best if they spoke right away before they each went their way. Mr Joshi's office was far from his and he knew how dicey things became with him. He hated that he had to work with him sometimes because Mr Joshi was always trying to gain the upper hand. He would ask him to come to his office and refuse to come to Farhaan's, indirectly implying that because he was senior in age and experience, Farhaan should bow to him automatically. Mr Joshi had previously been working with Abbu and Farhaan had just continued because it had been profitable and made sound business sense.

Now, however, his eyes kept wandering over to that pretty girl sitting at the table near his. Who was she and where had he seen her? She had a certain look about her – fearless and her chin jutted out every now and then as she spoke to her friends. Her skin was flawless and it glowed even under the harsh lights of the coffee shop.

'So tull me, Farhaan,' Mr Joshi continued and then stopped. Farhaan looked away from the girl quickly but it was too late. Mr Joshi had already seen why he was so distracted.

'You know that girl?' he asked him. Blushing, Farhaan shook his head.

'No, no,' he said quickly. 'She just looked familiar.'

Mr Joshi gave him a wry look. 'You're getting married next month and alruddy on the lookout for extra action?' he asked with a wink.

Farhaan stilled. He took a deep breath and tried to get his temper under control. Few people had seen him lose his temper and he prided himself on it. He shook his head.

'It's nothing like that,' he said curtly as the waiter brought their coffee and kept it on the table. He opened his file and realised that coming to this coffee shop had been a mistake. But he had been in a hurry to deflect Mr Joshi who would have asked him to come to his office and he had stopped at the very first coffee shop he had seen, not realising it was close to a college and probably full of students.

That girl who had been staring at him was probably just nineteen or twenty. What was wrong with him, and why had he been staring back? Was it just because she looked familiar or … she suddenly burst into laughter and Farhaan felt the hair on his arms prickle. The sound of her laughter shot straight to his gut, warming it and he looked away, annoyed.

Focus, Farhaan. Focus, he told himself. He had the

vaguest feeling that the young woman and her friends were checking him out but he opened the file and started going through the figures when he heard something that made him pause.

'... why is your sister hell-bent on ruining her life?'

He looked up. Suddenly, he remembered how he knew this girl. It was Ana's younger sister although he realised he didn't know her name.

He shut the file resolutely, deciding to go with Mr Joshi to his office after all to discuss things because he couldn't focus. Also, what did the other girl mean when she'd asked that question? How was Ana ruining her life by marrying him?

This was confusing and uncalled for.

'Mr Joshi, it's too noisy here. Coming here was a mistake. Let's just go to your office to discuss the financials,' he said.

The older man nodded, still giving him a knowing look as he sipped his coffee. Farhaan couldn't wait to leave. He wondered if he should speak to Ayub and ask if everything was all right with Ana.

He thought he had been the most courteous fiancé, going about his own way, doing his own thing, but he realised now it had nothing to do with courtesy. It was because the wedding was another chore on his list of tasks. Get married. Have children. He was not excited about it and he certainly hadn't given a second thought to Ana since the one and only time he had met her at her house.

But for the first time, he paused. Was this what he really wanted? Did he want to go through life, checking items off like a to-do list?

No, he thought decisively.

There was still a little under a month till he got married.

He was going to take a little more interest in his personal affairs and not end up like some of the people he had seen for whom life was a series of meaningless moments.

He looked up and glanced at her again. The young woman who was going to be his sister-in-law. She looked up at him just then and he realised she knew who he was. He smiled at her tentatively and to his surprise, she rolled her eyes and gave him a wry smile. He understood what it meant – that he had recognised her finally.

Mr Joshi clapped him on the shoulder as he beckoned the waiter for the bill.

'No, I've got this,' Farhaan said, pulling out his wallet from the back pocket of his jeans.

'No, no. You keep staring at the pretty girl. I'll pay the bill,' Mr Joshi said.

'Mr Joshi, it's not like that. She just looked familiar and I realised she's my fiancée's younger sister. That is all,' Farhaan said tightly.

'Yes, yes, shoor,' Mr Joshi replied, still giving him that knowing smile. 'After all, saali aadhi gharwali hoti hai.'

Farhaan counted to ten in his head and took a deep breath. In his mind's eye, he had just banged Mr Joshi's head on the table and bent close to him to tell him to mind his own business. 'But first, *you* stop staring at her!' he had snarled. Mr Joshi looked back at him, quivering, his nose running, tears springing in his eyes. 'Whatever you say, Farhaan. Whatever you say!' he said.

In reality, he smiled at Mr Joshi and rose to leave.

THIRTY-ONE

Haldi – One day before the wedding

Not too long ago, Tehzeeb had sat before the same mirror as she had readied herself for her wedding to Ayub. Ana remembered that her sister had been nervous but excited and there had been an undercurrent of anticipation in everything she did. She rubbed the centre of her chest, hoping it would stop the numbness and make her feel. But it didn't help.

The past few months had flown past in shopping with her sisters who had finally stopped telling her she was making a mistake. She had taken leave from work last week and Tehzeeb had insisted on treating her to some fancy spa treatment a couple of days ago. When Ana had been reluctant, Tehzeeb told her that she would be paying for it out of her own money if that made any difference to her.

Aslan was now nearly a year old and Tehzeeb had returned to her job a couple of months ago. Ana wondered how her mother-in-law had taken it but she didn't delve into her sister's life in detail. She had agreed to the spa thing reluctantly but as she lay there, her skin tightening as the face mask dried, she thought it was an apt metaphor for her heart too.

Athiya had joined them too and Ana realised it was good in a way because she would miss being with her sisters once she was married. Tehzeeb's in-laws were very cool and open-minded but she had her doubts about Farhaan's mother. After all, she remembered Luqman being apprehensive about speaking to her about the two of them.

Now, on the night of the Haldi, she was dressed in the dove-grey lehenga choli set that had been sent by Farhaan's mother. At home, the relatives who had come over to stay for the wedding had gasped when they had seen how pretty it was.

Ana agreed it was indeed very beautiful and in a subdued and classy way, unlike Tehzeeb's engagement gown that had cost lakhs. The accompanying note read that since Ana hadn't had an engagement, Farhan's mother had wanted to get something unique for her for the Haldi and she hoped Ana would like it.

Ana was supposed to wear the bare minimum today – both in makeup and jewellery. She was to look understated so that tomorrow, when she wore the wedding ensemble, she would be radiant.

But my heart is dead, she mused as she applied some colour to her cheeks. Tehzeeb was standing behind her, looking at her reflection in the mirror. Her jaw worked as though she was trying hard to stop herself from saying something. When other people who had been milling in the room left, Tehzeeb pulled up a stool and sat down beside her.

'Are you sure you can do this?' she asked Ana.

Ana shrugged. 'I'll live. It's not a big deal,' she said.

'You won't be living, Ana. You'll only be existing. Are you sure you want to spending time with her sisters

'Just let it be,' Ana snapped. She looked around for the jewellery that she was supposed to wear and she couldn't find it.

'What am I supposed to wear with this?' she asked. It was nearly time for them to leave for the function hall that Abbu had booked for today. Relatives had started leaving, booking autos and cabs and the house was emptying. Tehzeeb had promised Abbu that she and Ayub would bring Ana with them in Ayub's car.

Ayub was sitting in the living room, keeping Aslan busy.

Tehzeeb looked through the jewellery box and frowned. 'I don't know. I can't quite figure out what you need to wear with this. Gold would clash, so diamonds or pearls would have been best,' she said.

Ana rolled her eyes at herself in the mirror. Tehzeeb found it far easier to talk about solitaires and diamonds and pearls now that she was married to Ayub.

'Why yes, Api. Why don't you hand me that Kohinoor necklace that is lying there on top of the dresser?' Ana asked, mockingly.

'Ha ha, very funny,' Tehzeeb muttered. The doorbell rang just then and neither of them bothered to see who it was. People had been coming and going all evening. Athiya or Ayub would probably answer the door.

While Tehzeeb figured out what jewellery would complement the outfit today, Ana froze because she heard Luqman's voice. Tehzeeb, too, looked up in shock. She put the jewellery box on top of the dresser and went outside.

Ana's face had paled. Her stomach dropped and her mouth turned dry. Instantly, her hands had become clammy. She edged towards the door, wondering if she could bear to look at him now, when she hadn't seen him since the day he had been in the ICU. When he had failed to recognise her.

She stood at the threshold of her room, leaning forward to see if she could spot a glimpse of him. There he was. Dressed in a formal dark blue shirt paired with beige trousers, he looked a little flustered. She edged closer to hear the conversation and couldn't keep her eyes off him. He looked all healed and just like the man she had met on the plane, the one she had fallen in love with. And suddenly, her heart wasn't dead.

It had sprung to life on seeing him, beating so quickly that she almost gasped. She clutched the doorjamb and bit her lower lip. This was madness. Why had she thought she would be able to live under the same roof as him as his brother's wife? How could she have underestimated what he made her feel? She took in his features, happy to note that there was no indication of his accident. All the scars had healed, except the one in her heart. It had just been gashed open once again.

'Listen, man, don't be angry. I was just very busy at work,' she heard Luqman say. Tehzeeb had told her that Luqman hadn't spoken to Ayub in months which was strange. He hadn't answered phone calls and he had avoided meeting him too.

She couldn't hear Ayub Bhai's answer but she heard Aslan's chatter. Tehzeeb spoke softly, asking after his health.

'I'm fine, Tehzeeb,' he said.

Athiya emerged from Abbu's room and noticed Ana standing at the door, looking at Luqman longingly. Athiya's face clouded.

'I've come here to give this to –' he looked down and then up once more, '– to Ana.'

'What is it?' Tehzeeb asked.

'Ammi said she'd forgotten to send it with the outfit for today. Apparently, she wants Ana to wear it and asked me to drop it off at your house,' Luqman said.

Ana stared at him. He was here, in her house. He was just a few feet away from her. And she could do nothing. She was a fool. The biggest fool in the world to think she could make her marriage with Farhaan work.

She couldn't see Ayub Bhai or Tehzeeb's expressions. She wondered what they made of it when Athiya stepped forward, clearing her throat.

'Great. You can give it to her yourself,' she said. 'Ana Api, why don't you come out and take this necklace from your brother-in-law?'

Shit. That fool Athiya. What was she up to? But Ana couldn't just stay inside and pretend not to have heard, especially since she was already half out of the room.

She stepped forward. Everyone else around her melted away, blurred into soft focus but Luqman stood out in sharp relief, like he had been outlined with a pen. He stared at her, his eyes not leaving hers. Her heart jumped, no longer sluggish like it had been all these months.

'Here,' he said, handing over a box to her. Ana took it from him. She tried to look away but couldn't and he seemed to be suffering from the same problem.

'Dude, we have to leave now,' Ayub Bhai said, breaking the spell. 'We'll see you in the function hall in a bit, okay?'

'Thank god you're asking him to go and not asking me to make tea for him,' Athiya joked. Tehzeeb gasped but Ayub Bhai merely smiled, shaking his head.

'Okay, I'll see you all there,' he said, and turning around, he walked away. Ana could feel the energy in her body drain away with every step he took. She wanted to turn around, go back into her room and collapse on the bed.

Her sisters had been right. She should have put a stop to this right after his accident. Now it was too late. She would be getting married to his brother tomorrow.

THIRTY-TWO

Keep walking. Keep walking. Luqman muttered under his breath as he stepped outside the house. The jasmine tree that gave the house its name was full of lush blossoms and the air was heavy with its scent. He had parked his car nearby. He had been aghast when Ammi had given him the duty to drop off the necklace at Ana's house. Why couldn't Nouman go? But he was apparently ferrying relatives and doing other odd jobs which he, Luqman, still couldn't manage because he wasn't driving that much yet and Ammi didn't trust anyone else with the necklace.

He opened the gate and stepped out. He looked back at the house that looked like a tired bride, not unlike Ana herself. She had looked stunning in that silvery grey lehenga and he knew she was going to torture him once more in his dreams tonight. But there was something else in her eyes, a kind of pain that had surprised him. She looked exhausted. There were shadows under her eyes, like she hadn't been sleeping well either.

Cursing himself, he approached his car and drove to the function hall. Upon reaching, he parked his car in the basement parking area and got out almost reluctantly. This night couldn't get over soon enough, he thought as he noticed relatives who were starting to come for the event. Ammi and Farhaan Bhai would reach soon. Maybe he could skip the event by telling them that he wasn't feeling too well but he knew Ammi would be upset.

He was entering the hall when he heard a voice call out his name. He stopped and then turned around. It was the youngest sister and he recalled her name suddenly – Athiya. He wondered how he knew her name when he had met her for the first time just a little while ago.

She was walking towards him with determined strides and he frowned. 'Did I forget something?' he asked when she had neared. She stopped short and stared at him disbelievingly. Indicating they should shift to a quieter place, she moved to the side of the hall and he followed her. She turned around and he realised she was angry.

'You fool,' she snapped out. He reared back, shocked.

'What?'

'You love her. It's as plain as the nose on your face,' she accused him. Luqman felt himself turning red.

'What nonsense,' he muttered. Was he that transparent? How was he even going to survive till the wedding festivities got over? Akshay had reluctantly given him another chance to prove himself and he was being sent to manage one of the overseas projects for a couple of months before they would decide whether or not he could do it on a more permanent basis. He was due to leave next Saturday, six days from now. He didn't know if he could hold out that long.

Athiya was still staring at him with narrowed eyes. He had to get away from her.

'You didn't forget something. You forgot *someone*,' she said.

'What?'

'You forgot Ana,' she said, her voice lowered. He wanted to laugh at her. How could he forget her when she appeared in his dreams every night? As the wedding neared, in some of the dreams she was even his wife.

'I don't know what you mean,' he said. She stepped closer, her brown eyes lit up like sparks as she swallowed hard, looked around and then took a deep breath.

'I don't know if this is good for you or not but frankly, I don't care. Given the way you just looked at her and she at you, she's going to ruin her life if she gets married to your brother tomorrow,' Athiya said in the same low voice.

Luqman felt his blood turn cold but he waited for Athiya to continue talking. She didn't disappoint.

'You forgot her after your accident,' she said. He shook his head.

'I didn't. I remember her clearly,' he said. She looked shocked and then furious enough to hit his chest with both her palms.

'Then why are you doing this? Why didn't you speak to your mother like you said you would? You two had so many plans and now she's going into this marriage like a lamb to slaughter. Why would you do that to her?'

He paled. 'Plans? I was supposed to speak to Ammi?' he repeated. The churning in his stomach began in earnest and he needed to get away from there to think. His mind suddenly felt like it was in freefall.

'You still don't remember, do you? You met her on the flight and both of you were sitting together. You two talked throughout the flight and fell in love but since you didn't reach out to Api, she foolishly agreed to let Abbu go and see a boy for her. It turned out to be your brother and then when you heard about it, you came back from the

US immediately. You spoke to her on the phone late that night. I heard her speaking to you, dammit. And the next morning, while going home, you had your accident,' Athiya said.

Luqman stared at her and staggered back a little. Was this true? Little bits of jagged memories floated around in his head, struggling against something to come together. His head hurt with the effort and she looked at him, concerned.

'Fuck. I'm sorry. I shouldn't have said all this to you,' she said.

'But why didn't anyone tell me anything before? Who knew about it?' Luqman asked.

'Ayub Bhai and Tehzeeb Api knew about it. And me. That's it. No one else knows,' she said.

'Ayub knew? Why didn't he ...' Luqman trailed away, remembering that time when Ayub had visited him in the hospital. He'd foolishly avoided Ayub all these months thinking that he would remind her of Ana but if he'd just shared some of his concerns about her, like why she kept appearing in his dreams, he may have enlightened him.

'Does she also love me?' he asked suddenly. The memories would come eventually, he thought. Now that he knew there was a reason why she was so important to him, why he felt the way he did, he had to know about her feelings as well.

Athiya stared back at him. 'Of course. She loves you. She visited you in the ICU and you didn't recognise her. It broke her heart.'

Luqman remembered that moment clearly, when he'd woken up to something feathery soft and light that reached out to him, even over the pain.

'Why is she getting married to Farhaan Bhai then?' he

asked, frantic with the realisation that the love of his life would be marrying his brother tomorrow and he still didn't know what he could do about it.

'For the house,' she sighed. 'Abbu signed the joint development contract with Farhaan and Ana didn't want to upset him.'

'So she's willing to marry the brother of the man she loves?'

'I know, right? Tehzeeb Api and I have tried again and again to convince her that she's wrong. But she wouldn't listen,' Athiya said.

No wonder he had felt that sharp sting of recognition when he saw her now, that hard knock in the centre of his chest that left him breathless.

'Do you remember at least something now?' she asked him. He frowned.

'My mind doesn't remember but my heart does. And I've been beating myself up over this for the past few months, wondering what sort of person would be in love with his brother's fiancée,' he said.

Athiya exhaled. 'What a mess. What are you going to do now?' she asked.

His stomach hurt once more but he pushed it aside. He now knew the important thing he felt he had forgotten all these months, even though his mind didn't remember it yet. The anxiety of speaking to his mother was now a hundredfold.

'Athiya!'

Athiya looked startled. 'I have to go. I was supposed to come with Ana and Tehzeeb Api but I hitched a ride with someone and came here before them to try and speak to you. If you want to do anything, you should be doing it now,' she said.

He knew she was right. 'Thanks, Athiya,' he called out after her because she had turned around and gone in the direction of her relatives who were streaming inside.

He remembered clearly how Ana had looked at him in the ICU and his mind was still trying to come to grips with everything. He had wondered why she had come to visit him there. Even if it had been for courtesy, it had seemed too personal, the way she had looked at him.

Now he knew. And what a massive fool he'd been. Fate had dealt them both so many cruel twists but he was going to do something now. Even if it was reckless and foolhardy. He had to at least try.

THIRTY-THREE

Luqman went looking for Farhaan, realising suddenly that he had to speak to him before he spoke to Ammi. He had to clarify things with him, tell him the truth and hopefully get him on his side. Beads of sweat broke out on his forehead when he realised the magnanimity of what he was about to do.

His leg had healed but sometimes when he had walked a little too much, the pain twanged through him, like a string that had been pulled tight and let go. He was on the verge of running when he saw Farhaan sitting in the space which had been reserved for the bridegroom's side. The area had two adjacent halls, one for the bride's side and one for the groom's. He found Farhaan talking to some of his friends in the front.

Both halls had a flower-bedecked stage with huge throne-like chairs where the bride and the bridegroom would be seated respectively. The Haldi ceremony would begin after the daawat had finished and there was a sense of anticipation in the air among the guests.

Luqman reached Farhaan and looked down at his brother who was dressed smartly in a navy blue Pathani that had been richly embroidered on the cuffs and collar with silver thread. Farhaan looked at him in surprise.

'Is everything okay?' he asked. Luqman swept a glance around to see if Nouman was there. He didn't want his meddlesome brother around when he spoke to Farhaan Bhai. Thankfully his middle brother was nowhere to be seen.

'Can we talk?' he asked.

'Sure. Tell me what it is,' Farhaan asked, trying to get him to sit down beside him. Luqman shook his head.

'Not here. In private,' he stressed. Farhaan looked worried as he stood up.

'What's wrong? You're making me anxious,' he said.

'Please. Just come with me now,' Luqman said, knowing that the most private place they could talk without being overheard would be in his car.

'Fine. But let's make this quick. I don't want to worry Ammi,' Farhaan said, getting up to go with him. Without a word, Luqman took his brother to the lift and they went to the basement parking area. Farhaan continued to look surprised but didn't say anything as Luqman led him to this car. Farhaan got into the passenger seat and Luqman sat in the driver's seat. His heart was pounding now because the moment of truth was here.

He took a deep breath. 'Farhaan Bhai, you can't marry Ana,' he said.

'What?' Farhaan looked startled and shocked. Whatever he'd been expecting, it had certainly not been this. 'What's wrong with you?'

Luqman shook his head. His thoughts were still jumbled in his head but he was beginning to understand the different dreams he had been having of her now.

'I'm in love with her,' he said.

Farhaan stiffened. 'Is this a joke?' he asked, his eyes turning into cold slits.

Luqman shook off whatever reverence he held for his brother. There was nothing to do but tell him the truth.

'Hear me out. I've always liked her and even took her help last year to get rid of Maira's attention. This was done with Tehzeeb's knowledge, by the way,' he added since Farhaan looked angrier by the minute.

'When I travelled to the US, she and I had been on the same flight. She'd been going to Malaysia for a conference,' Luqman slowed down. The gaps were filling in now, so fast that it made him a little dizzy. He swallowed. 'In fact, we had been sitting next to each other.'

'And?' Farhaan asked tightly.

Luqman shrugged. 'We talked, Bhai. While everyone else ate and slept, we continued talking. But I was such an idiot. I didn't tell her anything. I thought I had time and I didn't even take her number. I remember her look of disappointment,' Luqman said, the moment flashing before his eyes with clarity. His head hurt but he continued.

'I thought I'd come back to India, take her number, speak to her father and ask him if he could wait until my older brothers got married. But Ammi sent out the proposal for you and you know the rest. That was why I came back early from the US,' Luqman said. 'To talk to Ammi.'

'But why didn't you?' Farhaan asked softly. He didn't look angry now, but anguished.

Luqman licked his dry lips. Here was the tricky part. 'I was going to when I had the accident,' he said.

'Oh!' Farhaan rubbed the side of his face wearily. 'But why wait until now, Luqman?'

'Because I didn't remember all this until now,' Luqman said miserably.

'What?' Farhaan was shocked once more.

Luqman nodded. 'I don't know how or why but the entire incident of meeting Ana and falling in love with her disappeared from my memory. So when I woke up, I had this constant feeling that I was forgetting something important. That I had to speak to someone about it. If it hadn't been for Athiya who pushed me to remember everything …'

'Who?' Farhaan asked sharply.

'Ana's younger sister. Apparently, Ana loves me too and she came to visit me in the hospital. I didn't remember our meeting and …'

'But why did she agree to any of this if she loved you?' Farhaan asked, baffled, his eyes wide now. Sweat had broken out on his forehead and Luqman turned on the ignition and switched on the air conditioning in the car. Cold air blasted their faces in a steady stream.

'Because of the joint development project deal that you signed with her father. She didn't want to disappoint her father,' Luqman said, almost bitterly.

Farhaan sat in the car, silent. Luqman wondered if he should elope with Ana tonight. Maybe find a masjid somewhere where they could get their Nikah solemnised. If not tonight, then Ana could stay with Tehzeeb and then they could get to a Masjid tomorrow. It seemed to be the only course of action.

'So, it's simple what we have to do,' Farhaan said, hitting the dashboard of the car, making Luqman jump.

'What?' he asked.

'Tomorrow, you are getting married to Ana instead of me,' he said.

'What?' Luqman asked, shocked. 'Ammi will …'

'Ammi doesn't need to know any of this,' he said. Luqman stared at him like he was crazy.

'Bhai, what are you suggesting?' he asked.

Farhaan sighed. 'Look, we're going to go to Ammi and I will tell her that I have second thoughts about marrying Ana. Then, Ammi is going to think I'm crazy. She will try to convince me that I am wrong. But I will tell her that I am not ready for marriage and I'll leave,' Farhaan said.

'What the fuck, Bhai? What sort of plan is this?' Luqman asked, his eyes wide in shock.

'Shut up and listen to me. This is the only way it's going to work,' Farhaan said. 'You're going to volunteer to marry Ana instead because a bridegroom leaving like this is going to spell doom for her future. Ammi will have no recourse but to agree.'

'And Ana? And her father?' Luqman asked.

'I'm sure Ana will be more than happy that she is finally marrying you. Her father, of course, is a different matter. You will have to call and talk to him. Get Ayub involved in this. I'm assuming he knows about this,' Farhaan said. Luqman nodded.

'Why didn't that idiot say anything before?' Farhaan asked.

'I don't know. I've been avoiding him because ... never mind. You think this will work?' Luqman asked.

'I have no idea but it's our only option. If you love Ana, you're going to have to do this,' Farhaan said.

'But lying to Ammi ...'

'I'll be the one lying to her,' Farhaan said.

'I'll be lying by not telling her the truth,' Luqman added. He frowned. 'And what did you mean when you said you'll leave?'

'Well, I'll have to get out of town for a bit or this isn't going to fool anyone,' Farhaan said. 'I can't possibly be at your wedding tomorrow just hours after walking out of it myself.'

Luqman stared at his brother for a few seconds. 'But where will you go? What will you do?' he asked.

Farhaan shrugged. 'I'll be fine. We can't waste any time Luqman. This is our only chance,' he said.

Luqman felt tears fill up in his eyes as he nodded. He wiped them away, feeling slightly foolish. 'Thank you for this, Bhai,' he said.

'You better spend the rest of your life thanking Athiya for confronting you today,' Farhaan said.

Luqman nodded. He leaned across and hugged his brother who hugged him back awkwardly.

'Chalo, let's go and talk to Ammi,' Farhaan said.

'Shouldn't we wait until the Haldi is over?' Luqman asked. Farhaan shook his head.

'We need to talk before that. Ammi needs to know this is something I'm very serious about. How will she believe me if I go to her after the entire function is over?'

Sighing, Luqman nodded.

'You should have called *me* the moment you heard about the proposal,' Farhaan said, shaking his head.

'I know. I should have,' Luqman said, hanging his head. He looked up at his brother suddenly. 'Are you going to be okay?'

'I'll be the black sheep of the family for once,' Farhaan said wryly.

'No, I mean, you were going to get married tomorrow and now, I ...'

'Really, I'm fine. Don't worry about me. It should be the least of your worries,' Farhaan said.

Luqman hesitated, knowing that couldn't possibly be

true. For the past few days, Farhaan had been rather busy shopping and doing all the things a bridegroom should be doing. He felt awful, but then, in the long run, he was saving Farhaan from an unhappy marriage.

'I mean it. Don't worry about me,' Farhaan insisted. Luqman merely nodded.

THIRTY-FOUR

Ana knew something was wrong the minute she entered the function hall, even though her head was bent demurely. Athiya had disappeared from the house and after a few calls, they found out that she had already reached the venue. Ayub Bhai was quiet on the drive over from the house to the function hall. Aslan fussed, asking for juice, asking for water, asking for snacks and Tehzeeb was in no mood to indulge him. They were all worried and tense.

'What is it?' Ana asked Tehzeeb when they entered the function hall and Tehzeeb led her towards the room at the back where Ana could rest for a bit until she would be brought out to sit on the stage.

'I don't know,' Tehzeeb said slowly. She sounded confused as well. Ana lifted her head and looked around. Was that panic on the faces of some of the people there? Her heart thundered. Had something happened to Luqman again?

'Api, please find out,' Ana said. She stopped and people started to look at her so Tehzeeb nudged her to keep walking.

'You wait here,' Tehzeeb said as she led her to the room and left. Ana's stomach coiled with anxiety. Where was

Athiya? She would have a better idea of what was happening. She remembered she had her phone with her in the shiny clutch that had come with the lehenga. She pulled it out and dialled Athiya's number with shaky hands.

It rang for a few seconds and Athiya answered. 'Where are you?' she asked without any preamble.

'In the room behind the stage,' Ana replied. She knew something was definitely wrong.

'I'm coming there,' she said and ended the call. Ana couldn't bring herself to sit down on the bed. She paced the room and caught her reflection in the full-length mirror that was there. She looked ill.

Athiya pushed the door open and walked inside. She didn't say anything to Ana but she knew the look on her face.

'What did you do?' she asked Athiya. Athiya narrowed her eyes and stared at her sister.

'What makes you think I did something?'

'I know that look on your face.'

Athiya rolled her eyes. She blew out a breath. 'Fine. I spoke to Luqman,' she said. Ana's face paled.

'What?'

Athiya crossed her arms and nodded. 'Well, someone had to since you two idiots are clearly hell-bent on ruining each other's lives!'

'But …' Ana couldn't comprehend this. What did it mean?

'Listen, he needed to hear this. He had to know how things were between the two of you,' Athiya said. Ana shut her eyes momentarily. Athiya was right.

'How did he take it?'

'What do you know, Api; he's in love with you even

without his memory of the flight returning fully,' Athiya said.

'What?' Ana was shocked.

'You thought he'd forgotten you, and he may have initially but that look on his face when he came home just now – anyone could see what he felt for you,' Athiya said.

'What's going to happen now?' Ana asked. She wanted to get out of this room, out of this lehenga. She wanted to scrub her face clean and go to sleep. When she woke up, all of this would be a bad dream and maybe she would still be on the flight with Luqman.

'I don't know. But I think something is happening on the boys' side. I caught a glimpse of Farhaan leading his mother away from a group of ladies and Luqman was with him,' Athiya said.

Ana's lips parted anxiously. Oh god. What was happening?

Tehzeeb walked inside the room then, her face grim. 'Ayub just got a call from Luqman asking him to come somewhere with him,' she said. 'I don't know what's going on but people from the boys' side are looking unduly anxious.'

'Athiya told Luqman everything,' Ana blurted out. Tehzeeb's eyes widened but Athiya looked at her defiantly.

'Someone had to act sensibly, Api,' she fumed. 'Didn't you see the way Luqman was eying her back in the house? He needed to know the truth.'

'Well it's no wonder that something big is going down now,' Tehzeeb said grimly.

'Y'all can thank me later,' Athiya muttered.

'I'll thank you now itself,' Ana said, pulling her surprised sister in for a hug. She had realised how stupid she had been, adamantly going ahead with a marriage that was doomed before it had even happened. How could she have been with Farhaan when one look from Luqman had all but slain her?

Athiya hugged her back and looked at her face. 'It's going to be fine,' she said.

'I hope so,' Ana whispered. Her heart was beating fast and she felt like it had suddenly thawed from the icy block it had been all these months.

'It will. Farhaan had quite a determined look on his face,' Athiya assured her. Ana nodded, wondering how Luqman's mother would react to all of this. They would know soon enough, she thought.

THIRTY-FIVE

Farhaan shot a warning glance to Luqman who looked like he was going to blurt out the truth to Ammi because she looked so anguished. They had managed to take her into one of the rooms on their side of the hall, and she had been worried at the look on their faces.

'Why are you doing this, Farhaan?' Ammi asked, her eyes wide and tears falling down her face. Farhaan steeled himself because he knew this was the only way that Ammi would accept Ana as her daughter-in-law but as Luqman's bride. His mother could never know the truth.

He glanced at his younger brother who looked pale. Luqman had been willing to become a family pariah, to walk away from Ammi and his own family, all for Ana. Luqman didn't even need to tell him what he'd been planning. He would have just come and told Ammi whatever he had told him half an hour ago and he would have probably eloped with Ana.

Farhaan had no idea what it felt like to love someone so much. He knew his eyes had never looked like this when he thought of Ana, but the impassioned gleam in Luqman's eyes, the desperation there, all this had been for one girl.

Instead of feeling bleak, oddly, Farhaan felt free. He

knew his mother was going to hate him for a few months at least. But for the first time in his life, he felt happy because he was being irresponsible for a good cause. He felt unshackled by the burdens of being the oldest son and he knew the scandal would tarnish their name for a long time to come but it was still better than what Luqman had been thinking.

'Ammi, I can't get married now,' Farhaan said flatly.

Ammi walked up to him and clutched the collar of his Pathani. 'Why are you doing this now? Why are you besmirching the family name? What has happened to you?' she asked, her voice thick with tears.

'Ammi, I never got to experience life like others. I was thrust into adulthood and responsibility the moment Abbu died. I realised that if I get married tomorrow, I will never be able to discover what I truly want from life,' he said. Luqman looked at him shrewdly and Farhaan realised that this was indeed the truth.

'Yeh kya bakwas hai?' Ammi asked, her brows furrowing even as tears rolled down her cheeks. 'How can you do this to us? Have you even thought of what this will do to poor Ana? What did she do to deserve this?'

Luqman's jaw worked. Not yet, Farhaan thought, hoping Luqman wouldn't jump in right now. It would look too convenient. They had to work on Ammi a little more, Farhaan thought with a pang. He felt bad doing this to Ammi but it was for the greater good.

'Ammi, I have to think about myself at least once in my life. I can't always be thinking of everyone else,' Farhaan said wearily.

'But Farhaan, the wedding is tomorrow. Why didn't you say anything all these days?' Ammi asked, her voice getting shrill. 'Is there someone else? A girl you like?'

He shook his head. 'Nothing of that sort,' he said.

'Then?' Ammi asked, her lips trembling.

He shrugged. 'Last minute panic maybe. I came here and I realised I just couldn't go through with this. Ammi, if I marry Ana, I'll be ruining her life.'

'And who will marry you after this scandal?' she asked.

He shrugged. 'I don't *have* to get married, you know. I am perfectly fine living on my own,' he said.

Ammi's face hardened. 'Fine. Go away then. I don't want to see your face,' she said.

'Ammi,' Luqman intervened. 'Don't say that. Please.'

'Then what should I do, Luqman? What has happened to him? He's the only person I could count on with my life and he does this to me on the eve of his wedding? How can he do this?' Ammi babbled, as Luqman pulled her towards him and hugged her.

Farhaan tried to keep his face blank but he was struggling to keep from going to Ammi and comforting her. It was his default response. He was the comforter and Ammi had always, always turned to him. He realised that this decision was going to cost him greatly because he too relied on Ammi's support and love. His eyes met Luqman's and he mouthed. 'Now.'

Ammi was still sobbing. 'What will we tell the people outside? What will we tell Ana's father? What face will we show to the world? Who will marry that poor girl? Farhaan, can't you see that you're ruining *your* life and hers?' she asked, turning to him. There was a hopeful look in her eyes, and she expected his altruistic nature to step up, take responsibility and do the right thing.

He kept quiet, hoping Luqman would do the needful. Luqman took a deep breath.

'I'll marry her, Ammi,' he said quietly.

Ammi turned to him in shock. 'What? How can you say that? She's your Bhabhi!' Ammi said.

Luqman seemed to be controlling the urge to tell Ammi the truth. Farhaan hoped his brother would rein in his normal recklessness and go with the script.

'Ammi, she would have been my Bhabhi if Bhai had married her tomorrow. You asked who would marry her. I'm willing to do it,' he said.

'But …' Ammi looked confused, but for the first time since they had come inside the room, she looked hopeful. 'How will we … what will we tell everyone? And what about Ana? Why would she agree to marry you instead of Farhaan? What will we tell her father?'

Ammi bit her lower lip and Farhaan took a deep breath. Slow. Take it slow, he thought. Luqman just needed to convince Ammi and he, Farhaan, could have no part in it.

'Ammi, people will talk for a few days and then forget about it. But yes, we need to ask Ana if she's okay with this. We'll ask Ayub to talk to their family and get their opinion,' he said. Yes, Farhaan thought. This was the best way to do it.

Ammi's face crumpled once more as she sniffled, trying to appeal to Farhaan once more. 'If your father had been alive, he would have been so ashamed of you,' she said to Farhaan. Farhaan struggled with his innate need to comfort Ammi and he straightened his back.

'This is for the best, Ammi. You'll realise it one day,' he said and walked away.

'Where do you think you're going?' Ammi asked, her voice rising to a shriek once more. Wincing, he turned around.

'I can't stay here. I'm getting out of Bangalore for

a few days,' he said, trying to look unapologetic. Ammi covered her face with her hands and burst into tears once more. Farhaan's resolve wavered but he looked at Luqman and nodded. Luqman's expression was pained too but he nodded back. As he left the room, he noticed the anxious expressions on the faces of his relatives. He knew they would talk about him for a long time to come once they learned what he had done. He saw people from Ana's family lingering at the entrance to their hall and he knew that they too had figured out that something was amiss.

He paused for a second on his way out when he spotted Ana's younger sister, Athiya. She stared back at him without any expression on her face. He was thankful to her for saving him from a loveless marriage with Ana. He couldn't imagine the sort of torture it would have been for Ana and Luqman if the marriage had happened.

He nodded to her slightly and she looked confused. Then, for some reason, her lips curved into a slow understanding smile and she nodded back the slightest bit. He walked to the basement where his car was parked, and he hoped he would be able to make a getaway before other relatives started to crowd around him to convince him that this was wrong.

This was right.

THIRTY-SIX

The next day

Ana stared at the Nikahnama before her, her fingers numb because she was holding the pen too tightly in her hands. She was exhausted and her mind spun in circles. No one had slept last night after the bombshell that Farhaan had dropped, walking away from the wedding, leaving Luqman to step in like a valiant saviour.

She still couldn't believe he had done that. Abbu had been so angry, so horrified that he had misjudged Farhaan. Ayub Bhai had sat down with Abbu on the sofa in the room and explained that maybe this was for the best. Maybe Farhaan walking away now before the wedding was better than him leaving Ana after they were married.

'But why? What's wrong with my darling Ana? Why would he do such a thing?' Abbu whispered in shock.

'He didn't explain much, Abbu. He's just gone off somewhere. He says he needs time and he'll come back to Bangalore when he's ready. Let's not waste any time. Luqman is willing to marry Ana,' Ayub Bhai reiterated.

Ana was sitting on the bed, unable to believe this turn of events. Ayub Bhai had merely given her a strange sort of look when he had walked inside, bringing Abbu with him. Tehzeeb had followed him and sat down with Ana because she didn't know what was happening either. The surprise on her face had been genuine and she and Ana had shared a look.

Abbu was holding his head in his hands. 'Ayub beta, you told me these were good people,' he said. Ana looked down at her mehendi-covered hands. What if Abbu didn't want her to get married to Luqman? But she watched as Ayub Bhai convinced Abbu this situation could be salvaged and hope was restored to her bleak mind.

Ayub nodded. 'They are, Abbu. I don't know what's gotten into Farhaan. He's … I've never seen him behave this way. But Luqman, I trust him with my life,' Ayub said.

'Is there some other girl? If he liked someone else, why did he agree to marry my Ana?' Abbu asked. Obviously, he wasn't going to let go of Farhaan that easily. Ana winced when she heard Abbu's words. They should have been directed at her. Farhaan had done them such a huge favour, she didn't know how they could ever repay him.

But Abbu had to agree too. His shoulders were slumped and she knew he was thinking of the scandal, the money, and oh my god, what would happen to Jasmine Villa? She didn't want to bring it up so she kept quiet.

'Abbu, you have to decide and inform them now. Luqman's family is ready to get him married to Ana. They will announce it tonight if you say yes,' Ayub said, reaching out and holding Abbu's hand.

'Do you think this is a good idea, Ayub? Will they treat my daughter well? How can I trust this family now?' Abbu asked.

'Abbu, Luqman is a gem of a person. He will not let us

down and he will keep Ana happy,' Ayub said. Ana knew he was laying it on thick, but what else could they do?

'Ana, I have to ask you what you think about this. After all, it is you who will be getting married,' Abbu said. Ana tried to keep calm and her expression normal. She looked down and didn't say anything.

'I don't care about any scandal. If you don't want to marry Luqman, just say the word and we'll leave right now,' Abbu said. Tehzeeb nudged her and Ana nodded. She wished she could tell Abbu the truth, even if it would leave her blushing. But she couldn't.

'Abbu, I trust Ayub Bhai and I'm happy with whatever you decide,' she said. Abbu looked at her thoughtfully. She knew he was thinking of Athiya and who would marry her if Ana refused to marry Luqman now. Because Farhaan walking away from their wedding would scar her reputation forever and affect her younger sister's prospects too.

So Abbu agreed and Ana's heart leapt. Oh my goodness, it was actually happening! After nearly six months of walking around like a zombie, her life had turned around so spectacularly.

When Abbu had agreed, one of Luqman's uncles came and spoke to Abbu, sounding apologetic and remorseful. Abbu didn't say much but merely nodded, cool anger emanating from his eyes.

And now, here she was on the following day, signing the Nikahnama. Last night had been chaotic after everyone discovered what Farhaan had done. The Haldi ceremony had obviously not taken place and instead, everyone was chatting and gossiping and Ana had gone back home with her sisters. She was dying to talk to Luqman, because if all this was happening, he had gotten his memory back. But

Ayub had left without giving her Luqman's new number and Tehzeeb had been too busy to ask for it from him. The three sisters had stayed up most of the night, talking about Farhaan's ingenious plan.

'I swear to god I wouldn't have thought of doing this,' Athiya said. 'That man is really something else.'

Ana knew she would owe her happiness to Farhaan her entire life. She hoped she would be able to thank him one day.

An uncle recited to her the terms of the Nikah and asked her to give her approval to which she demurely nodded but the uncle waited until she said the words. She felt a warm blush creep up her face and she looked down at the elaborate maroon lehenga that was splayed around her where she was seated.

In a few hours, she would finally be able to talk to Luqman, without the fear of anyone overhearing her, without worrying about any sort of recrimination.

She was his wife now.

THIRTY-SEVEN

Luqman had never dreamed that he would be taking his brother's place on his wedding day. Ammi had been inconsolable when they came back home from the function hall to see that Farhaan had packed a bag and left. She couldn't understand what had happened to her solid, dependable-as-a-rock son. How could he have done this to her, she moaned to her relatives who clucked their tongues sympathetically, although Luqman could have sworn a few of them looked rather gleeful at this turn of events.

Ammi had always praised Farhaan as the sort of son every mother should have. She had crowed about every achievement of his and Luqman knew there was a sort of pride in her demeanour whenever she talked about her sons, especially Farhaan. For those who thought that she needed to be brought down a peg, this must have been payday.

Luqman stood in his room, straightening his clothes. Ammi had come to him very early in the morning, much before Fajr prayers and her eyes had bags under them and were rimmed red. She sat down with him and brushed his hair back tenderly.

'Thank you for doing this beta,' she said softly. Luqman

nodded, wincing inwardly at the lies they were all weaving. But he wondered how things would have gone if he had gone to Ammi instead of going to Farhaan. Ammi wouldn't have been speaking to him now.

'I'm all right with it, Ammi,' he said. He was ecstatic and he couldn't wait until the Nikah was solemnised.

Ammi sighed. 'I wish he'd told me a little before. I wish it hadn't come to this. I feel sorry for the poor girl and how we're playing with her life,' she said. Luqman didn't trust himself to say anything so he kept quiet.

'You have to keep her happy, Luqman,' she said suddenly, grabbing his hands and holding them tightly. 'I don't know how we can face their family after this.'

'Ammi, it's going to be fine,' Luqman said.

'He even went and got all the wedding clothes for himself tailored. I can't believe he would do this,' Ammi murmured. Luqman nodded. Farhaan Bhai thought he could escape Ammi's ire in a few months. It would take longer to convince Ammi to forgive him.

'Will you … will you wear those clothes? Because I don't think you have anything that would be suitable,' Ammi asked hesitantly. Luqman gave it a thought. He and Farhaan Bhai wore the same sizes and their heights were the same. Bhai's tastes were more sedate though but he didn't mind at all. In fact, he felt honoured.

'I don't mind,' he told Ammi who looked relieved. She got up and left and as he wore the clothes that Nouman brought and kept for him Luqman couldn't wait to see Ana. Nouman had been shocked into silence. Farhaan's defection meant that he would have to take control of the office until whenever Farhaan returned.

'He's not answering his calls either,' Nouman whispered.

Luqman nodded grimly because he had spoken to Bhai when he returned home the previous night. Farhaan was not in Bangalore and he wouldn't say where he had gone.

Luqman glanced at the sherwani in surprise. It was a deep coppery brocade sherwani paired with white narrow trousers and a stole to complete the look. It was very unlike Farhaan. He never wore anything so flamboyant. He dressed quickly, glad that he could fit into it and at least it didn't look like he had borrowed it from someone.

As the quiet and subdued menfolk left for the masjid, Luqman missed his brother sorely. How could he get married without him? He had been dreading this day until last night. But now, his dreams were coming true and Bhai was not with him.

*

The wedding took place without a hitch. No one spoke about Farhaan but there were whispers amongst people, especially the wedding guests who had not been privy to the events of the previous night.

Nevertheless, Luqman was exhausted by the end of it. He had texted Farhaan, saying that it was done and that he missed him greatly. Farhaan had replied with a smiling emoji. Was this really Farhaan, he wondered. His brother rarely texted and never used any emojis.

Maybe it was because of the way the wedding had taken place that Ammi had foregone some of the different traditions and rituals that were done before they could take Ana home. He hadn't seen her yet. Where was she? Most of the wedding guests had left and he was exhausted after the sudden turn of events from the previous evening.

Last night, when he slept, he hadn't been plagued by dreams of her. His memory was now almost intact, and it showed him what he had forgotten all those months ago. Ana sitting next to him, smiling shyly, talking about her plans for life. He had been captivated by every single thing about her and going by the way she looked at him, he knew that she was thinking the same thing about him too.

When it was time for the bidaai, Luqman finally saw his first glimpse of Ana. She was stunning in a deep maroon velvet lehenga that glinted with gold sequins and delicate zari work and her head was covered with a dupatta that flowed down her shoulders. She walked towards him, her head bent a little but she straightened up as she neared him.

The look on her face hit him squarely in the chest. So much love. He was afraid that if he tried to react, he would end up doing something ridiculously dramatic like going to her and picking her up in his arms in front of everyone, so he looked away. He watched as she hugged her sisters and then her father. Her father held her the longest. He looked apologetic and sad but she nodded at whatever he was telling her.

Luqman couldn't take his eyes off her. His wife. Ana was his wife now. He would love her till the moment he died. And even after that. He would keep her happy for the rest of her life. Ana's father brought her over to him and he straightened, his breath catching.

'Luqman, my daughter is your wife now,' he said slowly. 'I trust you will take care of her.'

Luqman looked at her but her head was slightly bent now. He was overcome with emotion because he realised that Ana had to be very special indeed.

He had fallen in love with her twice.

THIRTY-EIGHT

Ana brushed the sides of her lehenga as she sat on the rather plain bed in Luqman's room. She didn't mind the lack of decoration and she knew it probably had to do with Farhaan's absence. Her mother-in-law was hardly being able to speak to her because she was so emotional and she merely patted Ana's cheeks and walked away when they reached the house.

There were no relatives around; the usual gaggle of people who hung around after a wedding; made bawdy jokes and made everyone uncomfortable were not there. Luqman's mother had told them that she wasn't in the mood to host anyone and she had a headache. Only Luqman's aunt stayed back with them.

Ana's mind was racing. She still felt like this was a dream and someone would wake her up and she would be marrying Farhaan. But no, she needn't pinch herself. She was sitting here in Luqman's room which hadn't been readied for another occupant. One of the walls had been fitted with a dark wooden wardrobe while there was a desk near the window. She could imagine him sitting there, working late into the night on his laptop.

The window looked out over a small patch of garden

and the branches of a tree brushed against the window softly. She could see its outline even in the near darkness. It was a regular room, painted in a standard ivory but she could see herself adding touches to it that could make it cosier. Her heart hummed with delight as she thought of Luqman and the life that lay ahead for them.

She was still waiting to see him. Earlier, when she had stepped inside the car, Luqman had got into the car from the other door to sit next to her. They hadn't talked because the person driving the car was Luqman's brother, Nouman. They didn't even look at each other because Nouman could see everything from the rear view mirror.

Ana realised she didn't even have time to feel emotional about leaving Abbu and Athiya or Jasmine Villa. She had been swept away in the drama of how this wedding had played out and she felt a pang when she sat in the car. But Luqman's presence kept her on edge. Just having him seated near her made her breathe differently.

When they reached home, Luqman's aunt led her upstairs to his room and she sighed when she walked inside and saw that it hadn't been decorated. She felt compelled to explain it to Ana even though she understood why it was so but at the same time, she didn't want to bring up Farhaan's name either.

'Apa didn't sleep all night,' she explained. 'She must have forgotten to tell the decorator to come and do up Luqman's room.'

Ana didn't respond because she knew she wasn't expected to say anything. The older woman helped her to sit down on the bed and made a lame attempt to spread the folds of the lehenga around her on the bed. Ana was embarrassed and wished she would leave. Her lips pursed, the aunt shook her head, said she would send dinner upstairs and left. Ana wondered where Luqman was and when he would be joining her. Her heart felt like it was tripping up in its haste to beat at an extraordinarily fast pace.

She pulled out her phone from her purse and dialled Tehzeeb's number. Her sister answered immediately.

'Ana, is everything all right?' she asked.

'Yes, yes it's all good. I … I'll be fine. I just realised I hadn't thanked you and Ayub Bhai for everything,' Ana said.

'There's nothing to thank us for and we didn't do anything. If anyone needs thanking, it's Athiya or you know how things would have gone,' Tehzeeb said warmly. Ana shuddered. She didn't want to think of what it would have been like to sit here, waiting for Farhaan to come inside and claim her as his bride.

'You're right. Okay, I have to go now,' she said, ending the call hastily when she saw a shadow at the doorway.

It was Luqman.

She stood up immediately, jewellery clinking, the heavy material falling to her feet gracefully.

Luqman stood just within the door, staring at her. He was still dressed in the elaborate sherwani and Ana wanted him to come inside and shut the door behind him. But she didn't open her mouth. She looked at him, just as he continued to look at her.

Someone cleared their throat and she started in surprise. It was that aunt. She had come from downstairs and was standing right behind Luqman, holding a tray in her hands. She cleared her throat once more, walked inside and kept the tray on a coffee table. She walked away but not before touching Luqman's cheek lightly and nodding.

To Ana's relief, she pulled the door shut on her way out. The sound startled Luqman who quickly locked it. Ana didn't even wait for him to turn, she ran to him and threw her arms around him, holding him tightly even though his back was turned to her.

'Ana,' he whispered, trying to turn around but she wouldn't let him as she tightened her grip around his waist. Tears were threatening to roll down her cheeks. He touched her wrists and her pulse raced.

'Let me see your face,' he said softly. She loosened her grip and he turned around, still in her arms. She pulled up closer to him and looked into his eyes. His face was finally just inches away from her. She took in his face, the one that had continued to star in her dreams ever since they met on the flight, the face that had stared back at her in confusion in the ICU, the face she so dearly loved. She touched his eyebrows lightly with the tips of her fingers, tracing his face, learning its shape and contours and he let her explore him.

Finally, he bent down to kiss her but she was already reaching up to do the same. Heat burst through her veins as their lips devoured each other. Finally, she was exactly where she was supposed to be. In Luqman's arms. She pressed into him, yearning, straining until his back was to the door. She couldn't stop touching him, her fingers running across his sherwani until she found the buttons. All this while their mouths remained fused.

His hands had pushed her dupatta off her head and travelled down her back until he found her warm skin. He unbuttoned the top few buttons. His touch made her shiver and press closer to him. He pulled away first and looked down at her, breathing heavily.

'Why are you crying?' he asked her, wiping away the

tears on her face with the pads of his thumbs. She didn't know when the tears had started falling down her face. She didn't know what she was doing anymore. She decided to let her body take control, let her instincts rule and pulled his thumb into her mouth, licking and sucking it while looking into his eyes. His eyes grew wide and she could sense his hardness growing between them. It sent an electric surge through her when she realised how she affected him.

His thumb slipped out from her mouth and she put her head on his chest, taking deep shuddering breaths. He stroked her back lightly, the half-open buttons letting a stream of air run over her heated body.

'We're together finally,' he whispered. She nodded, not sure she could look at him because she felt overwhelmed.

'Ana?' he asked. She looked up then.

'I was crying because … we had been so close to losing each other forever, Luqman,' she whispered.

Luqman nodded. 'I'm sorry for everything,' he said.

'Do you remember now?' she asked, feeling warm and safe in the circle of his arms.

He took a deep breath. 'When I came back from the hospital, almost immediately, I kept seeing you in my dreams,' he said. She listened to him in silence, his words healing the wounds that had been ripped open every time she thought of him and how easily he had forgotten her.

'I couldn't understand why I kept seeing you, because these were no ordinary dreams,' he said with a smile.

'Meaning?'

'Um, well, they were quite erotic,' he said, raising an eyebrow at her. She raised an eyebrow back at him. 'Obviously, I was freaked out because my memories of you started resurfacing slowly, the few times we had met before that flight, and I remembered just being vaguely interested in you. But it had been nothing like this, so I didn't know why you had this effect on me.'

'Hmm,' Ana said, pressing a kiss to the centre of his chest. This sherwani had to go, she thought.

'If it hadn't been for Athiya ...' he trailed off with a smile.

'And Farhaan,' she reminded him.

He nodded, looking solemn. 'I'll forever be grateful to the two of them,' he said. She felt the same way too. But she didn't want to spend her wedding night talking about their siblings.

'Luqman,' she said softly, playing with the buttons on his sherwani. They were still standing near the door.

'Hmm?'

'I'm done talking for now,' she said, looking up at him and pulling his face down to kiss him.

THIRTY-NINE

Somehow, they managed to get their clothes off, dropping them indiscriminately, somewhere in the vicinity of the bed. Luqman couldn't believe his luck, and how fate had conspired to bring them together. He picked her up in his arms, despite her protests about his leg, and laid her down gently on the bed.

'I have six months' worth of fantasies to play out with you. We're not going to miss out on any one of them,' he said sternly as he helped remove her bra. He loved that she was not even the least bit self-conscious about her body although it surprised him. The Ana he had met on the plane had been a little shy, a little reluctant, but god, he loved this fiery Ana too. The one who looked at him with such open desire. She was glorious. Her hair had tumbled around her shoulders and the sultry look in her eyes made his heart beat a fraction faster. It was already racing, and he didn't know how much more it could take.

As he helped remove her jewellery (which was challenging because she kept kissing his fingers, his face, his lips) he brought up this bold new avatar. She looked at him squarely in the face. 'What makes you think I didn't have any fantasies about you myself?' she asked.

He stared back at her, deciding that he could wait no longer and lowered himself over her, kissing her delicate collarbones gently. She arched and her breasts pressed into his chest. Moving slowly, he made his way down her body, stopping and paying special attention to her breasts. His fantasies did not hold a candle to reality, he thought, as she gasped when he pulled a nipple into his mouth.

She held the back of his head as he continued laving her breasts, his body keen to begin this sensual journey with her. As he moved lower down her body, she stiffened in surprise but didn't do anything.

'I feel like I'm melting,' Ana said breathily, her stomach quivering as he licked her navel.

'And I feel just the opposite,' Luqman growled, his mouth heading further below. He touched her between her legs and hissed when he felt how wet she was.

'You're scorching hot,' he said as he poised himself above her. 'You're so beautiful, you're like a dream come true. My dream.'

She held out her arms to him and he went to her willingly. She stiffened the slightest bit when he entered her but his touches and kisses had her melting into his arms. Her breathy sighs kept him raring to go, even as she clutched his butt with her hands tightly.

Her face went pink, her lips parted as she let out a prolonged moan and he collapsed over her, staring into her beautiful eyes.

They didn't talk but just continued looking at each other for long seconds that stretched into minutes. She clenched her thighs and he jerked a little in surprise because he was still inside her. He pulled out almost regretfully and disposed the condom, glad that earlier in the evening Ayub had reminded him about getting protection.

He came back to the bed as fast as he could, where she lay like a goddess, her hair spread out over his pillow. This morning, he had known that she would be his wife. But yesterday morning and all the mornings before when he'd woken up aroused, sick with guilt and shame, not understanding why she had so much control over him, he'd thought he hated her. But he hadn't. His subconscious was reminding him what his mind had decided to forget.

'I love you,' he said, snuggling close to her and kissing her softly.

She turned to him, her body covered with a slight sheen of sweat. 'I love you too, Luqman. But is this real? Tell me I'm not dreaming,' she whispered.

He pulled her close to him. 'It's not real. This is all a dream,' he said seriously.

'Huh?' she pushed back and looked at him, confused.

'The past few months, I've been waking up, knowing that everything that I saw, everything I did with you, was all a dream. That it wasn't real. It was awful waking up to that reality,' he explained. She stared back at him, understanding growing in her eyes about how he must have felt.

'I was so scared when I heard about your accident,' she whispered, touching his face with her fingertips lightly. Her face looked troubled and he never wanted her to have that expression on her face again. 'When Api called and told me, I left the school immediately and came to see you with her.'

'I remember,' he said, resting his head on the crook of his elbow. 'Did you touch me then?'

She nodded. 'I'd kissed your cheek because you were sleeping,' she said.

'I woke up because of that,' he admitted, sighing and pulling her closer, brushing her hair back from her face.

'I'll never forget that look on your face,' she said. 'When you didn't recognise me.'

'I'll spend my life making up for it,' he promised, his hands running over the dip in her waist and over her rounded hips.

'Luqman,' she whispered.

'Hmm?' he let his hands travel to her breasts.

'I think that food is for us,' she reminded him about the tray of food on the coffee table.

'Are you hungry?' he asked, as he bent his head close to catch the tip of her nipple between his teeth.

'I'm hungry for *you*,' she said, shutting her eyes in ecstasy as he continued his ministrations and she wrapped her legs around his waist. 'And I want you to devour me.'

'I am always at your service, ma'am,' he said, with a devilish glint in his eye.

FORTY

The next morning, Ana woke up first, yawning and stretching, waking to life parts of her body she hadn't even known existed. Like, what was the deal with the inside of her thigh? Why was it throbbing so much? Was it because Luqman had thought it was delectable and had bitten it a few times?

Outside Luqman's room, a bird chirped on the tree branch, and an early morning drizzle made the room a little dark and gloomy, but in a romantic way. She smiled and reached out, her hand connected with his head and she withdrew quickly. She wanted to look at him before he woke up and she turned to her side. He was lying on his back, his face peaceful and she looked her fill, reaching out to lightly swipe her finger across his cheek.

He frowned in his sleep and she was just about to lean in close to kiss him when he caught her unawares, suddenly opening his eyes and pulling her down beneath him. He looked at her with a sleepy, sexy smile on his face and her heart thundered.

'You startled me,' she accused him.

'And you were staring at me creepily,' he retorted.

'Just returning your favour,' she said.

He looked confused and suddenly something clicked in his head. 'Oh shit. You mean from the plane? Yeah, I watched you sleep but only for a little while. I wasn't being creepy about it,' he said.

She reached out and touched his chest, her hands learning the shape and contours of his body.

'It's not creepy when it's your wife staring at you sleep,' she said.

Smiling, he was just about to lower himself over her when she touched him between his legs, startling him.

'Are you sure you're up for doing this again?' she asked him.

Luqman's mouth dropped open. 'What?'

She shrugged. 'Just checking if you're wiped out from last night' she said, bringing her knee up and nudging his backside slightly. He jerked forward, eyes wide.

'I had no idea you were this insatiable.'

She rolled her eyes and touched his face tenderly but her words belied her actions.

'Well, now that you know … why are you still talking?' she asked.

She was so happy, she no longer wanted to pretend. She wanted the world to know her happiness and how Luqman was responsible for it.

'Wait a second, we need a condom,' he muttered as he got down from the bed. She felt like life was full of endless possibilities now with Luqman by her side and when he came back to her and kissed her, she held him close as the rain began to pound outside in earnest. It felt cosy, secluded, like it was only the two of them in the world, savouring each other, and Ana gasped loudly as he focused on pleasuring her repeatedly.

Later, they lay side by side, limbs still entwined. Outside, the rain had now become a downpour, which was standard weather for Bangalore in August. He brushed the hair away from her forehead and she smiled at him.

'I'm so happy now, it feels like my heart will burst,' he said, placing his hand on her heart.

She looked down at his hand and nodded. 'Your heart is in your chest, in case you didn't know,' she reminded him. He grinned and used it as an excuse to cover her breast with his palm. She moaned but shook her head.

'We do have to get out of this room at some point of time,' she said, pushing his hand away.

'I wish we didn't have to,' he muttered.

She sat up and pulled the sheet along to cover her body and he frowned. 'I thought you weren't shy,' he said.

'It's you. I'm not shy with you because you're the one I was meant to be with,' she said. His eyes grew dark and he tried to pull the sheet aside but she wouldn't let him. 'But we need to talk.'

'About what?' he asked.

'Luqman, we've gotten married based on a lie,' she said.

He was puzzled. 'No, there is no lie where our love is concerned.'

'I agree but don't you think your mother deserves the truth? Why should we let Farhaan take all the blame for this?' she asked.

'But Ammi will just get very upset, Ana. Why should we rock the boat? Farhaan Bhai did us a huge favour and I know we'll never be able to repay him, but if we tell Ammi the truth now, it's not going to help us,' he said. She could see that he was getting agitated because he got down from the bed and started looking for his clothes.

She didn't offer to help. 'Luqman, listen to me, please,' she said. He turned around and shook his head.

'Ana, you don't know Ammi. She's very traditional and she won't like it that the two of us had met each other before. She hates the very mention of the word 'love marriage'. Why do you think I was so anxious about talking to her about us?' he said.

She got down from the bed too, still clutching the sheet. 'But you were going to, weren't you? On the Haldi night, you had decided to come clean and tell her the truth!'

He looked up at her and walked back to the bed. 'I was going crazy with the idea of you getting married to Farhaan Bhai. And I was willing to go to any lengths to stop that from happening,' he said, cupping her cheek and rubbing the pad of his thumb lightly. She shut her eyes for a second and then opened them again.

'Right now, everyone in your family and my family hates Farhaan. This is going to affect our lives as long as we don't tell the truth,' she said, kissing the centre of his palm. He withdrew his hand regretfully.

'I don't think so. Ammi will forgive Farhaan Bhai soon. He'll come back and everything is going to be fine,' Luqman insisted.

'Are you scared of your mother?' Ana asked impatiently.

'No, but I don't want her to get angry again. Why can't we just enjoy what we have now, Ana?' he asked.

She stared back at him silently, knowing that pressing the issue would just make it worse. But it was true. Even as the two of them had slept the previous night, wrapped in each other's arms, dreaming of pleasant things and knowing that all their dreams had indeed come true, she felt regretful that Farhaan had borne the brunt.

'Okay, if not right away, then promise me that you will tell your mother the truth eventually,' she said.

He looked annoyed now. 'Fine. Whatever,' he said and yanked a towel from somewhere and went off to the bathroom to take a shower. She watched him leave with regret. She didn't want to argue with him but she knew that unless they told his mother the truth, they were living on borrowed happiness.

FORTY-ONE

Even as a child, Ana had always been the first to own up to mistakes, much to the chagrin of her sisters. She'd almost always gotten all of them in trouble when she needn't have told the truth of whatever they had done to Ammi or Abbu. She was reminded of their exasperated expressions when she watched Luqman getting ready in silence. She walked up to him, the sheet still clutched in her hand, trailing behind her. She smelled like him, she thought.

He glanced at her reflection in the mirror but didn't say anything.

'Don't be angry,' she whispered. He combed his wet hair, dropped the comb on the dressing table and turned around, his face still stony.

'Luqman, after everything that happened, it's a miracle we're together finally,' she said, acutely aware of her state of undress. He cocked his head slightly.

'And you want to smash this miracle to the ground by telling Ammi the truth,' he said.

'Okay, let's talk about this later. Let's not start the first day of the rest of our lives with this anger between us,' she said peaceably. His expression changed and he cupped her face with his palms.

'I'm not angry. I just … I think we deserve some time to ourselves where we're just glad we're together,' he said.

She didn't say anything but watched as he stepped out of the room. She hurried to the bathroom to take a shower and noted all the places he had marked her body with a warm sense of satisfaction. Their Valima was tonight and she wondered if her mother-in-law would continue to look like she was attending a funeral and not the wedding of her son.

She emerged from the bathroom, wrapping a towel around herself, and discovered that she didn't know where her clothes were. Her family had sent over the suitcases with her clothes a week ago. Shit. What should she do now? Should she wear the lehenga from yesterday?

She realised she didn't even have Luqman's number on her phone to call and ask him if he knew about her clothes. She padded over to the bed to hunt for her phone and ask Tehzeeb or Ayub Bhai for his number when her door opened and she yelped in fright.

It was Luqman.

He was wheeling in her suitcase from outside and he didn't make eye contact with her. 'Your clothes had been kept in Bhai's room,' he said shortly and walked off, saying he was getting the rest of the suitcases too.

Awkward, she thought as she unlocked the first suitcase and pulled out the first thing that came to her hand. A silk salwar suit in different shades of yellow. She dressed quickly before he returned with the other suitcases.

'Luqman,' she whispered but he continued to look down. 'I thought you weren't angry with me any longer.'

His jaw worked. 'I'm not angry. I … I just went to Bhai's room for the first time in months. All your stuff is there,' he said.

She didn't know what to say to that. He still looked stiff and guarded.

'It just made me realise that you were right,' he said. 'We'll talk to Ammi.'

Ana's mouth dried up at the thought of facing her mother-in-law with the truth but she was ready to bear the brunt of her anger now if she would forgive them soon enough.

'When Bhai returns,' Luqman added.

Oh. There was no saying when Farhaan would return. But still, this was better than never telling the truth to her family. She thought of Abbu too, and how much hate he was harbouring towards Farhaan. Abbu would be disappointed in her, and she internally quailed at the thought of meeting his gaze. But this had to be done.

'Ammi's asking you to come down for breakfast,' he said formally. Why was he behaving this way with her? Like they hadn't had explosive sex several times last night or this morning for that matter?

Before she could say something, he had already left the room. They had stayed awake so much of the night, talking to each other, filling the gaps between each other with love and memories. But she realised she still needed to know her husband better.

She walked downstairs slowly, wondering what her mother-in-law expected from her. This household was nothing like Tehzeeb Api's, with their servants and her perfectly coiffed mother-in-law who looked like she had just stepped out of a Pakistani TV show. Ana found Luqman's house more relatable although they were still several steps up from them in status.

Squaring her shoulders, she walked into the living room

where Luqman was seated with his mother, talking to her softly. She looked up when Ana walked in and smiled tightly. Ana nodded, said her salaam and then sat down on one of the sofas.

Luqman's mother said something to him in a low voice and he rose slowly and went outside. Where had she sent him, she thought, panicked. She kept her eyes lowered even though she wanted them to follow wherever he was going. She wanted the two of them to be on the same page and not fight. She wanted what they had with each other last night. But just as she had feared, last night had been a wonderful dream and this was the awkward reality.

To her surprise, Luqman's mother got up, came closer and sat down beside her. Then she lifted Ana's face and inspected her. Oddly enough, at that moment, inappropriate thoughts about Luqman ran through her mind and this made her blush. For some reason, this seemed to satisfy her mother-in-law. She moved her hand away from her face and spoke softly.

'I'm sorry for all that you went through,' she said. Ana kept her face lowered as she continued to talk. 'But I must tell you that Luqman is a wonderful young man. He will keep you happy. He will … he so bravely stepped up to take his brother's place.'

Her voice broke and she looked away. Ana realised that her mother-in-law thought she must be unhappy because she hadn't gotten married to Farhaan. That she had to make do with Luqman whom she thought was the consolation prize. Had she even *looked* at her sons properly? Farhaan was handsome, there was no doubt about it and he was probably a wonderful human being. But Luqman? Was his mother ignorant about all the girls who had been hovering around him all his life, drawn to his good looks and sexy personality?

Ana merely nodded. 'I'm hoping you will also keep him happy,' her mother-in-law said. See the love bites on his chest, Ana thought instantly, her face heating. She realised she was expected to say something so she cleared her throat.

'I'm all right, Ammi,' she said with the right amount of hesitation. It felt strange, calling someone else Ammi but she was Luqman's Ammi and now her life was entwined with his irrevocably.

Ammi patted her hand gently just as Luqman walked back inside with Nouman. Nouman barely glanced at her as he mumbled a salaam and sat down on the other sofa. Luqman looked at her strangely but didn't say anything.

'Come, sit with her for some time. I'm getting breakfast ready,' Ammi said, getting up. Ana stood up too.

'I'll help, Ammi,' she said, even though she wanted nothing more than to sit with Luqman and talk to him.

Ammi smiled and touched her cheek gently. 'It's okay. You stay here. I have help for now,' she said and walked away. The three of them continued to sit in the living room, making an uncomfortable tableau.

FORTY-TWO

Why wouldn't that fool Nouman get up and leave, Luqman thought savagely. But outwardly, his expression betrayed nothing. He glared at Ana once but she glared back at him. His gaze softened because everything about her delighted him. She gave as good as she got and what more could he want?

Nouman seemed to be unaware of the undercurrent of electric tension that reached out from him to Ana. He hemmed and hawed and then cleared his throat.

'Bhabhi,' he spoke, almost reluctantly. Ana turned to him in surprise.

'Since Bhai is not here, I, um, I will need to talk to your father about the Jasmine Villa project,' he said nervously. Ana frowned.

'Nouman, we got married just yesterday. Surely you can hold off discussing business until later?' Luqman admonished him. Nouman turned red and addressed Luqman a little angrily.

'It's fine for *you* to say that. I'm the one who has to figure out everything that he has left behind,' he said. 'I just thought I could get a head start and maybe talk to Bhabhi's father and ...'

'At least wait till the Valima is over,' Luqman said. His eyes kept returning to Ana and this was not lost on Nouman who looked at him strangely. He realised that to Nouman, it must indeed seem strange that he had adapted so easily to becoming Ana's husband.

'I'll speak to Abbu soon, Nouman Bhai,' Ana said softly. Nouman nodded and got up from there, saying something about taking care of the Valima details. The two of them were left alone in the living room. Ana picked up the newspaper which was on the coffee table and started browsing through it.

Smiling, Luqman joined her. The slightest stiffening in her body was the only indication that she had noticed he had come to sit next to her.

'Any interesting news?' he asked her softly.

'Hmm,' she replied in a noncommittal way that amused him because she was scanning the pages with a lot more interest than it required.

He placed his hand on her thigh and she jumped a little.

'What are you doing?' she hissed.

He shrugged. 'I'm your husband. I'm allowed to do this and much more,' he reminded her loftily.

'In our bedroom. Not here. And certainly not now when your mother thinks you're the consolation prize I have to live with,' she said. She looked pained immediately, like she had said much more than she should have. He felt the jolt of her words like a physical blow.

'What?'

'Nothing,' she said quickly.

He looked down at the carpet and exhaled loudly. 'What did you mean?'

'Nothing,' she insisted.

He took her hand in his and looked at her intently. 'You have to tell me what you meant,' he said. She looked away and then licked her lips.

'I think your mother thinks that since I was supposed to get married to Farhaan, I'm not happy marrying you. She was trying to convince me that you will keep me happy and that I should also do the same,' she said.

Luqman listened to this in silence. His insecurities about his big brother came back in full force and he withdrew his hand from hers. Big brother would remain the star in his mother's eyes even now, he thought. And the fact that he was indebted to him so hugely dawned on him just now. Did Ammi really think that Ana would have been happier with Farhaan Bhai?

Ana's warm hand covered his and he looked at her. 'I really don't see how your mother can think that. Farhaan is nice, in a nice guy kind of way, but she obviously has no clue about the girls running after you,' she said softly.

He didn't say anything but looked straight ahead.

'Luqman, it doesn't matter what your mother thinks. *I* know I've won the lottery,' she whispered, edging closer to him. Her thigh touched his and he wanted to pull away but he realised he was being unfair to her. She loved him, after all.

'Would you have really gone through with the marriage, Ana?' he asked suddenly.

She looked down. 'I don't know. I'm an idiot for thinking I could manage it but the more I think about it, I don't think I could have lived with myself.'

She rested her head on his shoulder and Luqman sat back on the sofa, his arm around her. He hoped no one would walk inside the living room. He didn't want to move away from her, just yet, even for the pretence they had to maintain for Ammi's sake.

The rain outside subsided and that was when he remembered. It was Monday and he still had a fucking job to go to.

'Shit,' he said, sitting up straight.

'What?'

He rubbed his chin anxiously. 'All this happened so fast, I forgot I have a job,' he said.

Ana grinned. 'I'll help you forget it a little more,' she said in a low and husky voice.

He shook his head. 'No, no. I can't. I'm in trouble with Akshay already and … oh fuck, I just remembered,' he said, covering his face with his hands.

'What?' Ana looked at him anxiously.

'I'm flying to the US this Saturday. I'd asked Akshay to send me on a long-term assignment! I can't believe I'd just forgotten about all of this!' he said, removing his hands from his face.

'What do you mean by long-term?' she asked quietly.

He looked at her helplessly. 'For good. I didn't want to stay here and see you as Bhai's wife,' he said.

Ana's eyes widened. 'But now?'

'Now, I have to go and talk to my boss once again, I've changed my mind. If he fires me, then so be it,' Luqman said.

'He won't fire you,' Ana said. 'But do you have to leave? What will I do when you're gone?'

'Let's figure that out once I've talked to him,' Luqman said, getting up and Ana stood up too. She looked anxious and nervous and he held her shoulders.

'We'll be fine,' he told her. '*Everything* is going to be

fine.' He leaned forward and kissed her forehead and she was just about to put her arms around his waist and pull him close when Ammi cleared her throat and they stepped apart.

Ana was right. This sucked. Ammi had to know that Ana had chosen *him* and that the two of them were deliriously happy together. Acting like strangers who had been forced to get married wasn't going to cut it any longer.

'Ammi, I have to go to the office. I'll come back soon,' he said.

'Arrey, but your Valima is happening today,' Ammi protested.

He nodded. 'Yes, but it's tonight. I have to go and talk to my boss anyway,' he said. With a regretful glance at Ana, he walked away from there and Ana, who seemed to have forgotten the pretence they were supposed to maintain, called out to him.

'At least have breakfast and go,' she said.

'I'll grab something on the way,' he replied. He realised that Ammi was probably surprised at their familiarity with each other but there was nothing he could do. It was difficult to hide your happiness when you were married to the love of your life.

FORTY-THREE

The Valima, or reception as people liked to call it, was hosted by the bridegroom's family and most people liked to invite their friends, business contacts, clients, customers or colleagues to this event. This was the reason why some of the people who showed up for Luqman and Ana's Valima didn't know that the bridegroom had changed and that it was no longer Farhaan who had gotten married.

They were mostly Farhaan's clients and customers who were a little taken aback upon seeing Luqman sitting on the stage with Ana, wearing a formal suit while Ana looked demure and quietly beautiful in a lehenga that was the colour of henna leaves. Deep green with whorls of gold zari everywhere.

So much had happened today! Luqman had gone to work and apologetically told his boss that he had gotten married over the weekend and that he couldn't possibly move away to live in the US. Akshay had looked at him in disbelief. But Luqman explained the situation – that his brother had stepped away at the very last minute and he had stepped in.

'How very like a Bollywood film,' Akshay had muttered. 'And you're telling me at the very last minute. Tell me Luqman, just what am I supposed to do with you?'

Luqman knew Akshay's ire was justified. In the end, Luqman had agreed to go on-site for a month until they had found a replacement for him there. While here, his job was definitely in danger because he didn't have anything to do, since he was already supposed to be on his way to the San Francisco office.

At the moment though, Luqman didn't worry about these things as he sat next to his wife on the stage. Their Valima was being hosted at a smart convention hall that had warm yellow lights and made Ana's skin glow like gold. He couldn't wait to be with her again tonight, touch her, hold her, taste her.

Ayub was busy like he'd been yesterday. He was the older damaad of the family after all, and he was playing his role as a host just as if he had been Ana's older brother. Tehzeeb had walked up to Ana a while back and the two sisters had been whispering with each other.

I hope Ana plays me up if they're comparing notes, Luqman thought and he squeezed her hand lightly. Ana stiffened but continued to whisper to Tehzeeb who had looked at him, then looked back at her sister and smiled slightly.

His life was nearly perfect except that he hadn't told Ana yet that he would be going away for a month. She was not going to be pleased.

He looked at her unobtrusively, at how willingly she showed her love to him and he felt like he needed to make up to her, for all the hurt he had put her through, albeit unwittingly. But first, he wanted this event to get over so he could finally focus on getting his life back in order. Nouman brought over an older man to meet him.

'Mr Joshi, this is my brother Luqman,' he introduced

him. Luqman stood up and shook hands with the man who looked a little bewildered.

'I thought this was ...' he trailed off.

Farhaan's Valima? So far, Luqman had met five such people who had come up to the stage and wondered where Farhaan was. Nouman looked tired of explaining what had happened to everyone and Luqman could see that he was losing his patience.

Ana, who was sitting beside him, merely smiled at the people who came. She didn't have to offer any explanations because the bride wasn't expected to speak.

'Congratulations,' Mr Joshi said, nodding finally, handing over a gift to him and walking away from there. Nouman wiped his forehead with a handkerchief and Luqman felt sorry for his older brother who was bearing the brunt of what both brothers had done.

'I'll kill him for doing this to me,' Nouman muttered as he walked away from there. The rest of the evening passed similarly, with people coming over to meet them, take photos with them and talk to them.

Luqman was exhausted. He hadn't slept much the previous two nights and he didn't look forward to going to work the next day. He was pretty sure he was the only bridegroom in the world who hadn't gotten a leave for his own wedding.

'The wedding is over, right? Why do you need a leave now?' Akshay had asked. Luqman had been tempted to quit over his increasingly high-handed behaviour but he restrained himself. He was a married man now, responsible for another person. Another wonderful person who was sitting next to him, smelling divine and looking fresh even after all these hours of torture. He couldn't take any rash steps here so he had to find another job if he wanted to quit this one. Right now, he wanted nothing more than to collapse on his bed, preferably with Ana curled into him.

When there was a lull and not many people were coming over, he leaned close and whispered to her. 'Why do we go through all this shit?' he asked.

She giggled. 'So that we never have to do it again?' she asked. He shuddered.

'Never,' he repeated.

'Relax, it will be over soon. Also, I do hope you remember that you're coming to Jasmine Villa with my family now. It's the custom in our house. The bridegroom stays over at the bride's house after the Valima.'

'What? I can't,' he protested. She frowned.

'Stop making a fuss, Luqman. I know our house is small and not up to your standards but if Ayub Bhai could come and stay there for Api ...' she trailed off, looking hurt.

'No, it's not that. You know me better than to believe that. It's just that I have work tomorrow,' he said.

'Work?'

He nodded just as someone else came onto the stage. The man was tall and somewhat familiar to Luqman but he couldn't place him. The man looked taken aback to see Luqman.

'But wasn't this Farhaan Ahmed's Valima?' he asked, holding a bouquet of flowers in his hand. Luqman sighed. Yet another friend/client of Bhai's. Bhai should have sent everyone a text to tell them that he wasn't getting married.

'I'm his younger brother. Farhaan Bhai isn't here,' he said. The man peered into his face and then glanced at Ana, who was talking to someone. He merely handed the bouquet over to him and walked away, shaking his head.

Luqman watched the man leave. But his wife's furious whispers made him turn towards her immediately.

'You already went to work today. Couldn't you take leave for tomorrow?'

Luqman looked out over at the people before them, most of whom were interested in heading straight to dinner. Ammi was sitting on the ladies' side of the hall, not really acting like a host. She had delegated the job of feeding the guests to the other women in the family because she knew everyone would ask her about Farhaan.

'Ana, we'll talk at home,' he said, knowing it would look odd if they argued on the stage.

'Yes, we'll talk at *my* home,' she replied softly.

'Um, my home is your home now,' he retorted.

'Your home has to earn me first. Just because I got married to you doesn't make your home mine,' she replied.

Rolling his eyes, he turned to her. 'I'll be sure to inform the home that it has to prove itself to you and earn you,' he replied.

'It's not like you can't go to work from there,' she said finally.

'You're right actually,' he said.

'I know I'm right,' she replied. He smiled. He loved this banter and he loved everything about her. But a sudden annoying thought occurred to him and he knew he couldn't voice it now. If he was going to stay in her house tonight, he would actually have to sleep.

FORTY-FOUR

Luqman took a sip of tea and grimaced when he kept it back down on the coffee table. Ana grinned and then burst out laughing because Athiya had laced it liberally with salt. He glared at Athiya who was laughing away.

'Is this the way to treat the son-in-law of the house?' he asked in mock anger.

'This is *exactly* the way to treat the son-in-law of the house,' Tehzeeb confirmed as she came and sat down beside Ana. The Valima had gotten over a while ago and it was past midnight now. The relatives who had returned to Ana's house had finally left and Ana's father had excused himself to go to sleep.

'Don't trouble him too much,' he'd said with a twinkle in his eye. That should have prepared him for what lay ahead but he hadn't taken his father-in-law's words seriously.

'Are you saying that Ayub went through all this?' he asked. Ana glanced at her brother-in-law who was sitting on the sofa but was fast asleep, just like Aslan who was lying on his chest. Tehzeeb looked at him too and smiled, the love on her face evident for anyone to see.

'No, he didn't,' Ana admitted. 'Athiya wanted to but I told her that he may mind it.'

'And you decided I wouldn't mind it so you told Athiya to go ahead?' Luqman asked, eyes narrowed. Ana shrugged. He was cute when he was riled up. The few times he wasn't hot but actually cute enough to make her want to ruffle his hair.

She saw him looking around her house, probably wondering where they were going to sleep. She had assumed that Abbu wouldn't want to go ahead with this custom of the bridegroom coming over to the bride's house, given the way the wedding had taken place but Abbu had thankfully accepted Luqman as his damaad and wanted everything to proceed smoothly, as it should.

Their house had only two rooms which meant that they were going to sleep in her old room while Athiya slept outside in the living room.

'Should I plug my ears with cotton?' she whispered to her when they went to the kitchen to get him a fresh cup of tea.

'Whatever for?' Ana asked, lifting her lehenga a little as she walked across the kitchen floor. The kitchen was a mess, she realised and she felt a pang when she thought that it wasn't her mess any longer.

'In case you guys make a lot of sex noises?' Athiya asked, as she poured tea from the jug where she had strained it earlier.

'Ha ha, very funny,' Ana said, but her heart pounded suddenly. She was a little sore from last night and, well, even this morning, and she wasn't sure she wanted to have sex with her husband while her sister slept outside and her father was not too far away.

Thankfully, Athiya was already on to something else, talking to herself as she tried to hand the tray to Ana.

'What are you going on about?' Ana asked, pushing it back to her. Athiya frowned. 'Arrey, you take it and go. Have you seen how I'm managing this stupid lehenga? I'll trip and fall on my face if I have to carry a tray while wearing it.'

'Hmpf. I was just making plans on how else I could trouble him,' Athiya said. It was an old custom of sorts, that the bridegroom was teased and troubled during the time when he stayed over at the bride's house. She and Athiya had let Ayub Bhai go scot-free because they had been a little intimidated by his wealth and weren't sure he would appreciate being doused with cold water as he stepped out of the room. But they had been so wrong about him. Ana was quite sure he would have been very sporting about it.

'Okay, so there's some mithai that we can serve him. I'll chop garlic and sprinkle it on top to make it look like chopped cashews,' Athiya said with a gleam in her eye.

Ana rolled her eyes. 'He has office tomorrow. Don't do anything that might make him fall sick,' she said.

'Oho. So much concern for him already?' Athiya said.

'Obviously,' Ana said, with a smile.

They went to the living room where Tehzeeb was taking Aslan from his father's arms and waking him up gently.

'Hey, we have to go home,' she told Ayub, brushing his cheek tenderly. He woke up, blinked and then smiled at her in a way that was so intensely personal that Ana looked away and found herself looking into Luqman's eyes.

He was looking at her in exactly the same way and her breath stopped. She couldn't turn away even as Tehzeeb and Ayub were saying their goodbyes. Athiya went to see them off and Ana shook herself out of her stupor just then. She held out her hand to him and he took it and got up.

She smiled as he pulled her close, her happiness complete. 'I love you,' she whispered to him.

'Ugh. Go inside already,' Athiya muttered when she returned to see Luqman holding her close. 'I'll get cotton for my ears.'

'Shut up,' they muttered together, Ana led him inside to her old room and stopped in surprise. She had no idea when Tehzeeb and Athiya had done this. Maybe after Tehzeeb had heard from her that Luqman's room hadn't been decorated at all, she and Ana had decided to give them a proper wedding night, at least here.

The bed had been covered with jasmine buds and the fragrance was delicate, yet overpowering in its own way. Rose petals had been sprinkled around artfully and there were candles lit around and placed in various nooks and corners.

Even Luqman was surprised. He stepped inside the room and shut the door. He put his arms around her waist and pulled her closer from behind.

'There is no way I'm sleeping on that bed tonight,' he whispered in her ear.

'Huh?' Ana asked, turning her face slightly, confused. He kissed her and she turned around fully, kissing him back the way she'd wanted to, all day.

'Let me rephrase,' Luqman said when she let go of his face. 'There's no way I'm having sex with you on that bed.'

Ana rolled her eyes. 'Because Athiya and Abbu are outside?' she asked.

He nodded. She'd actually had the same thought but now that he was backing out, she decided that she wanted him anyway.

'It's not just that. Your sister sleeps here. I don't want to … um, you know,' he went on apologetically.

'Will it help if I tell you that I slept here too? Until two days ago?' Ana asked.

He narrowed his eyes and shook his head. 'It just feels weird,' he explained.

Nonsense, she thought. But she had an idea of what to do. Her heart raced at the thought of seducing her husband like this but it just added to the excitement.

Sighing, she stretched and pulled away the dupatta and dropped it somewhere. 'Oh, okay. Too bad then. I thought you'd help me out of this outfit I've been wearing all evening,' she said.

She unbuttoned the top slowly, peeled it from behind her shoulders and let it drop from her body. She was wearing a pretty lacy black bra underneath and Luqman froze.

'Err ...' He stared as she walked around him acting like it was completely normal to walk around in her bra and a lavish skirt as she removed the jewellery slowly, deliberately.

'Ouch,' she whispered as she removed her earrings and rubbed her earlobe. 'It's a little sore. The earrings were so heavy and big,' she added meaningfully. She glanced up at him as she bent forward to remove the necklace, making sure he got a good look at her cleavage. She already felt like she was on fire but continued with the act.

She removed the bangles and they slid off her slim wrists and clattered on the side table. He was definitely affected, she knew, but now that the jewellery was out of the way, she had to proceed with even more abandon. She stood up and dramatically released a sigh as she slowly unknotted the string that held her lehenga up.

'Uff, this was so heavy too,' she said, shimmying out of it as it dropped on the floor. 'I need something lighter to wear.' She opened her hair out and shook her head, exhaling loudly.

She would *never* have been able to do this with anyone

else, she thought. Never. Continuing her act, she walked around him again, in just her bra and panties, ostensibly searching for a nightie.

'I wonder where it is,' she said, deliberately bending down to search for it. She straightened up and turned to him. His mouth had dropped open slightly and she could see his chest rise and fall. He seemed to be in shock as he stood unmoving.

'A little help, Luqman?' she asked, beseechingly. His jaw worked and he shook his head. She pouted.

'You won't help?' she asked, pushing her breasts out the slightest bit. That did it. Broke his control and he strode forward and pushed her back, pressing her against the wardrobe, bracketing his arms around her shoulders. His face was flushed and he was breathing heavily but he still didn't say anything.

Realising she was almost naked while he was still in his suit turned her on madly and she stepped closer to him, making sure her body aligned with his in all the right places. He drew in a breath when the top of her thighs touched his erection.

'You witch,' he whispered, leaning close and kissing her cleavage. He licked across it and stepped back, shaking his head.

Ana's eyes widened. What the hell!

She pressed closer to him. 'I'm going to touch you until you're out of your mind,' she whispered.

'Ana, your sister is just outside!' he whispered back, trying to stop her as she undid the knot in his tie.

'So? Your brother is also just down the hall in your house. I'm sure he's also fully aware of what's happening inside our bedroom,' she retorted as she threw his tie away and started attacking his shirt. He held her wrist and she realised she couldn't budge. She narrowed her eyes. He let go, brought his arm around her waist and held her close.

He shook his head. 'We're not having sex on that bed. I said it and I meant it,' he said. Anger and hurt burst through Ana and she pushed back or tried to. Rejection sucked, she thought. This was why you shouldn't put all your feelings out on display. It makes you weak and vulnerable. She tried to step away from the circle of his arms but he wouldn't let her move.

'I can literally read everything on your face,' he whispered, bending close to her, his hand creeping down her body to skim across her panties, slowly pulling them down. Her breathing ratcheted up and she licked her lips.

'It's not what you think. I want you so bad, I can't think straight, let alone think about your family outside,' he said, still working her panties down until they were on the floor. 'But I didn't say we're not having sex tonight. We're just going to be doing it another way.'

'What? How?' she sputtered because his fingers were tracing her nipple under the bra and it budded immediately. She arched back as his mouth covered her breast, leaving an electric wet spot on the bra when he lifted his head.

He swallowed, then he peeled it off and threw it down. He removed his clothes quickly without any of the striptease that she had done but Ana didn't care. She was so hot for his touch that she ... she nearly yelped when he picked her up and bent her over the desk. Her hands scrabbled to hold on to the edge of the desk as she heard the crinkling of a condom wrapper and then he was pushing inside her. She shut her eyes as the delicious sensations began to build inside her.

'I hate to tell you this,' she gasped breathlessly as his hands came around under her and his fingers twisted her nipples, 'But you're fucking me against Athiya's desk.'

He stilled for a few tense seconds, and she could feel his sweat drip on her back. She could feel him shudder as he bent forward and pushed her hair and kissed the back of her neck, while still embedded inside her. Ana's thighs quivered and her mouth was dry. Would he actually stop?

His fingers dug into her hips as he picked up pace again and Ana sighed as pleasure took over.

FORTY-FIVE

One week later

Luqman almost missed his flight this time as well but it was because he had a wife now and he was unwilling to leave her. He had been dreading his flight all week, especially since Ana had been livid when she found out that he was going away for a month.

'I don't even get a honeymoon and you're going away for a *month*?' she had asked him, the day after their Valima when they were trying to settle back into a routine of sorts.

'I promise I'll make up for it when I come back,' Luqman said. They were at the dining table, conversing softly over dinner and Nouman who had just come back from the office nodded in their general direction and walked away.

'I don't think he likes me,' Ana said.

'*I* like you. A lot,' Luqman said. Ana made a face at him and then toned down her expression and made it look demure because Ammi had just walked in. She had insisted that Ana and Luqman eat together because she probably thought they needed to spend time together and get to know each other.

Ammi had also been displeased when she heard about Luqman's travel plans.

'Why can't you take Ana with you?' she asked.

'Because it's a work trip and Ana doesn't have a visa,' Luqman explained patiently.

Ana kept her head down and didn't say anything. Luqman thought that they should start behaving like a proper couple now, because acting distant and polite in front of everyone else was painful. But Ana had said that they needed to tell Ammi the truth before they could be themselves and Luqman had agreed to talk to Ammi after he came back. They had no idea when Farhaan would return and they would just be delaying the inevitable by not talking to Ammi.

As he said goodbye to Ana and his mother that evening before heading to the airport, he felt like he was leaving a huge chunk of himself back in the house. All day, he had been trying to get Ana alone in their room but she had been avoiding him. He even stupidly asked her to help him pack at which Ammi frowned because he barely packed whenever he travelled and he almost certainly didn't ask for help from anyone.

But she never came inside the room so he couldn't talk to her in private. She stayed outside with Ammi and it frustrated him. Nevertheless, he could see her expression change when he got into the cab and pulled out of the driveway. He took out his phone and texted her – 'I love you'.

She texted back instantly – 'I hate you'.

He smiled. He knew she didn't mean it because immediately after that, there followed a flurry of 'I love you's' from her. Until he had boarded the flight and even then, he kept up a conversation with her on Whatsapp.

Ana had wanted to go to Jasmine Villa and stay there for

a few days and Ammi had told her to go ahead. He realised that Ammi was still not comfortable with Ana because of her guilt about Farhaan Bhai. Ammi must have thought that with him gone, it would be a good reason for Ana to stay at her father's place for a few days during this time.

Nouman was supposed to speak with Ana's father about the joint development project and what they intended to do about it. Since Luqman didn't concern himself with the family business, he didn't want to get involved so he stayed out of the way. But he knew that Nouman had been putting off the task of talking to Ana's father because he was busy handling everything else. Even though Farhaan was one of the most organised and orderly people around, the business stumbled without his calming presence and Nouman felt like he was making a mess, no matter what he did.

There were still times when he couldn't believe that Farhaan had walked away from all his responsibilities so calmly and hadn't even turned back to see what had happened. This was so unlike his staid and responsible brother that it was beginning to worry him a little now. Farhaan lived for his work. Or that's what he had thought.

Ever since his father died, he had seen Farhaan manage the family business without ever taking a holiday, without complaining about how much pressure it was for someone so young and without ever getting into any sort of messy personal situation. He'd been so focused on his work that it was incredible that he would leave, just like this. Luqman consoled himself that maybe this was a good thing for his brother too. Maybe his brother needed the break, needed to be on his own for a bit.

He hadn't spoken to Farhaan since the Haldi night and there were no more texts from him either apart from that smiling emoji. He was getting anxious too, but Nouman was in full panic mode, unable to figure out what to handle – clients, projects or finances – and he was trying his best to cope but he was clearly a follower, not a leader.

When the stewardess told him sternly that he had to switch off his phone, he put it away reluctantly and started counting the days until he was going to return. Of course, that was ridiculous. He hadn't even left and he was thinking of when he would return.

He shut his eyes and smiled, replaying the many different moments he had spent with Ana. He was a changed man because of her, of the things she did to him, knowingly and unknowingly. They may have stayed together for just a week but it felt like they'd been together, forever. The level of unspoken understanding between them was freaky. He just had to look at her in a certain way, or she just had to cock her head the slightest and he could guess what she was thinking.

He briefly thought of how disastrous this would have turned out if she had married Farhaan. There were times he still couldn't believe how close he'd come to losing her and he could never quite figure out why she would almost go ahead with the wedding with Farhaan when she clearly loved *him* so much.

She constantly surprised him in a number of different ways. Her striptease on their Valima night in that small stuffy jasmine scented room would remain in his memory till he died, he thought, running his finger under his collar. A couple of days later, without even a hint of coyness, she'd suggested they save water and shower together.

Luqman had always thought this was silly and impractical when he'd seen it in movies or TV shows. The stupid people could slip on the tiles and break their heads, he used to think. But when he stood under the steaming shower head, watching her body get wet, water sluicing down the valley between her breasts, her nipples beading, her eyes dark with desire for him, he stopped thinking as he reached for her.

Enough with the sex thoughts, he told himself sternly as the plane took off. Now, if only his mind would comply.

FORTY-SIX

Ana folded Athiya's clothes and put them away in the wardrobe. Athiya was such a disaster when it came to managing the house. In the one week that she had been away from Jasmine Villa, Athiya had washed the clothes in the machine and put them out to dry but never got around to folding them so they lay in heaps on her bed. She was in college at the moment for her final exams and was due back in some time.

The house itself seemed to have brightened up now that she was back here and that included Abbu who seemed relieved to know that she would be staying a few days here.

'I hope Luqman is keeping you happy, beta,' he told her gruffly, watching for her nod and then walked away to the doorstep where he sat in the evenings, thinking of Ammi. What did old people mean when they asked this, she wondered. Even her mother-in-law wanted to know this. How could anyone define happy in this context?

Does it mean if he's satisfying you in bed or vice versa? Because they had been married for just a week and her husband had already gone to the US for a month. How on earth was she going to tell anyone how happy he made her? Just having him tucked behind her made her sleep so much better and now that he wasn't there, she could barely function.

That first night when he'd left, she lay awake all night, holding his pillow to her chest and sniffing it for traces of his scent. She was such a goner when it came to him. When the pillow wasn't enough, she scrounged around in the laundry bag and found the T shirt he'd been wearing this morning. She scrunched it into a ball, disgusted with herself but she fell asleep, the ball tucked under her chin, her dreams vividly occupied by her husband.

Ana looked around her old room, thought of the last time she'd been here and blushed when she remembered how she had behaved with him. So wanton, so unafraid and brazen! And he'd loved it. He loved her, she thought with a dreamy smile.

Poor Athiya who studied at her desk had no clue what they'd done leaning against it, she thought, her face heating up. Even now, she recalled the sounds he'd made as he grunted against her, how he'd felt inside her, hot, hard and relentless, and she shut her eyes in agony. How was she going to last for a whole month without him?

She was going to rejoin her job in a couple of days and she hoped that would take her mind off him and help the days move faster. Out of habit, she went to the kitchen and started preparations for dinner. Athiya would come and make tea. That was her job.

Abbu walked back inside and sat in the living room as she went about her work and she knew he was thinking of her.

'I've missed you, Ana,' he said quietly when she finished kneading the atta and came outside.

'I missed you too, Abbu,' she said. He smiled, his eyes twinkling as he shook his head slightly.

'You've been too busy to miss me,' he said.

'I'll always miss you,' she insisted, rubbing her hands clean of the bits of atta that had stuck to it. She looked around the house, wondering what was going to happen to the joint development project. Would Abbu go on with it even after what had happened with Farhaan? She didn't want to bring up the subject, however, so she didn't.

It was strange being back home when her heart was no longer here and she wondered if this was why Tehzeeb didn't stay here for too long when she came to visit. At most, she'd stay overnight and leave the next morning. She should text Tehzeeb and ask her to come and stay here. It would be like old times. Almost.

Out of a sense of duty, she called her mother-in-law every evening and they would exchange a painful but brief conversation that revolved around what they'd eaten or cooked that day. Ammi would ask if she had spoken to Luqman and she would say yes.

Half her time was spent texting him, video calling him, and missing him. She told her mother-in-law about going back to her job and Ammi had been quiet at first.

'I thought you had quit your job,' Ammi said after some time.

'I took leave, Ammi,' Ana said. 'I am supposed to begin on Monday.'

'Okay,' Ammi said. Ana knew from experience with Tehzeeb's in-laws, how important it was to get this out of the way, right at the beginning. Her mother-in-law had better not expect her to sit at home to cook and be a housewife, not after her master's in psychology.

Athiya came back from college and she made tea like always, grumbling and muttering under her breath about child labour and how much they owed her for making tea all her life.

'You act like we asked you to make tea from the time you were in diapers,' Ana said finally as she took a sip of the hot ginger tea that Athiya was famous for making.

'If you had known that I could make tea then, you'd have made me do it,' Athiya snapped, but without any heat.

They watched TV for a little while but Ana was itching to go inside to talk to Luqman.

'Bah. Go already. And shut the door if you two are going to be sexting or doing x-rated stuff on video call,' Athiya said.

'Shut up, you fool,' Ana whispered as she got up and went inside. She checked the time on her phone. It was 7 p.m. here and early morning there but she didn't care. She shut the door when she walked inside and started the video call.

Luqman answered, sleepy-eyed, jaw covered with a light stubble, hair falling on his forehead. He was sleeping without a shirt and Ana eyed him appreciatively as he mumbled something. He kept the phone against the headboard and rubbed his eyes.

The clean lines of his body called out to her, and this physical ache for him was almost deliciously painful. She took a deep breath, wishing she could reach out through the phone and touch him.

'I want to bite your chest,' Ana whispered. He blinked and looked more awake then, his eyes becoming alert and wide.

He rested his chin on his hands and looked at her in that way of his, eyes running over her face like he was memorising every detail.

'I want to suck on that tiny spot below your ear. The one that makes your nipples hard,' he said, his voice louder than hers and just the tenor of it made her wet. The fact that she was insanely turned on by her hot, shirtless husband who was in another continent, annoyed her more than anything else.

'Can't you finish your work fast and come back sooner?' she asked, putting her head down on Athiya's desk. She was sitting on the chair in front of it.

'If I could have, I would have done it long back. I already told you the situation when I left. It can't be expedited, Ana.' She sighed but didn't answer.

'Are you sitting in Athiya's room?' he asked her huskily.

She nodded. 'It's my room too,' she said. He ignored her.

'At her desk?'

She nodded.

'The one we ...'

She nodded even more. 'Dammit, how am I supposed to go to work now with this image of you in my head?'

'What image? I'm fully dressed, unlike you. How am I supposed to go to sleep with this shirtless image of you in my head?' she shot back. He grinned and preened a little more.

She didn't tell him that her strangest and deepest fear was that they had cheated fate somehow and had managed to get married to each other. But what if fate had something worse in store for them? She didn't voice it because she didn't want to worry him but she couldn't stop thinking about it. What if they had been granted just that one week of happiness together? By snatching it away from under fate's nose, had they just made things worse for themselves?

FORTY-SEVEN

Ana felt like she had changed monumentally when she left for work after a few days. She had returned to Luqman's home because all her things were there and the next morning, after she got ready, she asked Ammi hesitantly about the nearest bus stop. She didn't want to waste money on autos and cabs and even though she was married to Luqman, she didn't want to use any of his money. Not yet anyway.

He'd kept money for her in his room with a note that said the money was for her and to please use it as and when she needed it. Since she hadn't gone inside her room when he'd been packing, she knew he had left that note or she would have thought he had forgotten the money and gone. Anyhow, she didn't touch any of it.

Ammi looked at her in horror. 'Why do you want to go to the bus stop?' she asked. She looked up and down at Ana who was no longer wearing any bridal finery but had switched back to a plain blue cotton outfit with a brightly coloured dupatta.

'My office is quite far, Ammi,' she replied as she finished her tea. She got up and went to the kitchen to wash the teacup.

'So? Nouman can drop you,' Ammi said. Ana turned around in surprise.

'No, no! I don't want to trouble Nouman Bhai any more than necessary. Also, the school is nowhere near his office. He'll waste half the day going there and coming back here,' Ana protested.

'Then you can take a cab and go,' Ammi said. 'But today, Nouman can drop you. You're a new bahu. We cannot have you travelling alone in buses and autos.'

Why? What will happen to me? Will I get tarnished, Ana wanted to ask, but kept quiet wisely. Nouman was not pleased with this new development, but the more Ana protested, the more Ammi insisted so she agreed rather reluctantly.

She got inside the car beside him in the passenger seat and he started the car, staring straight ahead. She didn't know why he was so aloof with her but she didn't know what she could possibly do about it either. So she kept quiet, checking her phone and texting Luqman.

'Bhabhi, I have to pick up some papers from a client's house. It's on the way. I hope you don't mind,' he said suddenly.

'Not at all, Nouman Bhai,' she said softly, looking up from the phone at him. He was looking straight ahead. Her heart sank at the thought of being late on her first day back at the school but there were some compromises she had to make. If Nouman had been a little friendlier, she would have told him to drop her off somewhere midway so she could take an auto from there.

He took a few turns and reached a three-story building painted in light green. He dialled a number and spoke to someone briefly, informing them that he was downstairs.

'Okay,' Nouman said and ended the call. He barely glanced at her as she said, 'I'll be back in a minute.' He got out of the car and shut the door and walked ahead, stopping near the entrance because his client had come outside. The man and Nouman walked up to the gate, talking among themselves. Nouman took a file from the man's hand and nodded.

Bored, Ana looked away. Nearby, there was a construction site and some children were playing in the sand. She observed them for a while, smiling to herself when she saw their antics. Dressed in torn shorts and muddied vests, the children were throwing sand at each other. She heard Nouman approaching the car and realised that the client had walked with him towards the car while still talking to him. He was a middle-aged man who glanced at her a couple of times so she sat straighter. She checked the time on her watch. She had already known that she was going to be late today because the school was even further from Luqman's home. But at this rate, she was going to reach there only in the afternoon. Maybe she should just call it a day and come back early the next morning.

But she didn't want to do that. She had informed the school management that she would be joining back today and she wanted to do that even if she was going to be late. She pursed her lips and stared straight ahead. Nouman was taking his own sweet time with this man she thought impatiently. She checked her phone again for messages from Luqman.

He had texted her earlier that he was going to sleep soon as he had an early morning meeting. But he had wished her luck in joining work once more and he promised her they would figure out a way to make her commute more manageable once he got back to India.

Finally, Nouman shook hands with the man and got back into the car. He started the engine and drove away without looking at her even once. No explanation, no small talk. The atmosphere in the car was downright cold.

'I can take an auto from here,' Ana said, an hour later when they had reached the main Sarjapur Road. Being stuck in traffic with Nouman in this silent-as-a-tomb car was her least favourite thing in the world, she decided. She wondered if he somehow blamed *her* for Farhaan leaving.

'No, I'll drop you at the school gate,' he replied stiffly.

'Nouman Bhai, that will take another twenty minutes at least. You're already late for work,' she protested.

'Since I'm already late, a few more minutes will not make a difference,' he said, still looking ahead.

Fine, she thought. She looked through her bag for her ID card and her things just to have something to do. When he reached the gates, he stopped the car and only then, turned to look at her.

'How's Luqman?' he asked her suddenly.

Startled, she couldn't figure out why he was asking *her*.

'He's fine. Don't you talk to him?' she asked. He shook his head.

The three brothers were indeed quite strange, she thought. Nothing like the three of us. She loved her sisters and all three of them were constantly involved in each other's lives. She would have it no other way.

'Tell him to come back soon,' Nouman said shortly and drove away when she got down. What a strange fellow, she thought. But she put him out of her mind when she walked into the school and got pulled into her work.

She enjoyed talking with the parents and the students who came to her. It was such a wonderful feeling to have someone open up to her, talk to her and she worked hard to draw them out slowly, helping them understand themselves. It wasn't her job to give them answers but to help them arrive at the answers on their own. It was frustrating at times but also very fulfilling.

The teachers in the staffroom were formal and distant with her but one of the women had heard that Ana's bridegroom had changed on the day of the wedding and their curiosity had overtaken their politeness and they crowded her when she walked inside for a cup of tea.

Ana had been surprised at first but she sat down and told them the official story that her bridegroom had walked out on the eve of the Nikah and Luqman had stepped in. Everyone listened to her wide-eyed.

'But you were okay with this?' asked one of the teachers. Ana had to keep her face passive as she answered Minimol.

'I had to think of my family and what it would do to them, especially since my younger sister is also unmarried,' she said.

'Wow. It sounds like something from a movie,' another teacher said.

Oh, you have no idea, Ana thought.

'Are you happy with this man then?' Minimol persisted. She was the chemistry teacher for the high school students.

So happy, my heart feels like it will burst, Ana thought. So happy.

She looked down a little demurely. 'He's nice,' she said with a small smile.

FORTY-EIGHT

That evening, when she returned from school, Ana was tired but happy. The commute was awful but she would manage, she told herself as she waited for the door to be opened. It felt strange to come back here to Luqman's house instead of her own. There, she didn't have to think ahead much apart from figuring out dinner and what to make but here, she was still wary of entering the kitchen and doing as she liked.

Ammi had politely but gently made it clear that she would manage the kitchen and Ana needn't worry about cooking or anything else for that matter. The door was opened by Asma, one of the young women who worked for them and helped out with cooking and cleaning. Asma's mother had been working in Luqman's house for the longest time and she now continued the tradition, going back home only at around 7 p.m.

'Salam, Didi,' Asma said. Asma was shy and had barely spoken to her in the few days since she'd come here to stay.

Ana smiled, replied with her own salaam and was about to head upstairs to her room when Asma stopped her.

'Didi, Apa has asked you to come to the living room,' Asma said.

'Oh, okay. Tell her I will just take a shower and join them,' Ana said, walking on when Asma stopped her again.

'She wants you to come right now,' Asma said apologetically.

Surprised, Ana walked back downstairs, wondering what could be so urgent. Sighing, she walked back to the living room and saw that Ammi was seated with Nouman. They both had a strange sort of look on their faces.

Ana greeted them both but neither replied with the standard 'walaikum salam'. They sat stiffly, staring at her. She was just about to sit down on one of the sofas when Ammi spoke, her voice sharp like a blade that could whistle through skin cleanly.

'When was the first time you met Luqman?' she asked.

Ana felt her stomach drop to the floor. Why were they asking her this? 'I d-don't remember,' she said.

When Ammi stared at her with that fixed gaze, she felt the need to elaborate further. 'He's Ayub Bhai's friend. He was there at Tehzeeb Api's engagement,' she said, looking between Ammi and Nouman.

'So you just knew him as a passing acquaintance before you married him?' Nouman asked. His tone was even more strange, subdued but with a lot of hostility behind it.

Warily, Ana nodded, not trusting herself to speak. Her mouth was dry. Had they found out the truth somehow? But how was it possible? Only her sisters, Ayub Bhai and Farhaan knew about them.

'We know you're lying,' Ammi said finally, her eyes glinting with what Ana realised was hate. Her stomach roiled and she fought back the bile that rose inside her.

She licked her dry lips fearfully. She had wanted to come clean to Ammi about her and Luqman but he had said that they would talk when he came back. How had they learned the truth?

Nouman stood up suddenly. 'What sort of a woman are you?' he asked, his nostrils flaring.

'What do you mean?' Ana asked, refusing to cower before him.

'You string along both my brothers? Fool one and marry the other?' he asked.

Ana's mouth dropped open. 'How dare you say something like this to me!' she said.

'You were on Luqman's flight when he went to the US last time and you had him under your spell with your smiles and your charms,' Nouman spat out.

Ana's face flamed but she didn't back down. 'I'm married to your brother. You can't say such things to me,' she said.

'Oh, I will,' he said quietly.

She turned to Ammi, hoping to make her listen to reason. 'Ammi, please listen to me. I tried to explain to Luqman that ...'

'*Don't* take my son's name,' Ammi said, her voice swift and lethally soft. Ana froze, realising that it was no use explaining anything to them.

'Because of you, my Farhaan left home,' she said, her voice breaking. 'We haven't heard from him in days.'

'And Luqman? How did you get him to dance to your tunes? Did you seduce him on that flight? Are you the cause of his accident? Did he come back early for you?' Nouman sneered.

Ana felt hot tears filling up in her eyes. How dare he? How dare he accuse her of such things! Her chest heaved but before she could reply, she heard Abbu's voice from the entrance of the room.

'Ana?' he asked. Her face paled as she turned to him. He was holding a file in his hands which had a sticker on it that read 'Jasmine Villa'. Why hadn't Abbu said anything about coming here if he'd wanted to speak to Nouman?

'Abbu, what are you doing here?' she asked, her voice breaking. She didn't want Abbu to see any of this but it was already too late.

Abbu's lips parted but he didn't seem to have any words. 'You've certainly trained your daughters well, Mr Yusuf. Especially when it comes to trapping the sons from rich families,' Ammi said softly.

Abbu's eyes turned dark with rage but before he could say anything, Ammi continued.

'First, you let Tehzeeb seduce Ayub and then you made sure your daughter tried her luck with both of my sons? Luqman and Farhaan? If it hadn't been for the man who had sat with the two of them on the flight six months back, we'd never have known about their deception!' Ammi said.

Ana covered her mouth with her trembling hand but she couldn't think of what she could say. Who was this man? How had he known who she was?

'Is this true, Ana?' Abbu asked, his voice low and pained.

Ana shook her head wildly. 'No, no, it's not like that Abbu,' she said.

'Then what is it like?' Nouman asked, his voice harsh and loud. 'You seduced Luqman and then you didn't want to marry Farhaan, so you convinced him to leave us and go away? Haroun recognised you both from the Valima and when I met him this morning, he told me that he was quite sure you were the same girl from the plane.'

Nothing made sense to Ana.

'You're not making any sense,' she said to Nouman. She

had to make them understand that she and Luqman had been in love but their faces were set. But Abbu's face, she couldn't bear to see him like this.

'Abbu, please listen to me. I …' she turned to him. If Nouman and his mother weren't going to listen to her, then she had to convince Abbu at least. But Abbu didn't listen to her. He dropped the file on the sofa and turned around to walk away.

Ana realised that tears were running down her face as she followed him out. She could barely see where she was going but she followed him blindly.

'Abbu, please listen to me,' she called out but he walked ahead steadily, unmindful of her pleading. Ana followed him, not even sure of what she was doing anymore.

Abbu ignored her. His back was straight but she had seen the hurt and anguish in his eyes. She hated the fact that she was the one to put it there. She was totally losing her shit on the road and people were staring at her but she didn't care. She wiped her face with her dupatta and followed him but to her shock, he had hailed an auto and was getting inside.

'Abbu, wait for me!' she called out. The auto driver looked at her uncertainly, paused to see if she was going to get inside.

'Let's make this clear,' Abbu said, his voice soft but lethal as he leaned out of the auto. 'From today, I have only two daughters. Tehzeeb and Athiya. I don't know who you are. You are nothing to me.' And then he tapped the auto driver's shoulder.

The auto drove away. Ana crumpled on the road in pain, her world turning dark.

FORTY-NINE

Luqman hadn't checked his phone all day. He had an intense KT session today with the guy who was going to replace him in the San Francisco office and he didn't want any interruptions. As he sat with the young chap, Joginder, he felt the slightest pang at what he was leaving behind. This was promising to be an exciting project with a chance to work on cutting-edge technology in a way that was still not forthcoming in India at the moment.

But he didn't want to ask Ana to move to the US with him. Not right now. Not if it meant she'd have to leave her family and come away for an unknown stretch of time. He was drained by the time the day ended and the Knowledge Transfer session was still not over. It was going to take at least another week and maybe then he could hurry up with the rest of it and go back home.

Ana had texted him when she left for work earlier. He wondered how her day had gone. She had probably messaged him but he thought he'd go back home and see it. She was also probably busy or tired from the commute. Maybe he'd try to convince her to get a job closer to home so she wouldn't have to travel all the way across the city. As he let himself back into the apartment where he stayed, he yawned.

He took a hot shower, willing himself not to think of Ana soaping him luxuriously, kissing him as the water sprayed over their faces. He wrapped himself in a towel, grabbed a shirt and track pants and only then picked up his phone.

Nothing. He frowned. How was this possible? Usually, she left him voice notes, messages and selfies but there was nothing. On Whatsapp, the last time she'd been online was around 18 hours ago. Why hadn't she contacted him? He was feeling restless suddenly, an urge to know that all was well with her.

He started a video call and waited for her to answer. It rang and rang and ended. He tried once more. The same thing happened. He checked the time. It was 11 p.m. now which meant that it was probably mid-morning there. Was she busy at work? She could have texted him to say that she couldn't talk now. He wished he'd timed it correctly and called her when she'd gotten back home. Now, he was free and she was busy.

With uneasy thoughts running through his mind, he tapped open the gallery on his phone and looked through her pictures, something he did every night. He flipped through each photo and then with a sigh, he put it face down beside him and fell asleep.

The sound of the phone ringing woke him up some time later. When he checked the time, he saw that it was 3 a.m. Frowning, he peered into the screen, his heart racing when he saw that it was Ayub.

'Hello,' he answered, blinking away the sleep from his eyes.

'Listen, you need to come back right now,' Ayub said without any preamble.

'What? Why? What happened? How's Ana? Has

something happened to her?' he asked, his chest hurting suddenly. He rubbed his chest with his palm, trying to regulate his breathing.

Quickly, succinctly, Ayub told him what had happened. No, he thought in shock.

'Where's Ana? How is she?' he asked, a sick feeling spreading through his stomach. She had kept telling him to come clean and he hadn't listened to her and now ... what Ayub was saying didn't make any sense. How had Ammi and Nouman found out about them?

'Listen, Ana didn't want me to call you,' Ayub said, hesitantly.

'What? Why?' Luqman asked, standing up, his heart pounding.

Ayub was silent for a few seconds. 'She's beyond upset Luqman. I've seen her go through a lot ever since this whole thing with you started and when you had your accident, she was devastated. But this ... I've never seen her like this.'

'Like what?' Luqman whispered. The pain lanced through his gut and made him wince.

'Broken. She's broken. Abbu left her crying on the road. He's told her she's no longer his daughter. She had left home with Abbu trying to make him understand what happened but Abbu didn't listen. He came home and told Athiya and she called us. Tehzeeb and I went to your house immediately but she was two streets away, sitting on the road, weeping as people surrounded her.'

The images that Ayub's words formed shocked Luqman.

'Why didn't she want you to call me?' he asked quietly, his breaths coming slow and uneven.

'I don't know. I honestly don't know how her mind works. We took her back to our home with us and she's sleeping in the guest bedroom right now. But she told me not to call you,' he said.

'She's mad at me,' Luqman said.

'I don't know. She sounded weary. She sounded like she'd had enough,' Ayub said.

Luqman's panic increased when he heard these words. Fuck this job, he thought. He didn't care if he got blacklisted but he couldn't sit here while his wife suffered alone.

'I'm leaving on the first flight I get,' he told Ayub.

'Good. Don't call her. She's left her phone back at your house. She was sitting on the road with nothing and I don't know what would have happened if we hadn't reached there,' Ayub said.

'How could Abbu do this to her?' Luqman asked, incensed.

'Well, from what I gathered, Nouman said all sorts of things to her, and your mother said that Abbu had trained his daughters well to seduce the sons of wealthy families,' Ayub said.

'Fuck no. How could Ammi say such a thing?' Luqman asked.

'I don't know man. I don't know,' Ayub said. He sounded tired too. He hung up and Luqman sat back on the bed, holding his head in his hands. How had he allowed this to happen?

How had Nouman found out about them? Ayub hadn't explained what had happened. Rage filled inside him as he dialled Nouman's number and waited for him to answer.

'What?' Nouman said as he answered the phone. Luqman was taken aback at his rude attitude.

'Who do you think you are to talk to my wife like that?' Luqman asked, his tone low and angry.

'So she went tattling to you? I was wondering when you would hear of it,' Nouman replied, his tone smug and annoying.

'Listen, you little shit. She's my wife,' Luqman said, struggling to control his emotions.

'Don't talk to me like that,' Nouman replied. 'Your *wife* played you and Farhaan Bhai. You're such a fool. Really. I'm so glad she didn't try anything underhanded with me when I went to drop her at her school.'

If Nouman had been here, Luqman would have strangled him, he thought viciously. How was any of this Ana's fault? He was the one who should have been blamed. Nouman continued talking, unaware of Luqman's murderous thoughts.

'If it hadn't been for Haroun, we would have all fallen for your great act of sacrifice,' he said.

Luqman paused while killing Nouman in his head. 'Haroun?'

'Yes, Haroun. The guy who was seated with you when Ana seduced you on that flight some months back,' Nouman continued. Luqman struggled to remember who it was. He tried and tried but couldn't recall anything about this man. And then it came to him in a rush. The annoying man who had followed him to the coffee shop to tell him that Ana had been into him.

Luqman shut his eyes. 'How do you know him?' he asked.

'He's a client. He was invited for the Valima and when he came, he was taken aback to see you instead of Farhaan Bhai,' Nouman said. Luqman didn't want to hear any more but Nouman continued with vicious relish.

'Then I had to pick up some papers from his house and

I was dropping your wife to her school. Does she even teach there or is that also a big lie? Anyway, he saw her sitting in the car and he told me he remembered where he had seen her before.'

Luqman's head was pounding. He didn't say goodbye but he ended the call and tossed his phone on the bed. It was time for reparations. He had to go back to India right now.

FIFTY

Ana wasn't sure how much time had passed since that awful day when she had been kicked out of both homes. She didn't even recall how she had reached Tehzeeb's house. She opened her eyes and stared at the ceiling, her ears listening in to the quiet ticking of the clock on the wall. It was driving her crazy. She wanted to yank the clock and smash it on the ground, stomp on it until it broke into pieces.

Sighing, she turned around in the bed and saw Tehzeeb walk inside. She was wearing a white and maroon kaftan which probably meant it was night. Ana placed her hand on her chest and it felt like whatever was inside had crumbled into so much powder and dust. She felt empty. She wanted to feel something, anything. But a sort of coldness had crept over her, covering her, freezing her.

'Ana,' Tehzeeb spoke softly and Ana cringed. She hated this tone that people used. It was reverential and funereal. She didn't want her sister's pity. She didn't want anything from anyone.

'Please eat something?' Tehzeeb spoke in the same soft tone. Ana didn't have the energy to shake her head but she looked away.

'I'm not hungry,' she managed to say.

'It's been two days,' Tehzeeb said. 'You can't continue like this. You need to at least drink some water.'

'I drank water sometime back,' Ana said. She had woken up, her throat lined with needles and she had gulped two glasses thirstily, wincing as the water ran through her cracked lips.

'Yes, but food ...'

'I can't. Please don't force me,' Ana murmured.

'Listen, darling, you need to face the world and ...'

'I don't need to do anything,' Ana said, hating that she had nowhere to go but her sister's house. How long could she stay here? She didn't have much savings, but maybe she could borrow some money from Tehzeeb and rent a small room somewhere. Maybe she could live in a PG. Yes, that would be the cheapest option, she thought.

'Yes, but ...' Tehzeeb sighed unhappily. 'But you have to take care of yourself too.'

'I don't want to. I want to punish myself,' Ana said.

'But ...'

'Please, Api. I'll get out of your hair soon. As soon as I figure out what I need to do with my life,' she said.

'Ana, you're not alone,' Tehzeeb said in a whisper. 'You have us and Athiya and most importantly, you have Luqman.'

Ana closed her eyes and opened them. She exhaled loudly. 'We were so stupid,' she muttered.

'Everyone is stupid in love,' Tehzeeb said. Ana shook her head.

'No, you don't understand. We were never meant to be together. We did this to ourselves. We played with fate and we didn't even understand the signs when Luq ... he met with the accident,' Ana said. Saying his name, talking about him, even thinking about him was painful.

'Don't say that. It's not true,' Tehzeeb said, sounding shocked. She brushed the sweaty strands from Ana's forehead.

'Listen, you've been holed up inside this room for two days. Take a shower. Eat something. You'll feel much better,' Tehzeeb said softly.

'You really think that, Api?' Ana asked, turning to her. She had never felt this bleak before.

Tehzeeb nodded. 'Just the motions of everyday routine, getting up, washing your face can make you feel much better.'

'Or are you just saying all this because I stink?' Ana asked. Tehzeeb smiled. Ana didn't. Tehzeeb got down from the bed and pushed open the heavy curtains. Ana blinked. It wasn't night like she'd thought it to be. Light streamed in from outside, filling all the corners of the room but her heart remained a stump. Dark and burnt. She couldn't forget Nouman and his mother's taunts. She couldn't forget Abbu's hurt and pain.

'Come on. You need this,' Tehzeeb said, yanking her from the bed. Ana sat up reluctantly and covered her eyes against the light. She felt grimy, sticky and unwashed. Taking the towel that Tehzeeb had in her hand, she walked to the bathroom, every step hurting some part of her body. She realised that the words that had been thrown at her in accusation had affected her physically. She felt like she'd been pummelled and attacked.

She stood under the hot shower gratefully, as the water soothed the pain in her body. But no matter how hot the water became, it couldn't touch the ice around her heart.

That remained frozen. Feeling like there was something at the back of her throat, an urge to throw up, she wrapped a towel around herself and stepped outside. Api had thoughtfully kept some clothes for her and she wore them quickly.

She wanted to fold her body within herself. She felt cheap, used, like a prop. Steeling herself, she looked around the guest bedroom and decided that Api was right. She had to face the world eventually. Her hands automatically went for her phone but then she remembered she hadn't brought anything back with her.

Would Api go and get it for her, she wondered. That was too much to ask of her and who knew what her mother-in-law would tell her sister? Did she have it in her to face that house again? To walk inside and take her things back? Things she needed, because without her phone, how could she communicate anything to anyone?

'Api, can I borrow your laptop?' she called out, not willing to leave the room just yet. She could probably send an email to the school, telling them she had fallen ill and would join as soon as she felt better. Of course, she was never going to feel better, was she?

'Api?' she called out, and pushed open the door, still reluctant to leave the room. To her shock, she saw Luqman climbing up the stairs, holding a bag in his hands. Her heart pounded painfully and she was tempted to shut the door. She didn't want to see him. What was he doing here? How had he known to come … of course. Ayub Bhai would have told him, despite her telling him she didn't want to talk to Luqman right now.

Tehzeeb must have known that he would have been arriving now. No wonder she had pushed her to freshen up and look like less of a bhootni.

Annoyed with the machinations of her sister and brother-in-law, Ana watched as her husband felt her gaze on him and he looked up. Their eyes connected and his warmed with love, but she felt nothing. Her face remained expressionless as he reached her. He walked inside the room, deposited the bag on the floor and took her in his arms.

Still nothing. The ice refused to budge and she didn't hug him back. He stepped back and looked down at her, his face sorrowful and everything she had dreamed of, but she looked away.

'You shouldn't have come,' she said softly.

'I quit my job,' he replied. He lifted her chin gently with the tip of his finger. Ana felt the slightest crack in her armour but she sealed it over, swiftly.

'You shouldn't have,' she said. He frowned.

'Ana, I'm so sorry for ...'

She turned away, unable to listen to his words. She didn't want to see him or hear his voice. He reminded her of everything that had gone wrong in her life. Abbu was not talking to her, had said she was as good as dead to him, because of this man, her husband.

'Luqman, you should leave,' she spoke in a staccato voice.

'Leave where?' he asked, bewildered. She turned slightly and glanced at him.

'We were a mistake, Luqman. From the very beginning,' she said. He frowned.

'What?'

She nodded, even that small action sending a shooting pain up her head. She winced.

'We should have let things be. My biggest mistake was in agreeing to marry Farhaan when I loved you,' she said.

'Loved?' he asked, his voice low. She didn't look at him. She had to finish speaking before she could or she would lose courage.

'This is what we get for crossing fate,' she said. He walked up to her and turned her around.

'What nonsense are you saying, Ana?' he asked angrily. His eyes softened when he saw her expression. He bent his head and kissed her.

She felt the touch of his lips on hers and shut her eyes. The pain was back and it was better than the numbness. She pushed him back, shaking her head.

'We were a mistake,' she repeated. 'We shouldn't be together.'

He held her shoulders and shook his head. 'How can you say that? After everything we've been through?'

'Exactly. No one should go through so much shit for a relationship. We're not good for each other, Luqman. It's better to cut our losses while we can,' she said, removing his hands from her shoulders.

Luqman went silent. His mouth dropped open.

She didn't want to listen to his explanations. She didn't want to hear his apologies. He had nothing to apologise for. This was plain and simple. They shouldn't be together.

'I want a divorce,' she said.

FIFTY-ONE

Athiya was restless as she paced the floor of her room. She thought Ana needed one tight slap across her face. But then that was how she reacted to everything – with anger and passion. How could things have gone so wrong for Ana? She had been so happy just a few days back!

Now, Tehzeeb had called to tell her that Ana had asked for a divorce. Not much shocked Athiya but this certainly had. It didn't matter one bit to her that Ana's divorce would affect her own marriage prospects. She wasn't planning on getting married anyway. But she had been shocked that Ana had made this decision.

What was wrong with her? Yes, Abbu was angry and she had never seen Abbu this angry, ever. But that didn't mean he genuinely meant what he said. If she didn't know any better, Ana was his favourite. Maybe that was why the deception hurt him even more. That didn't mean that he wouldn't come around eventually.

She had wanted to go to Ana the moment she heard how Tehzeeb and Ayub had found her. She couldn't believe that Abbu had been callous enough to leave her on the road like that. It just showed how angry he was with her that he hadn't been thinking straight. He had sat glumly in the living room, clutching his head and muttering to himself that he was glad Ammi wasn't around to see what her daughter had done.

What *had* she done?

Nothing. She hadn't done anything wrong. She had, in fact, nearly been a martyr, willing to sacrifice her life's happiness by marrying Farhaan and giving up Luqman forever. Thank goodness that hadn't happened. She had seen how she looked at Luqman and she knew that sort of love didn't come easily.

That was why she couldn't believe her sister had asked for a divorce. This couldn't happen. Someone had to do something. But according to Tehzeeb, Ana had refused to listen to reason, having sent away Luqman when he had come to her after learning of what had happened.

This love business was too complicated and messy, she thought. She had already decided she was never getting married because seriously, she wasn't interested in these power games that mothers-in-law wielded over their bahus. But that was secondary. The whole love thing itself was fraught with so many emotional dangers and she had seen how Tehzeeb and Ana looked when their respective husbands weren't with them. She never wanted to be so dependent on another human being. The pain wasn't worth it.

But she had to stop Ana before she did something rash. What could she do? She thought hard, pacing the floor, thinking of different ways in which Ana could listen to her. It all came down to just one person. Abbu.

Abbu was Ana's hero. He was everything to her. She remembered the dressing down her normally mild sister had given Tehzeeb during her engagement, all because she feared that Abbu would find out and be disappointed in her. The only person who could change her mind was Abbu. But who would change Abbu's mind?

She wasn't scared of Abbu but she knew when there was no hope in bringing up Ana with him. The very moment she had heard what had happened, she'd tried to talk to Abbu but he had silenced her with a motion of his hands.

'I don't have a daughter called Ana. Don't talk about her to me,' he admonished her.

She had wanted to roll her eyes. You couldn't just negate your children like that, she thought but as the days passed, she realised Abbu was very serious about it. He truly meant it. That was naïve of him, Athiya thought, if he thought he could forget his own daughter.

The idea occurred to her suddenly, when she had become tired of pacing the room, thinking constantly. Farhaan.

If Farhaan told the truth about what had happened, then Abbu would know that none of this was Ana's fault. In fact, Ana had gone as far as to almost marry Farhaan just to keep Abbu happy. He had to learn about that and she knew it had to come from Farhaan.

She wondered how she could contact him. She didn't have his number and according to what Luqman had said, he wasn't answering anyone's calls or replying to text messages. She walked outside and saw that Abbu was dozing in the living room. Warily, she reached for his phone. Abbu had an old Nokia phone that had seen much better days and although she had gotten tired of telling him to upgrade to a decent smartphone, she was glad he hadn't.

She unlocked it quickly, scrolled down the contacts list and found Farhaan's number. Saving the number on her own phone, she went back inside and shut the door slightly. With shaky hands, she dialled the number, knowing that it was most likely to be switched off but to her surprise, the phone rang and he answered.

'Hello?' his voice was low and firm. Athiya rubbed her elbow suddenly, wondering why it was tingling.

'Um, hi,' she said, trying to stop her own voice from getting wobbly. What was wrong with her? She decimated guys with just a glance and here she was, becoming nervous about talking to this man.

'Yes? Who's this?' he asked in that same cultured voice and this time, she felt the tingling in the area of her tummy.

Straightening up, she took a deep breath. 'This is Athiya. Ana's sister,' she said.

He was silent and she thought that maybe he had ended the call. 'Are you there?' she asked.

'Yes, but why have you called me?' he asked, sounding irritated.

'Listen, I have no interest in talking to you but there's a major crisis going on here and I think only you can fix it,' Athiya said.

'What do you mean?' he asked, sounding alert.

Sighing, she quickly told him all that she knew. He listened in silence and then she asked again if he was there.

'I *am* here. I'm just thinking,' he said.

'There's nothing to think. Just come back and speak to Abbu. Tell him the truth,' Athiya said.

'It's not so easy, Athiya,' he said, his voice low. She felt that odd fluttery tingle in her tummy once more when she heard him say her name. Frowning, she snapped at him.

'No one said it would be easy. But it's what needs to be done. Ana and Luqman love each other but because of what your mother and brother said to her, Abbu has disowned her. And she thinks that she shouldn't be with Luqman anymore. It's as simple as that. You need to set things straight,' she said.

'Athiya,' he said softly, and her breath caught in her throat. 'Your father also hates me. What makes you think he'll listen to me?'

His voice was doing funny things to her and she didn't want to let him know that, especially the way he said her name like it was a personal invocation. Maybe this quiet and subdued charm worked on other women. Not her.

'Don't patronise me, Farhaan. Stop making excuses. If you want to save your brother and Ana's marriage, just grow the fuck up and come back. Set things straight,' she fumed and ended the call.

She held the phone a little too tightly in her hand and she realised she was breathing hard. She blinked as she tossed the phone on the bed.

Clearly, this hadn't worked. Farhaan was not going to come back from wherever he was. How was she going to help Ana?

Her phone pinged. She picked it up and saw that it was a message from Farhaan.

'Thanks for letting me know. I'll try and figure out something soon,' it read. She made a face and threw the phone face down on the bed once more.

FIFTY-TWO

Luqman's headache hadn't let up for what seemed like months now, although it had been only a few days since he had returned to India. But so much had happened in the interim that it still made his head spin. He had moved out of his house, rented an apartment and was living there.

Waiting for Ana.

He knew she didn't mean it. She couldn't. But her eyes looked so dead and her words were so final. He blinked as he strained tea for himself in a mug, refusing to think of that moment when she'd told him that she wanted a divorce. She'd turned away from him after saying that, walked inside the room and shut the door.

He had no other choice but to leave, thinking that she needed some time. But it had been three days since that momentous day when he had spoken to her, when he had held her in his arms and she had been like a block of wood. He hadn't heard from her and the reports from Ayub and Tehzeeb were not encouraging.

He took the mug with him and went to the tiny living room. It was bare, except for a couple of plastic chairs and the boxes he had brought back with him. As he sipped the tea, he tried not to think of the ugly scene that had taken place with Ammi and Nouman when he'd arrived home. But those moments, that day kept playing on a loop in his head.

Ammi had been surprised to see him but she'd turned her face away in anger when he had tried to speak with her. Nouman's sneering face had reminded him of the things he had said about Ana and he'd walked up to him and punched him in the face. Ammi had screamed and started shouting that Ana was a witch who had carried out jadu-tona on her sons. They were fighting with each other because of her.

He'd turned to Ammi, shaking in anger. 'Ammi, Ana is not at fault here. You should have spoken to me before accusing her,' he'd said, trying to control his anger. Nouman, nursing a bleeding nose, snorted in contempt.

'You hit your brother over a two-bit girl? She was two-timing you and Farhaan Bhai. How could you be so blind?' Nouman asked through a mouth full of blood. Luqman wanted to pummel him. He wanted to hit him several times more. But he stopped himself because he already regretted what he had done. Clearly, hitting Nouman was not going to help his or Ana's case.

Still, he'd clenched his fists, breathing hard. 'I wish you hadn't been so quick to judge her, Ammi. Why did you decide that it was her fault? Why didn't you speak to me?' he'd asked Ammi. He hadn't wanted to look at Nouman.

'I don't want to talk about that girl. Aisi kameeni ladki maine zindagi mein nahi dekhi,'Ammi had spat out the words. Luqman felt like she had slapped him across his face. Licking his dry lips, he'd ran upstairs and filled up a bag with her clothes and things. She wasn't going to stay here and neither was he. He was going to talk to her and they would live separately. If they had each other, nothing else mattered.

He'd come downstairs and found Ammi helping Nouman wipe the blood from his face. She'd shaken her head when she noticed the bag in his hands. 'Don't do anything rash, Luqman. Think about it.'

'No, Ammi. You don't know the truth. I've been in love with her for months. When I found out that you wanted to get her married to Farhaan Bhai, I came back immediately because I wanted to stop you,' he had said. His eyes had strayed to the sofa where he saw Ana's handbag. He'd recognised it immediately and walked over to it, picking it up.

His heart had pounded painfully when he thought of what she must have gone through. Her phone was also probably inside it.

'Why didn't you say anything then?' Ammi asked, eyes narrowed.

Nostrils flared, he'd turned to her. 'I *was* coming to talk to you. But then I had the accident. And I had … I faced some memory loss. I forgot that I was supposed to talk to you about her. But I kept thinking about her all the time.'

Ammi frowned. This was distasteful to her, but he hadn't cared.

'I remembered everything on the Haldi night and I went and spoke to Bhai,' he'd continued. Ammi was frowning but he continued.

'This was all Bhai's plan. He said that the only way I could get married to Ana in an acceptable manner was if he stepped down,' he said. 'I was coming to talk to you and to tell you that I loved her. I was willing to elope with her if need be but he told me this was better.'

Ammi had looked as though she couldn't believe it. Luqman was exhausted. He didn't have the energy to deal with his mother and brother and he was desperate to see his wife. To console her and tell her that they would always be together no matter what happened.

When Ana had turned him away, he didn't know what to do. He felt lost, walked around aimlessly and sat at a park bench for a couple of hours, his head pounding in pain. Ayub called him repeatedly until he had got exhausted of the ringing and answered, telling him where he was. Ayub came to him and they sat in Ayub's car and talked.

'I can't go back to that house,' Luqman said.

'Fine, then come and stay in my house,' Ayub said without a pause. Luqman shook his head.

'Your house is Ana's safe space. I don't want to invade it and make her uncomfortable,' he said.

'Uncomfortable? You're her husband,' Ayub said.

Luqman pursed his lips, knowing his eyes were filling with tears. He had messed up big time. Ana had wanted them to come clean. They could have controlled the story if they had told it themselves. Ammi would have been shocked and horrified but she wouldn't have assumed Ana was to blame.

He closed his eyes. 'Yes, but she asked for a divorce,' he whispered.

Ayub was stunned. 'But ...'

Luqman sighed. 'I'm hoping she doesn't mean it, Ayub,' he said, looking down at his hands. He wanted to break down and cry but he controlled himself.

'Shit. What will you do, Luqman?' Ayub asked, as though wondering aloud.

'I don't know. I just can't go back there,' he said.

Ayub nodded. 'Then maybe we should find you a place to stay,' he said. Luqman felt better at the thought of doing something. He was going to find a house for his family. For himself and Ana.

Even though his heart felt like it was crowding his chest, he and Ayub worked out a plan and got around to finding a place for him. The apartment was in a building not too far from either Jasmine Villa or Ayub's house. He moved in with his meagre belongings – he'd gone home once more and taken away his things from there. Ammi had watched everything in silence, her mouth pinched and angry. He knew she didn't believe him but he didn't care.

Ayub had helped him with the shopping for basics like a bed and chairs and things for the kitchen. The landlord was a friend of his and Luqman was grateful for how quickly he'd been able to move in with Ayub's help.

Tehzeeb had visited him yesterday with Aslan and Ayub.

'How's she?' he asked, his voice hopeful, his eyes alight.

She looked down. 'I don't know, Luqman. I've never seen her like this. It's like she's reached the end of her rope. She hasn't gotten over the shock of what happened in your house and what Abbu said to her,' she said softly.

Luqman rubbed the back of his neck angrily. 'I punched Nouman by the way. That asshole deserved a lot more for the things he said about Ana. But I'm also angry with Abbu,' he said.

Tehzeeb nodded unhappily and shrugged. 'I don't know why Abbu did that. Ana is his favourite among the three of us and ... she may be called Ana, but she's his pride and joy.'

Luqman shook his head. 'Whatever his reason, he shouldn't have done that to her.'

Now, sitting alone as he sipped his tea, he thought of this empty house and wondered when the only person who could make it into a home would join him.

He saw her in every room, wandering about, inspecting cupboards, checking the bathroom. He saw her pull aside the curtains that he hadn't hung up yet because he didn't own any. He saw her turn to him, love shining in her eyes. He saw her hold him close to her, soothing him as he calmed her. They were each other's anchors. How could she think she'd be able to live happily without him?

But then, what if she was truly tired of everything? What if she wasn't willing to give him another chance? What if she really wanted to be free of him?

He'd give her whatever she asked. Even this. Even if it killed him.

FIFTY-THREE

Farhaan was not sure where he should go first. To his house, to speak to Ammi or to Ana's house to speak to her father. In the end, he remembered the urgency in Athiya's voice and he headed to Jasmine Villa, directly from the airport.

When he left Bangalore on the Haldi night, he had gone to Hyderabad. He'd stayed in a hotel and caught up with a few friends whom he hadn't met since college. From there, he had headed to Chennai and then Mumbai. He felt completely free since he had left home. Without the burden of the responsibilities of the house and the business on him, he felt like a different person.

No one asked any questions and he was glad. He didn't know what he could tell them anyhow. Everything had just been too bizarre. He didn't know anyone in either Chennai or Mumbai so he was spending each day like it was a vacation. But this soon got tiresome for him. As a workaholic for almost all his adult life, he didn't know what to do with all this free time.

The calls from his family kept coming but he ignored them constantly, knowing that it wasn't the right time to go back. He didn't know when it would be but it couldn't be so soon. He needed to give time to Ana and Luqman to settle down and for Ammi to forgive him. He did feel a little bad at leaving Nouman with all the work but he felt that his brother was capable enough of figuring things out on his own.

He had been planning to go on a Ladakh bike trip when the unfamiliar number had rung and he had answered it without thinking. When he finished talking to Ana's sister, he rubbed his forehead thoughtfully. It was time to go back home and fix things. It wasn't going to be easy but the mess at home needed him. He was a problem solver and this was yet another thing that he had to take care of, especially if Ana and Luqman's marriage depended on him.

He pushed open the gate to Jasmine Villa and walked inside, wondering what Nouman had done with the project. Athiya hadn't mentioned anything to him because she was worried about her sister. But the project should have begun by now and it hadn't. He rang the doorbell, wondering if Ana's father would listen to him. He had taken a real liking to Farhaan and he felt a little sick at how his betrayal must have hurt him. Farhaan had seen something in Yusuf Hasan's face and his demeanour which reminded him of his own father.

The door opened and he took a sharp breath. It was Athiya. The youngest sister. The one who had called him and given him a dressing down. He hadn't given her much thought but now that she stood before him, he remembered the time he had seen her in the café when he was with Mr Joshi. Or even how she had looked on the Haldi day when she had smiled at him. She had looked resplendent, like a bride herself, even though she had been dressed rather simply.

She was not beautiful like Tehzeeb and neither did

she have Ana's quiet prettiness that made one stop in their tracks. But surely, there was something about her that made one pause. She was fiery and that look in her eyes made him smile at her. She didn't smile back.

'Finally. Come inside,' she said, reaching out to pull him inside the house. The contact of her hand on his arm almost felt prickly, he thought. There were spots of colour on her cheeks too, maybe because of the familiarity with which she had behaved. But she looked back at him defiantly as she fixed her dupatta over her shoulders, inadvertently bringing his gaze down to her chest. He looked up immediately.

'I just hope you're not too late,' she said as she worried her lower lip with her teeth. He stared at how her teeth sank into her plush lip, the simple act firing up his veins and arousing him all of a sudden. He looked away because of this strange reaction he was having towards her. He wanted to touch her lips with his fingertips and soothe the spot with his own lips.

He wanted to kiss her.

Dismissing the absurd thought from his head, he nodded.

'Where's your father?' he asked.

'Abbu has gone out,' she said. What? They were alone in the house? This was not appropriate, he thought wildly.

'Maybe I should come back later,' he said, turning around to leave.

'No, wait!' Athiya said, holding his elbow. He turned back and looked at her hand pointedly and she dropped her hand. 'Abbu will be back now. He's just gone to the nearby masjid for namaz.'

'I'll wait outside then,' he said.

'Did you come from the airport?' she asked. He nodded because she was looking at the trolley bag he had with him.

'Then just sit here in the living room. I'll make some tea for you,' she said.

'Athiya, it's all right. I can wait outside. That's the right thing to do,' he said. She looked exasperated.

'Do you *always* do the right thing?' she asked, her hands on her hips. He tried to look away, because the movement accentuated her full breasts that were barely covered by her dupatta. She was wearing a short knee-length white top with a flared pink shalwar and a flimsy pink dupatta and the overall effect would have been casual with any other girl.

But she wasn't any other girl.

'I try to,' he responded shortly.

'Sit,' she ordered him and turned around, walking to the kitchen. Rolling his eyes, he sat down on the sofa, glad that she wasn't sitting with him. His thoughts were turning inappropriate and she was just a kid, he realised. Why on earth would he have such thoughts about her, he chastised himself. The door opened then and her father walked inside. He hadn't seen him yet, so Farhaan stood up and Yusuf Hasan stared at him in shock. He looked tired, his eyes had sunk in deeply and there were lines on his face that made him look much older than he was.

'What are you doing here?' he asked sharply.

'Uncle, I came to tell you the truth,' he said, going to him and taking his hand. He withdrew his hand immediately, his nostrils flaring.

'Why did you come here? Please leave,' he said. He looked angry and upset and Farhaan didn't want to upset him further but this had to be done.

'Uncle, you don't know the whole story,' he told him.

'I know enough.'

There was a finality in his tone that should have sent most people scurrying but Farhaan hadn't transformed his family business into the top real estate agency in the city by running away when faced with challenges.

'No uncle, you don't know everything,' he said.

'Abbu, please listen to him,' Athiya said, as she emerged from the kitchen, with a tray that held two teacups.

'You go inside,' her father ordered her but she didn't listen. Instead, she walked around the sofa and kept the tray on the coffee table. She had covered her head in an attempt to look modest but her eyes continued to radiate her passion.

'Abbu, you broke Ana Api's heart. Do you know that she had asked Luqman Bhai for a divorce?' Athiya asked.

Her father looked startled. She turned to Farhaan, shaking her head. 'I've been trying to tell him this for days but he wouldn't listen. Please sit down, both of you.'

For some reason, her father complied and Farhaan sat down as well.

'Uncle, it's important that you know the truth,' he said and he quickly related everything to him. When he finished talking, Yusuf Hasan looked troubled and beads of sweat had popped up on his forehead.

'But your mother ...' he said softly. Farhaan shook his head.

'My mother is a very traditional woman and she can be blind when it comes to her sons. I'm sorry about the things she said to Ana and to you. But please, you have to forgive Ana. She and Luqman belong with each other and my brother loves her very much.'

He looked up and his eyes met Athiya's who looked back at him, compassion in her eyes and she smiled a little and nodded encouragingly. But to his surprise, she spoke, her eyes lighting up.

'Abbu, you wouldn't listen to me all these days but Ana Api was willing to marry Farhaan because you were so happy, especially with the whole joint development project. She didn't even care for her own happiness as much as she did for yours, which I think is very stupid, considering how you treated her,' she said in a rush.

Farhaan stared at her. Overkill. That should have been her middle name. Her father winced and rubbed his forehead.

'I need to think,' Yusuf Hasan said and got up to go to his room. He stopped at the door and turned around. 'Thank you for coming to tell me the truth.'

Farhaan nodded and stood up as well. He had the strangest urge to continue sitting in the living room. He wanted to talk to Athiya, drink tea with her, hold her, kiss her. Stop right there, he ordered his mind.

'At least have your tea and go,' she said with a smile.

He shook his head. 'No, I better leave now,' he said. He had to get out of here before he acted on these strange impulses. He wondered if it was probably because of the various things he'd been doing all these days which were all out of character for him.

She walked up to the door with him and he couldn't resist turning around and looking at her. She smiled at him then and his heart knocked about in his chest.

'Thank you,' she said softly. 'I hope this works. I just want to see those two stupid lovebirds happy together.'

He nodded curtly and walked away. As he opened the gate and stepped outside, he looked once more in her direction. She was standing at the door, the warm afternoon sun outlining her and she looked like an angel. She lifted her hand to wave at him slightly.

He didn't wave back.

FIFTY-FOUR

Ana couldn't forget the expression on Luqman's face when she had told him she wanted a divorce. The shock, the horror and the resignation on his face broke her even more. She knew she was right. The two of them were not good for each other. There had been more than one sign and they had ignored them all.

Sending him away had been the hardest thing she had done. Her heart squeezed painfully in her chest when she shut the door on his face. She had hurt him. Badly. But what else was there for them to do? How could they be together when his mother and her father thought such things about them?

It had been five days since he had walked away and she didn't know which was worse – the fact that she didn't want to talk to him or that he hadn't reached out to her. He hadn't sent her even a single message or text to convince her that she was wrong. Of course she wanted to talk to him. Of course she wanted to hold him close and tell him that they'd figure out everything as long as they were together.

But she had sent him away and he had really gone. It took all her willpower not to ask Ayub or Tehzeeb if they had heard from him or to even ask how he was doing.

She could barely sleep at night and she had taken to sitting outside in the hall on the first floor of Tehzeeb's home. She had startled Tehzeeb's mother-in-law once when she emerged from her bedroom to get something. Ana was always a little wary around her because she had been rude to her sister all those months ago. But compared to what her own mother-in-law had said to her, she seemed like a saint.

Aafreen Ahmed sat down beside her and patted her back. Ana had already cried her heart out with her sister but she found that she could still summon tears which fell down her face readily. She knew that Tehzeeb had told her mother-in-law everything and she was grateful to them for letting her stay there. But she sobbed quietly and Aafreen Ahmed hugged her.

'Shh,' she said softly, enveloping her in a cloud of her expensive perfume (that she wore even at night?) and made soothing noises. She set Ana back and looked at her critically.

'Is this how you plan to spend your life? Crying over a man?' she asked. Ana looked at her, not sure how much she knew about her own daughter who had been in love with Luqman for the longest time. She realised Aafreen was still waiting for an answer.

'No, but ...'

Aafreen Ahmed sighed. 'I know what's happened is not ideal. And I really didn't think Salma Apa would be so vicious,' she said. Ana didn't know what to say to that. She hated thinking about her own mother-in-law and the horrible words that had spouted from her mouth, the hot gleam of hatred in her eyes.

'I didn't know anyone could detest me so much,' she whispered.

'Leave her be. Tell me why you sent away Luqman,' Aafreen said.

Ana looked down at her lap and lifted her shoulders slightly. 'I … I don't know, Auntie. I think we weren't meant to be together. And after what Abbu said …'

'Your Abbu deserves a dressing down too. How could he just leave you like that on the road and go away?' she said.

'No, Abbu is …'

'… is not perfect. I agree he was angry with you. But this is not done. He could have taken you home and scolded you. He could have decided not to talk to you when you were at home with him,' she continued.

Ana didn't know how to respond, so Aafreen continued.

'Listen, I also haven't been the perfect mother-in-law. You know what happened with us too, right? But I don't think Salma Apa is like that. She's very set in her ways. Very traditional. You should just ignore her and move on in your life with Luqman,' she said.

Ana nodded and got up to go to her room. She didn't want to discuss this with anyone and so she went to sleep where she dreamt of Luqman. As always.

In the morning, she was debating how to tell Ayub and Tehzeeb that she wanted to move out. They had been nothing but gracious hosts and she didn't want to outstay her welcome. But her phone rang just as she emerged from her shower and she walked up to it, her steps quick, thinking it was Luqman. She was going to ignore it, of course, but it would prove to her that he was thinking of her.

It was Abbu.

Eyes wide, she answered the phone cautiously.

'Ana,' he said.

She held her breath. 'Yes, Abbu,' she said after a pause.

'Can you meet me at home now?' he asked.

She nodded and realised he couldn't see her so she said, 'Yes, I'll come,' and she ended the call. Had Abbu forgiven her? But even as she dressed quickly, she realised she could be wrong. Why would he forgive her all of a sudden? Was he calling her to tell her how much he hated her? How completely he has disowned her? Was he asking her to come and take away whatever things she'd left in Jasmine Villa?

Tears sprang into her eyes but she wiped them away resolutely. If that was what Abbu wanted, then so be it. She decided she wouldn't come back here. She was going to find a PG and she had to stop behaving like a martyr. It was a wonder the school hadn't fired her already. Luqman had brought her things like her phone and some clothes that he had found at home with him when he came to see her that day.

She was touched by his thoughtfulness but she pushed him away from her mind now. She got ready quickly and went to Tehzeeb who was feeding Aslan. Ayub had left for work already and she was glad she didn't have to see his hurt expression because she refused to listen to him about patching up with Luqman.

'Api, Abbu called me now,' she said and both Tehzeeb and Aslan looked at her, startled. Aslan smiled and waved at her. He was just shy of turning a year old and she knew Tehzeeb and Ayub were planning a big birthday bash for him.

'Api,' he called out to her. He had started calling her Api too, after listening to Athiya and it amused everyone enough to let it be.

'What did he say?' Tehzeeb asked, helping Aslan sit up and she adjusted her clothing. She kept saying that she had to stop breastfeeding him but he wasn't taking to the bottle easily.

'Nothing. He's asked me to come there,' Ana said, looking down.

'Okay. Do you want me to come with you?' she asked. Ana shook her head.

'I'll see you in a bit,' she said and left. She was nervous and would have liked to have Tehzeeb's moral support but she knew she had to face Abbu alone.

When she reached Jasmine Villa, she felt her composure crumble. She had missed her home, had missed walking inside its jasmine-scented tiny patch of garden and she saw that Abbu was sitting on the steps, like he always did every evening.

It was mid-morning now, the sun streaming inside the garden, lighting up everything beautifully, Would she be seeing this for the last time? She paused just inside the gate and he noticed her and stood up.

She was breathing hard, and somewhere in her mind, she registered that her stomach hurt with all the different feelings that were rushing through her. Her mouth was dry.

Abbu stepped forward, his arms held out to her, and the relief that he had forgiven her was so intense, that she burst into tears as she rushed into his arms. He held her tightly and she kept crying, unable to stop the heaving sobs that seemed to be wrenched from the very core of her being.

'I'm sorry, Abbu,' she said, gasping finally. He shook his head and held the back of her head.

'No, no, I'm sorry, Ana beta. I don't know what came over me. I don't know how I could have done that to you. I should have at least listened to you first,' he said.

Ana kept sobbing and he held her tighter.

'Come,' he said, leading her inside to the living room where she sat down on the sofa, still sobbing.

'Where's Athiya?' she asked, when her crying finally subsided as she looked around for her sister.

'Out somewhere. She'd rung Farhaan and asked him to come and talk to me,' he said.

'What?' Ana asked, surprised. She wiped the tears from her face. She still couldn't understand what was happening. 'When?'

'Yesterday afternoon. He came and told me everything. I just wished I had listened to you before being so harsh with you. Will you ever forgive me, Ana?' he asked.

Ana's mouth was dry. 'There's nothing to forgive. I had wanted to come clean to you but ...'

Abbu shook his head almost wryly. 'Your sister told me that you were going to marry Farhaan because it would make me happy. And she said it was stupid of you and I agree,' he said.

Ana didn't say anything. She wiped her face with the edge of her dupatta because she found that tears were still streaming down.

'Ana, your happiness matters. And Luqman makes you happy, doesn't he? Athiya told me that you had asked for a divorce from him. How could you do that, beta? After everything the two of you have been through?' he asked.

Ana froze. She looked at Abbu, and shook her head.

'Abbu, why did we have to go through so much? Isn't it a sign that we shouldn't be together?' she asked. Abbu smiled and shaking his head, he took her hand.

'No, it just means that you had more hurdles in your way than others. Life is a journey, beta. You're lucky if you have someone to hold you, comfort you, and just be with you on that journey. Just because the terrain gets rough, it doesn't mean that you let go of each other. In fact, you have to hold each other even more tightly so you can cross the rocky path together,' he said.

Ana sighed. 'Abbu, you and your pop psychology,' she muttered but she saw the smile on his face and she found that she couldn't resist letting one blossom on her face too.

'Since a certified psychologist like you couldn't figure out your own problems, I had to step in,' Abbu said, patting her hand.

Ana was silent as she weighed her options. She wanted to go to Luqman but she couldn't bear stepping inside that house once more.

'I can't go there, Abbu,' she said finally. 'I know what we did was wrong but the things she told me, told you ...'

'Luqman is not there. He left his house,' Abbu said. She looked at him in surprise.

'Then?'

'He's rented a place for himself nearby. I called Ayub and asked him to text me the directions. Take it from my phone and go to him now,' Abbu said.

Her heart started beating madly, and once more, she felt alive at the thought of seeing Luqman. At the thought that they would be together. Abbu was right. She couldn't abandon him the moment things went south. He had quit his job and left his family. For her.

She had to go to him now.

FIFTY-FIVE

Luqman had been looking for a job these past few days. He had savings which meant that he could afford to take a little time but he knew he couldn't take too long. As it was Akshay had been livid when he had quit the job before he flew down to India and he didn't want his reputation to precede him so it was best he get something new, and soon.

He opened his laptop and checked his email to see if there were any responses from the places he'd sent out his resume. He sat in the makeshift living room and wondered what was going to happen to his life. This was day seven without Ana and nothing seemed to be getting better. What was she doing now? Why hadn't she contacted him yet? What was going on between them? He couldn't believe that they had reached this standoff after just three weeks of marriage.

Last night, however, he'd been surprised to see Farhaan's name pop up on his screen. He answered the phone and learned that he was back. He had gone straight to Ana's father and told him the truth. Then he'd gone home to Ammi.

'She told me you had moved out,' Farhaan said.

'Yes. I can't stay in a house where my wife is treated

unfairly,' he said, wondering if Farhaan would try to change his mind. He wasn't going back there without Ana.

'I told her she was wrong to blame Ana. But she doesn't seem to be thinking clearly. She's refusing to change her mind about her,' Farhaan said.

Luqman scowled. 'Fine. I also refuse to come back to that house until she and Nouman apologise to Ana,' he said. Farhaan sighed.

'You know Ammi,' he said. Luqman grunted.

'Yes. And she's being completely unreasonable. How did you get to know about all this anyway?' he asked.

Farhaan paused. 'Athiya called me and said I had to come and speak to her father about the truth,' he said.

Luqman pondered over his brother's words for a bit. What would it matter if Farhaan spoke to Abbu? Ana was still refusing to meet him, refusing to be with him. His heart heavy, he had hung up. He ran his hand over the beard that had sprouted on his face and he sighed. He should shave but he didn't have any motivation to even get up from the living room. He looked around, thinking that he should fix up the place but there was a nasty part of him, telling him why bother. Why bother with anything?

He looked up, startled when the doorbell rang. Placing his laptop gingerly on the makeshift table, he went to the door, wondering who it could be. No one had visited him here except Ayub and Tehzeeb. The door didn't even have a peephole so he opened it cautiously.

Ana stood outside, her face drawn. He stared at her face, not willing to believe that she was really standing here before him. He wanted to reach out to her, to hold her in his arms but he stopped himself. Why was she here? He was afraid to feel optimistic about their relationship. Not after what she had said to him.

He stepped back and pulled the door open wider. She walked inside and he breathed in her light perfume, something that was unique to her and it made him want to pull her into his arms. She looked around cursorily in silence.

'What are you doing?' he asked her finally. Had she come here to end things between them? Could she really do it? He held his breath as he waited for her to speak.

She didn't reply but finally pulled aside one of the plastic chairs and sat down on it. He didn't sit down but he looked at her expectantly.

'Ana, I asked you a question,' he said. His heart was beating erratically. If he thought he looked like shit, she didn't look any better. There were circles under her eyes and her face was pale. But he had never seen a more beautiful sight. His wife, in his house, finally.

She looked at her hands that were on her lap and then she looked up, drawing a breath.

'I'm sorry,' she said.

'For what?' he asked sharply. She was sorry she was ending things between them? Dammit, no. He hadn't thought it would really come to this. He had hoped she would change her mind about them, that she would give him a chance.

'For the way I treated you,' she said softly. He looked at her, into her eyes and he saw her apology there, but also, love. Overwhelmed with gratitude, he sank to his knees and she, startled, as she got up from the chair to sit down before him.

'I thought you had come to end things between us,' he whispered. She shook her head, her hair coming undone. She looked so beautiful at that moment that he sat down on the floor, held his head in his hands and cried. He knew he should be a man, take charge of things, hold her in his arms, but he was so tired.

'Shh,' she soothed him as she edged close to him and held his head to her chest. She arranged herself so that he was leaning on her as he cried and held on to her. She was crying too. He lifted his face and wiped her tears, hiccupping. She did the same to him.

They looked at each other for long moments, exchanging wordless promises. He moved away from her embrace because her proximity wasn't letting him think clearly.

'I know you came here because Farhaan Bhai spoke to your father,' he said. She nodded. He moved back from her, even further, needing to make her understand how much she had hurt him.

'Ana, *you* decided everything. *You* decided we couldn't be together and *you* wanted a divorce.' Even the words were painful.

She slid forward and covered his mouth with her palm, shaking her head. 'I'm sorry. I just ... I just thought it was best for us at that time,' she said.

He moved her hand away. 'Ana, when things go wrong, as they will, we have to talk it through and be in it together. You can't just walk away from me or decide things for us on your own,' he said, holding her wrist. Her pulse was beating rapidly and she nodded fervently.

'I'm sorry. I didn't realise what I was doing. I know I hurt you very badly,' she said.

'You broke my heart,' he said, letting go of her hand and rubbing his chest. 'It hurts. Physically.'

Swallowing, she moved closer to him and kissed his chest. His pulse leapt. Other parts of his body came to life as well. He slid his palm around the nape of her neck and looked at her intently.

'I don't have a job,' he said softly.

'I have one. I think,' she replied.

'This house is very small.'

'It's home,' she said.

They looked at each other again and this time, they both moved. He held her face and kissed her. She kissed him back, straining to get closer to him as she rocked into him and reached under his shirt to touch his chest. He gasped as her fingernail raked over his nipple.

'Do we have a bed?' she whispered as his lips traced her jaw.

'We do,' he replied, wrapping his arms around her.

'I want to see it,' she said. He held her shoulders and his eyes bore into her.

'You just want to see it?' he asked, cocking his head slightly. She rolled her eyes and bent forward to kiss the side of his neck. 'You know that we don't really need a bed.'

'I know that better than anyone else but I also want us to be comfortable,' she said, raising an eyebrow. His heart felt like it had unfurled, all the hurt erasing slowly as he saw the return of the old Ana. There were so many different aspects to her and he looked forward to learning all of them.

He kissed the tip of her fingers as he rose gracefully, carrying her with him. She gasped as she held on to his shirt.

'Luqman, your leg!'

'It's fine,' he said as he carried her inside the room. Thank goodness the room was not messy. The bed occupied the space centrally and he was glad he'd remembered to use a bedspread. Her arms were looped around his neck and he lowered her onto the bed gently. She didn't let go of him, so he had to settle down on top of her.

Her chest was rising and falling with each breath. She traced his beard and frowned slightly.

'Didn't feel like shaving,' he explained, working on the buttons of her kurta.

'I like it,' she said softly, rubbing his beard with the tips of her fingers. Even her simplest touch was seductive and sexy, he thought.

'But it's going tomorrow,' he said as she lifted her neck to give him better access. He parted the kurta, his hands covering and squeezing her breasts and she whimpered.

'We'll see,' she said with a groan.

He was hard and aching for her. It felt like it had been forever since he had been inside her.

'I missed doing this with you,' she said as he went to work on her shalwar, yanking the string free. Her hands roamed over his back and slid under his shirt, bringing him closer.

'I missed everything,' he said, pulling the cup of her bra down and lowering his head to lightly graze her nipple with his teeth. She hissed and arched into his mouth.

'Everything,' he repeated and sucked harder. Her ankles locked around his hips and she moaned loudly but he didn't relent.

'Stop, please,' she whispered, loosening her grip around his hips, her heels pushing into the bed.

He lifted his head and looked at her. His Ana was back with him finally. He got rid of his clothes as soon as he could. She pulled him down and rose above him, her legs straddling him. He could feel her wetness on his belly and it only made him harder. He looked at the picture – hair open and streaming down around her shoulders, naked and willing, and he wanted to own her completely.

'This is the first day of the rest of our lives,' she leaned forward, whispering into his mouth and she lifted herself, letting him slip inside her. He gasped as she struggled to fit him at first but then began to move slowly, seductively. Her hands caught his and she surged over him.

'I love you, Luqman,' she whispered as she started to move faster, her skin turning pink and he smiled through his grimace because he was so close to coming.

'What?' she asked, her breath catching in her throat. He slid his hands around her torso and spanned her ribcage with his palms.

'I've fallen in love with you twice, Ana. But I'll love you forever,' he said. Her eyes shone with tears as she collapsed over him, her breath gusting against his neck.

'Forever,' she repeated.

EPILOGUE

One month later

'You don't have to watch this, you know.'

Athiya started when she heard Farhaan's voice come up from behind her. She squared her shoulders and glanced at him.

He looked different. Ever since he had returned from wherever he had gone, she realised she ended up thinking about him more than she wanted to. She was especially glad he had come back when she had spoken to him and had convinced Abbu to forgive Ana. It was another matter altogether that he hadn't been able to get his own mother to change her mind.

'Well, someone has to,' she replied, turning back to the demolition crew that was just getting started. When he returned, Farhaan had set things into motion and made sure that the Jasmine Villa project continued as before. She was aware that there was some friction about it at home, especially from his middle brother, the asshole who had made the big scene about Ana in the first place. But she liked that he didn't care about it and went on doing what he was supposed to.

She braced herself even as she looked at her beloved house that would soon cease to exist. Both Tehzeeb and Ana had refused to come for this. They said they wanted to remember the house as it had been, and they couldn't bear to see it razed to the ground. The construction crew had been informed to work around the jasmine tree because it had been planted by her mother and they were as close to it as they were to the house.

Abbu and Athiya had finally moved out of Jasmine Villa into a small apartment nearby where they would stay until the apartments here were readied. Athiya hated the idea wholeheartedly. They were going to have to live with complete strangers here, and their home, their safe space would never be the same.

But Abbu had decided and he was insistent that he wanted to do this. Farhaan walked away to talk to someone and she looked at him, realising to her dismay that she was actually admiring him. Well, he did make for a striking figure, she thought as she saw him take those long strides towards the construction crew. He was wearing a white polo shirt with jeans and a pair of shades hung from his fingertips loosely.

Abbu, who had been inside the house, walked out and stood beside her, giving an imperceptible nod to Farhaan. He put his arm around her and she leaned into him, breathing in his familiar attar fragrance.

'It's going to be fine, you just wait and see,' Abbu said. It sounded like he was convincing himself more than her.

Athiya didn't say anything. Her sisters had come here. All of them felt the same way, like the house was a person too, an extension of their family and their lives. People like Farhaan who worked on houses day in and day out wouldn't see it that way. For them, everything was just a business transaction.

She smiled when she thought of her nephew Aslan who had run around the tiny patch of garden. Aslan would not know what it would be like to sit here in the evenings as the birds made their way home, as the air was infused with the scent of jasmine. But did the future generation even care about all that? She knew she shouldn't. All this emotion was for losers.

But was it, she asked herself. She saw how Ana had looked when Luqman had come to pick her up. Her entire face lit up and she would have kissed him if Athiya and Abbu weren't there. Ana behaved like she hadn't seen him in days when it had just been a few hours but even though Athiya thought they were overdoing it, she was happy for them.

They were happy together. Very happy. Ridiculously happy. They were living in an apartment nearby and Ana had made it into a cosy home already. Luqman had found another job and both he and Ana were busy but they were making it work. She and Abbu visited them often and while Ana was thrilled to see her, she knew that Luqman missed being with his family.

His mother hadn't forgiven him and he hadn't forgiven her either. That was a tricky situation, she thought. Ana had sat down with her and told her that for the moment, the two of them were taking each day as it came. Given all they had been through, that was miraculous enough. But Ana told her that she knew her husband missed his family too.

Athiya glared at the lone member of his family who stepped away and signalled the construction crew. Farhaan visited them apparently, and Luqman was glad that at least his brother was with him.

'Isn't it weird for you?' Athiya asked her. Ana shrugged.

'I don't know. I don't think of it that way. It's not like we were engaged or anything and Farhaan Bhai is ...'

'Farhaan Bhai?' Athiya asked, eyes growing wide.

'Well, he's Luqman's older brother and that's what he calls him,' Ana said with a smile. Athiya had just rolled her eyes.

'Is it done?' Ana messaged on their Whatsapp group. She had set up one for only the three of them. No Abbu, and no husbands.

'It hasn't even started yet,' Athiya replied. She stared straight ahead, waiting for the crucial moment when her house would go down, when there would be nothing left of their memories and dreams but dust and debris.

In the end, it was rather anti-climactic as the crew went about their work. Athiya turned away, unable to see her house being reduced to dust. It would take hours, of course.

The sun shone down brightly at them as the sounds of clanging and smashing went on. Athiya didn't want to see how this was affecting Abbu. She felt a little nauseous herself. She took deep breaths and texted her sisters that their house was being demolished.

They didn't reply but she knew they had seen it. She looked up from her phone to see Farhaan staring at her, a strange expression on his face. She narrowed her eyes and wanted to look away but found that she couldn't. A kind of connection was brewing between them and she didn't know what it meant.

She didn't want it. She wanted to remember the pain of losing her home. But the more she looked at him, the more she seemed to forget what her problem was. Farhaan smiled slightly and it changed his demeanour immediately. She stiffened the slightest, but she didn't smile back.

He fixed the shades on his face and nodded curtly.

She looked away.

ALSO IN THE JASMINE VILLA SERIES
BY ANDALEEB WAJID

ALSO IN THE JASMINE VILLA SERIES
BY ANDALEEB WAJID